SHAMAN CIRCUS

Gail Gray

ISBN: 978-0-9842594-6-5

Library of Congress Control Number: 2010900353

Cover Art by Steve Viner

Cover design by All Things That Matter Press

Printed in 2010 by All Things That Matter Press

This book is dedicated to Brian K. Ladd
and
the amazing energies in writing groups
as they transform wannabes into published authors.

Acknowledgments

Thanks to Brian K. Ladd of the Reedy River Guerilla Writers Group for his constant support and inspiration.

Thanks to Brian, Raewyn Lowe, Chris Patrick, and Deb Harris for editing. Thanks to the Reedy River Rats.

Thanks to Scotty Tillotson of Scotty and the Disease for his Halloween performance as Baron Samedi one night at Coffee Underground which served as the initial inspiration for the character, Jacob Laguerre and the concept of *voudou* following Katrina.

Thanks to my children, Beth and Jeff, and my granddaughter, Kendall, for putting up with the long hours I spend at the computer in research and in writing.

CHAPTER ONE — RED DUST ENCHANTMENT

Jacob Laguerre spit on his hands, knelt and buried them in the mound of red clay dust at his feet. He scanned the cave he'd built of banana tree leaves. Sweat soaked his shirt. The trance was already on its way – ahead of schedule again. He shuddered. *Why do I continue to do this? Why do I give in?*

His hands moved of their own volition, swirling in the dust. A low deep song, NIN's *Discipline,* erupted in whispers from his lips as his shoulders unclenched, as the liquid energy of someone else poured through his body. He didn't welcome the intrusion - but he'd made the choice - the dust was the invitation. Jagged, mini-electrical eruptions, tapped at his nerve endings, a cosmic SOS. They bundled the synapses in his brain, the wiring no longer his own. He was just a passenger.

Anything could happen now. Despite himself, he craved this strange unearthly passion, cursed by a deep gut knowledge. It coursed through him in tremors. Brick dust. *How can brick dust, rubedo powder, make me do such things?*

***

Alex Hampton stared at Lily as she slept. He held the blindfold in his hands. Tendrils of light alternating with shadows, flickered across her face, intense as strobes highlighting the too high cheekbones and the hint of circles beneath her eyes. The car slid beneath the overhanging cavern created by huge ancient oaks laden with Spanish moss...a lie, an invitation to dusk, invading in a subversive assault. Alex watched the light slide down her hair in syncopated techno beats, igniting it into flames or bloody rivers, snapping into black holes. She lay half-turned away from him, her shoulders squared-off, as if even now, even as she slept, she required an invisible glass wall. The light pulsed. Her skin, as pale as gesso-covered canvas quaffed strobes. Epileptic triggers of void, repeat, repeat, repeat, light, shadow made him high or dizzy. Repeat. Again. Repeat.

"Is this really necessary?" Alex asked Laney Deschenes, a fellow anthropology professor. He didn't bother to hide his irritation. Even the fact Laney drove made him feel inadequate.

Laney turned his attention from the road to peer into the back seat. The alternating shadows made his black face disappear from time to time. *Now you see me, now you don't.*

"If you want to be a witness, yes," Laney said. "They don't trust you…or anyone else. You're damn lucky to be invited. Lily will understand."

Alex wasn't so sure. This was his gig. Maybe he'd made a mistake bringing her along. He wanted to see her eyes. He needed to read in their teal stillness how this trip would make everything right. He wanted to lean over the barrier of her back to kiss her, but her lips turned down at the edges. He refused to bless the fact with a kiss. Instead, he pulled back, his muscles taut, strung so tight he thought he'd snap. She'd witnessed too much pain, this serious woman beneath the adventurous, flighty girl. He wondered if she'd still be his wife when the blindfold was removed.

"You must have patience," Laney said from the front seat, nodding his head toward Alex. Laney turned and peered over his glasses at Alex. "There'll be many things you won't understand."

Alex wanted to be reassured by Laney's compassionate tone, but the lack of being in control of the scenario was overpowering. The oaks and Spanish moss were behind them now. More exotic, crowded vegetation lined the roadway. To Alex it seemed predatory, glistening with the remains of another afternoon gully washer, strands dripped like saliva from leaves he didn't recognize and couldn't name.

"I know you feel the academic world rejected you," Laney continued, as if unaware of his friend's growing discomfort. "It's not uncommon, especially in the fields of shamanism. Sometimes it takes years before the scientific establishment accepts new findings such as yours, especially when the culture he's researching pulls you into events."

"But I had no choice. I had to become involved."

"Yes, as it often happens in politically disruptive times," Laney agreed. "And that's another point; who knows what political motivations were behind the dissension you received? I'd say it proves the point. You touched a nerve… all the more reason not to discount what you witnessed with your own eyes. You can't take it personal."

"But this affects my tenure, my position, grants for further research trips," Alex emphasized.

"Yes, it does. But many of the best scientists in their field have been driven out of one university after another, only to end up becoming chairs of their departments at much bigger universities, all because of such struggles. They end up in the cat bird seat, their papers held in acclaim because they didn't give up. It all hinges on how much you believe in your work."

"I just don't know," Alex said in a defeatist attitude. One he'd adopted lately whenever pushed.

"Like you, at one time," Laney said, "I considered hanging it all up. I could have gone into theoretical physics for all the flack I received. A field where you expect such controversy, but my passion lies with people, not theories. Perhaps we each have our turning point, where we're forced to choose: succumb to the system or build a new one. Perhaps this is yours." Laney looked in the rear view mirror to examine his friend. Alex, once an inspiring professor, was now a grayscale shadow of himself, his signature shade these last few months, his eyes lackluster, more pewter than blue. His hair was limp and ravaged into a ponytail, as dull as a day forgotten. It accentuated facial angles and a square chin, a saturnine appearance found in men ten years his senior. He wasn't a man meant to be a stoic. He didn't wear it well. "You can't risk defying the established hierarchies and not expect retaliation. But now, you have a rare privilege." Laney reminded him.

Alex glowered at his friend, despite wanting to believe.

"You are about to enter a world few have understood." The black professor pinched the bridge of his nose, as if a pain on his part could alleviate his friend's, but Laney couldn't protect Alex any longer. "Don't you see, your presence here is allowed because you refused to follow the established routes? Your academic derailment may be, instead, a gift."

"I'm not even sure I'm an anthropologist anymore," Alex repeated his current mantra, running his hands over the black silk of the blindfold, with all its implications. *Initiation.*

The car slid to a halt. The large black man leaned around. He wore a look of exaggerated patience. "Let me finish, Alex. You feel self pity because you've been misquoted, ridiculed, slandered for your choices in research. But you're not alone. What you'll witness is an entire culture, hundreds of thousands of people, who've been misrepresented, abused by the media, by the world's assumptions. They don't view you in the same way academia or the scientific world does. They view you with hope. But still, you'll have to earn their trust. After so many years of oppression, trust isn't given naively here."

Alex felt like a child chastised for whining.

"You asked to witness what very few have witnessed," Laney said. "You've been granted that wish. The future is in the hands of the gods. All you can do is trust." Gone was the nondescript voice of Alex's colleague, a man he'd known for eight years, the man who introduced him to Lily. Laney's voice boomed with a resonant air as if he were an accomplished actor, not an academic who spent most of his life in research. Alex noted an accent…Haitian, Jamaican perhaps, but knew his friend had grown up in Boston.

3

Alex looked over to where Lily slept, wondering about her purpose for coming. The feeling in the pit of his stomach told him this was more than field research jitters. He'd made so many mistakes these past few months; he couldn't trust his own judgment. He wondered if he could even trust Lily or Laney. They seemed, no, *were* different ever since they'd begun the trip. Or was it he who had changed? He'd lost all perspective. This was a last-ditch effort to get it back.

The sensation of lurching forward stirred Lily awake. She woke slowly, gave Alex a brief smile, genuine, as if the past months hadn't shaken their world to desperate reactions. The smile even spread to her eyes. The opaque gaze was restored to the dagger points of challenge he'd fallen for at their first meeting.

"Do you think this will help us?" he asked her.

"In the form of the royal *We*? I don't know. I think we each have to find our individual way first, before we can have an 'us'." She sat up, brushed the hair absent-mindedly from her face and looked at him, a slightly confused look on her face.

Laney leaned between them, interrupting their talk, and handed Lily a blindfold. "A small inconvenience, just for a short time."

Lily accepted it without argument.

Alex wanted to voice his objections, but instead brushed Laney's hand away.

"Calm down, my friend." Laney said. "It's just a measure of protection for them as well as for you. In case you change your mind." Laney smiled at him, the smile of his friend.

"Okay, okay." Alex held out his hand. "Yeah, right. Patience. But it better be worth it."

CHAPTER TWO — THE RITUAL

When they took the blindfolds off, Alex saw the sun had already set. A full moon illuminated a narrow dirt road bordered by lush plants and low trees jostling each other for head space. A heady mix of fragrances mingled in his nostrils…jasmine, mimosa, chamomile, bringing back memories of summers in South Carolina. But the heat here was more oppressive. Already he was breathing heavier than normal. Rivulets of sweat ran down his back. There was a hush, as if the landscape held one finger to its vibrant lips and whispered…*sssshhh*. Secrets were harbored in the folds of light and underbelly of vegetation reclaiming its turf. Aromas and sounds fused with humid droplets to kiss the skin as if open-mouthed, taking possession…a gentle reminder: here no one is in total possession of their own psyche.

***

"Where's Lily?" Alex scanned the landscape. As his eyes adjusted to the dark, he saw Laney a few feet ahead, but no one else was within close proximity. Further up, Alex heard voices. He looked for Lily, but even in the moonlight, figures were indistinct.

People walked in twos or threes, speaking quietly. Occasionally he'd catch snatches of conversation spoken in a variety of languages. The content eluded him.

"Where is she?" Alex asked Laney, as he spun around. He'd been uneasy on the way but now he was afraid. No one back home knew where he and Lily were. Anything could happen here. Already his friend, Laney, was different from the person he trusted.

"It's okay." Laney took hold of his elbow. "She's with the women. We're on their turf now. Let's respect their customs. Relax. You'll be reunited soon, but in the meantime there's much to witness."

Even though Alex wasn't convinced, he allowed Laney to lead him down the path until they reached a warehouse. As they waited in a line of people, Alex peered over the heads of those in front of him, but couldn't see inside the door. Younger black men, impatient, jumped up on a loading dock to avoid the line. The odd mix of the atmosphere was unlike any Alex had encountered, an odd paradox. At times he experienced the same rush he felt standing in the crush of a ticket line for a band who inspired him, that tribal thrill which runs through music fans, makes them antsy and on the verge of losing control. And at other times Alex felt the odd hush similar to the experience in the entrance of a great cathedral, museum or antiquity…outrageous, unbridled excitement coupled with reverence – the Dionysian versus the Christian, the sacred and profane coursing through a dimly lit crowd.

Once they entered the dark vaulted room, the attendees were assaulted by the thick smell of oil and machinery. He felt himself pushed along by the crowd. It made him even more uneasy, like at a huge arena where one wrong move could erupt into a panic with people being trampled. As they wound downstairs, the air grew close and dry. Not what he'd expect underground. The lighting, even from bare bulbs, was so sparse he held onto the walls to feel for each step.

They descended three levels before reaching a small plateau. He was led into a long narrow room. Huge burlap bags bulging at the seams lined the walls. Odd antiquated machinery guarded the room in rows of tired angry sentinels offset by the aroma of coffee or raw cocoa beans. *Medellin, Colombia, Haiti.* People sat on stacked burlap bags or the floor. Many stood, while others, mostly younger men, talked with each other and acknowledged those they knew.

A fire flickered in a pit centered in the room, the flames licking and spiraling over tiles emblazoned with cryptic symbols. The mood was charged with anticipation as the crowd watched a young man in a white dress shirt feed the fire. He looked totally out of place in this sultry underground den preparing for a rare and private ceremony and surprised Alex when he spoke in an English accent. "If you will all find a place to be comfortable, we will begin in a moment," the Englishman said as he threw powders on the fire. Bright colors flared leaving hazy spirals of smoke. Alex recoiled as pungent smells filled his nostrils, forcing him to breathe in through his mouth.

He looked around for Lily. He couldn't see her or see any other women in the room. This was not what he expected; he'd imagined an open field, old mystics and women, not a room full of young men, many of whom could be thugs. Spasms twisted his gut as smells in the room overpowered him: smoke, sweat and whatever commodities were held in the sacks, along with a roasted scent, of meat, of flesh.

A door, previously hidden in a solid stone wall opened and a group of people walked in, conversing as if at a party, some in native costumes. Alex spotted Lily among them, chatting with Laney. Lily didn't look around or seek out Alex. He felt invisible.

What the hell was going on? His paranoia grew. *Was she hypnotized or just pissed he'd brought her here?* He looked around, fist-clenching panic constricting his chest. It snaked up his esophagus and gave a vindictive squeeze to his windpipe. He wanted to grab her and bolt. *What had happened to him? At one time this was his milieu: odd adventures, new discoveries, access to the secret weird rituals of off- the-wall cultures. Had Lily done this to him? Or had he done it to himself, locking himself up in a classroom, forgetting what it was like in the field? He'd imagined feeling like an addict taken off methadone and tasting heroin again. Instead he was acting like a child afraid to take the first puff on a Camel.*

Somewhere off in the dark end of the room drums interrupted his self doubts. A second man entered the circle gathered around the fire in measured slow steps. Onlookers stepped aside and allowed a path, as though they knew he who was. He unceremoniously walked over to the fire, paying no heed to the people on either side or those gathered three or four deep around the perimeter, and stood for a long time looking into the flames. Alex, disconcerted, looked to Laney for affirmation. The man was nothing like what Alex had expected from Laney's paper and descriptions. The man, acting as if he were alone, ignoring all those who'd traveled here, looked more like a college student in a first year play or a SNL guest doing a bad Halloween take-off. Young, wearing an old beat up top hat along with a long leather coat, the sleeves torn off, symbols, drawings and graffiti drawn all over the coat, flaunting his rebelliousness. Nothing in his dress or demeanor offered the reverence Alex had expected. Long dreads fell rampantly from beneath the hat, a row of knotted cords, matted rope with a life of their own. Around his neck was a string of bones. The wooden stick he carried, festooned with red ribbons and bones, shook in odd jerky motions. At the end, a small voudou doll danced and jerked from its jute noose. He couldn't have been more than twenty-five years old. At first it seemed like a joke, a farce. Alex was disappointed and more afraid than before, sweating from the close quarters and the jostling of onlookers. Alex stepped from one foot to the other, looking towards the exit, trying to control an unsettling nervous agitation, especially regarding Lily.

But when the mood of the crowd shifted, swelling, filling the room in a tsunami of anticipation, as if it would rush forward and engulf the man if he didn't act, he replied in chant, long drawn out symbols of unrecognizable words, powerfully expressed, the raw emotion painful to Alex. The crowd let out a communal release of breath, as if they'd been holding it all along, joined as one being, one related organism waiting just for this moment.

In response, a duet between one man and all those gathered, his posture changed, his stature appeared to grow as he unleashed one of the most distinctive voices Alex had ever heard, operatic, racked with emotion, with an odd undertone, like a bruised whisper, as dark brown as a cello's lowest string vibrating in sympathy.

The whole room quieted. The voice soared over the room, a dark cloud of menace. Catalyst or cataclysm? It was hypnotic, not in the generic metaphoric way, but irresistible and hypnotic, like the first sight of the ocean after a long absence through a gap in the rocks or the novice glimpse of a woman's naked body. At first, Alex hardly listened to the words but instead was drawn into the cadence of what was part song, part poem, part dirge, part chant. Never had he been so moved by a voice. Not at the hundreds of concerts he'd attended. Chris Cornell, not even Goeff Tate could match it.

Alex wondered if it was the acoustics of the underground room. He knew Celtic priests often searched for particular stone structures for their ceremonies. The placement of the dolmen and upright stones naturally amplified the human voice so as to lend it more power.

Alex hadn't eaten or drunk anything that could have been drugged, yet he had the distinct feeling he was in an altered state, overwhelmed by a split-brain mentality which happens only in highly charged situations, experiencing and observing at the same time.

His editorial mind raced, cataloging every nuance of the event, while his conscious mind, caught up in the trance the shaman's voice induced, was mesmerized.

Mass hypnosis? He'd experienced it at concerts… at Ministry thanks to their strobe lights; at Metallica, thanks to the energy of the audience. But he didn't connect with this audience. These were not his people.

In fact, he felt alone, singled out even. He realized he was no longer afraid of what was around him, but of what he would find inside.

Things passed through his mind in flashes of illumination: his fear of change, his possessiveness of Lily, his inability to show his true self to the grimace of the public eye.

The chanting pulled him back to the fire. The man, who looked part *voudoo* shaman, part rock singer, danced around the fire, shaking the stick. Sometimes he chanted, sometimes he was silent. When he stopped and stared into the flames, his arm falling to his side, the red ribbons of the staff splayed out on the stone floor like rivulets of blood, those observing sucked in their collective breath, watching the man as he entered a trance, oblivious to anyone else in the room. Waiting. Once again they waited.

At one point, he raised his head, dropped it back until the hat fell off. He released a deep-gutted scream so primitive, so universally despairing, the hair on the back of Alex's neck stood up. Chill bumps broke out on his arms, even in the sweltering heat. The scream went on for longer than it seemed anyone could breathe as it echoed off the walls in a wail exhorting the depths of all human suffering.

Alex felt a scream of his own bubble up in his throat like bile, like a curse. He fought to keep it down. His hands shook with the effort and he let himself drop until he landed on burlap sacks, grateful for the comfort of something solid, tangible beneath his butt and hands. He needed something to hold on to so he wouldn't be swept away in that scream. Tears streamed down his cheeks.

He saw others in the room were also overcome. Some had even sunk to the floor and sat with their heads bowed. He could not see Lily. *How had it affected her? Never in their time together did he need to hold her hand or look into her eyes as much as he did this moment. Was she affected as much as he was?*

The scream stopped; the following silence brutal. The shaman, for now Alex truly believed him to be a shaman, shuffled around, turning and twirling, like a dancer of some Native American tribe, humming quietly to himself, a lullaby to soothe a bruised soul, a hymn to quiet a frightened child. As he twirled, the ribbons swept up from the floor and spiraled in the air until they seemed part demonic, flaunting their color, and part ethereal in flight and dance. Aerials. The ribbons performed aerials...and then the voice lifted and floated with them. Not the powerful sonorous voice of the earlier shaman, but now a lilting sing-song voice, light and airy and somehow innocent; as if the scream could exorcise the shadow and a rebirth was taking place.

CHAPTER THREE — MONGOLIA

Alex scanned the view from his office window. Students bustled across the quad, chatting on cell phones or to each other, some hurrying to their next class. At one time, this view excited him. Young new minds to open up to the world he loved. Now he saw the reality. He was a scam. Only six years into his teaching career and he was already out of touch with the breakthroughs in his field. He couldn't keep up with all the new studies, hadn't been in the field for three years, and with each day fell into a deeper sense of detachment.

Even the walls of his office, filled with the reminders of his successes and failures in the field, taunted him. Each memento brought back moments of high excitement and enthusiasm. Where had it all gone?

The beribboned stick from the Turkic-Tungis in Mongolia, the wall filled with ritual masks from New Guinea, Guatemala, dream story stones, an Inuit eagle feather—each one representing new awakenings and insights. Each one mocked him now. *Slacker.* A pair of masks in particular spoke to him. They always had spoken in some way or another.

He picked up the staff from his desk. A craftsman had carved a horse's head in its handle and a hoof in the base. It was festooned with colorful ribbons woven in silk. When had he stopped it seeing it on his desk, stopped seeing the magic… stopped remembering? The gift was now covered in dust. He thought back to the life-altering events of his second field study during grad school. He'd been fortunate to accompany Fred Gillespie, a well known ethnographer on Mongolian shamanism. For a few months, they'd traveled through the Mongolian Dakur steppes with a small tribe made up of five families. He had worked hard assisting with setting up the yurts, their octagonal tents which were often furnished with beautifully made cupboards, tables and rugs. He'd been assigned to follow and interview one boy, Etern, who, despite being only eight, was one of the best goatherds. The boy had undergone a serious illness the year before, leaving him with tremors, dissociative and pressured speech patterns, and vivid dreams. The tribe's shaman had declared the boy was chosen by the spirits as his successor. Alex wandered with him alongside the goat herds and, in the evenings, cataloging the occasional rituals. Almost at once, Alex was adopted by Etern's family and invited to share their yurt with Etern's parents and younger sister. This gave Alex the opportunity to record much about their daily life. He noticed the boy became especially animated during rituals and often mimicked the shaman's steps perfectly the next day while just the two of them were away from the camp with the herd.

However, one day things had not gone well. The tribe had argued about where to head next, with a stronger, more virile member suggesting an alternate route instead of their traditional passage to the west. Tensions had built throughout the day. It was around the cooking time of the evening meal when Etern tripped on a tent stake and fell onto a guide rope which held up the awning over the opening. The awning collapsed. The pole fell and hit the fire sending a copper pot of boiling rice over the boy and his family. The camp erupted into chaos. Alex was the first to reach the boy where he fell. A length of rope had caught the boy around his neck. As the panic-stricken child struggled due to the burns from the steaming rice, the rope tightened around his throat.

In an odd instinct Alex could never explain later, he sang the childhood lullaby, *"Rock-a-Bye-Baby."* As he wiped the now cooling rice away, singing in a low voice close to the boy, Etern ceased struggling. Even after all these years, Alex recalled the look in the boy's eyes. Nothing had ever wrenched his heart so deftly. In seconds, the boy's stare went from absolute terror to defeat. He could stop breathing at any moment. But as Alex continued the song, gently trying to tease the rope loose, he watched as Etern's reaction changed to trust. As the boy relaxed, so did the rope. Alex was able to untangle the rope and free it from the boy's throat. Etern took a huge gulp and then, as a harsh coughing jag erupted, Alex gently cradled him in his arms to alleviate the boy's fear.

It was a busy evening for the shaman, Batuur, and his female assistants, but after Etern's family was asleep, Alex, Fred, and Hosbayar, the field translator, sat outside the family's yurt. The shaman performed what Fred explained as a brief ritual of healing for the family.

Alex was mesmerized by all aspects of the ritual, each part instinctively designed to put not only the shaman, but also the onlookers, in a trance. Batuur wore a ceremonial costume of layer after layer of cloth strips which spun like rainbows as he twirled. The falling, flying and rippling of the ribbons was mesmerizing, like watching flames or acid trails. On his head was a metal skull-cap helmet adorned with feathers signifying the freedom of flight—to the imagination, to ideas, to the spirit world where answers could be found. Iron bells and clappers hung across his shoulders, their oddly-toned sounds slightly unsettling until one learned the rhythm of his dance was repetitive and a melody formed in the mind. A silk sash at his waist was adorned with small brass mirrors. Hosbayayer whispered to Alex, "See how the mirrors are hung to turn outward. They are to frighten away evil spirits."

Alex soon realized, however, the most important ritual tools were the stick and bell Batuur used to drive his frenzied steps into dance. It was a stick adorned with colorful ribbons he used to beat a large brass bell in a complex but repetitive melody. The music drove the dance, the dance the music, and soon Alex was as hypnotized as the shaman; he could feel the energy vibrating in the desert and he thanked all the synchronicities which brought him to such a place at such a time.

Fred tapped Alex on the shoulder, pulling him out of his reveries. "What you're witnessing is very unusual, especially in these times," he said. "The Communist rule of Mongolia has persecuted and killed many shamans who can't stop healing even though they've been ordered to by the local invaders, some of whom are just thugs and thieves who were once nearby tribesmen but were kidnapped as boys. Many of their families were driven off the land, and the boys grew up learning survival meant doing what they were told."

Alex watched with a new appreciation for the fortitude of these highly spiritual and from what he'd seen, peace-loving people.

"How do they manage?" Alex asked.

Hosbayar was quick to enlighten Alex. "Our people have strength in their close ties to each other and in leadership devoted to the good of the tribe. Both our local tribal leader and Batuur work hand in hand. Batuur, at the moment, is taking the greater risk with you here. Other foreigners, who didn't understand the restrictions of the invading government, have caused trouble by speaking about what they've witnessed of shamanic rituals, as if we were just another tourist attraction. His life is in danger each time he performs the tasks which give us courage."

Hosbayar spoke. Alex watched his expressions, shifting in the alternating shadows and light of the fire, and realized conversations such as this were dangerous to the tribe.

Fred added. "It's very different from our religions. These people don't live separate from their faith. It's an integral part of everyday life, and they trust as much in the gods' protection as they do in the physical aid of their tribe. They feel lost without the guidance of someone like Batuur. But now, most of his rituals are very private and only among tribe members who are extended family. With the recent political climate even the nomads have had to change their ways and leave behind some of their spiritual traditions. So what you've seen here is very sacred."

Hosbayar leaned forward to speak to Alex. He appeared much older than he did in the daylight, as if one of the ancestors had, indeed, attended the ritual. His skin, deeply lined from years in the sun, stretched across prominent cheekbones common with others in the tribe, who'd experienced years of starvation under years of Chinese and Russian persecution.

13

"In rushing to help the boy," he said "you inspired Batuur to enact one of his full rituals. He's been reticent in normal daily rituals. As you have seen, they have been more subdued. Batuur and other shaman must even be careful about wearing the ceremonial dress. But today was a day of great conflict and danger for the tribe. It challenged him to be true to his craft. He told me he must perform because of your courage and knowledge in rescuing the boy."

"Watch how he moves," suggested Hosbayar. "The word, *Batuur*, means hero, and many of the tribes view him as the hero of southern Mongolia. Twice he was captured and tortured to reveal the names of other shamans. Twice he escaped before they could kill him. He was once taught by Ghoste, who is considered to be the most powerful shaman in all of Mongolia. If Batuur had revealed the whereabouts of Ghoste, leading to his death, it would have unraveled the morale of many of the Mongolian tribes, even here in the south."

"The traditions are similar but not identical," Fred said quietly.

"Yes," Hosbaya added in a whisper Alex could barely make out. "In the northern steppes, shamans with the reindeer herds, like Ghoste, beat on a drum, some of which are made with the skins of human skulls, with those of eight year old boys the most valuable."

Hosbayar stared at Alex to see his reaction. The implication was not lost on him and he wondered if Etern would have been allowed to survive if the freak accident had occurred in the north. The thought of it made him shudder even though he was close to the fire. The young anthropologist realized he'd been naïve to consider the Mongolians held the same approach to human life as Westerners. From now on he'd need to suspend all assumptions.

Batuur circled in front of them, oblivious to anything but the beating of the stick on the bell and the supposed communion with the gods. His face, transformed took on an otherworldly expression. He cocked his head to the side, as if listening to voices. Alex sat enthralled, the music thrumming through his solar plexus. Swept up in the rhythms, he also tried to focus on what Fred and Hosbayer told him, functioning with two sides of his brain at once; one side, the scientist, absorbing their commentary, the other side caught up in the trance effects of the music, the swirling colors produced by the silk ribbons— the total mesmerizing effect of sound, movement and colors.

"Here in the southern part of Mongolia," he heard Hosbayar continue, "the horse is the totem and a gong or a bell is the primary tool or "bridge" the shaman utilizes to traverse the axis mundi and speak with the spirits." The interpreter gave him a relieved look. "Flesh and human bones are not quite as revered here."

After the ritual Batuur joined them and spoke. Hosbayar translated. "Batuur says the spirits used the boy. They use him frequently as the catalyst for releasing the tribal tension. This time it was the disagreement over which route to take. Changing a course can mean disaster in the desert of the steppes. But there are times when it must be changed for the benefit of the tribe in regards to weather, resources, and trade. The shaman says the boy's actions often reunite the tribe. Baatur believes that because of Etern's emotionality, the boy seeps up the various energies and conflicts in his body and often does something awkward which wakes the tribe up to their fragility which brings them back together in some way. Batuur read the portents of the events: the boy's fall, the rice burning the family, and the boy choking. These symbols of starvation, according to Batuur, were sent to warn the tribe by the spirits. Because the rice was scattered, if the tribe took the new route, there would not be enough food or water. They would not encounter other nomads to trade with to ensure our tribe would survive. So, the message tells us to alter our route in the future; this is not the year to do so. We'll be safer if we meet at our usual sites."

Alex sat back on his haunches and was amazed at how the shaman had tied so many conflicts within the tribe together using the boy as a focal point.

"That is not all he said," Hosbayar turned to Alex and winked, his furrowed forehead now relaxed and his eyes sparkling in the stove light. "Batuur asks if you've ever been very sick or nearly died or had a seizure."

Alex wondered what that was all about and why Hosbayer was smiling. The anthropologist thought back, more out of respect for the man than the question. "Yes, when I was a boy," Alex said, remembering it all suddenly in full detail. "I had scarlet fever. I was in fourth grade. The illness was almost of unheard in the '70's, but that's what it was. I ran very high fevers and hallucinated. It was very bizarre. I can still remember it vividly. I had to go stay with a minister's family in the country for a while to get my strength back."

Hosbayar translated Alex's words to the shaman who nodded his head in agreement. The shaman's eyes beamed at the younger man as if he knew something Alex didn't. Then with a little reverent bow, the shaman handed him his drumstick covered with ribbons.

Alex thought he wanted his opinion of its craftsmanship, for indeed, it was very strikingly embellished with anthropomorphic equestrian symbolism.

"Exquisite craftsmanship. Very beautiful." He also knew how valuable wood was in the desert. He handed the staff back to the shaman waiting for Hosbayar to translate his comment.

But the shaman interrupted them both, shook his head and hand dramatically, both indicating, *"No,"* then took Alex's hand and curled the shocked man's fingers around the shaft. The shaman spoke rapidly, his voice louder and more animated as he continued.

"He says you were chosen by the spirits to be a shaman of your people when you were ill and they showed you the visions." Hosbayar waved over their shoulders as if to indicate a great distance. "He wants to know what type of shaman you are in your land. He says the staff is for a gift, because your actions, your chanting of magical words saved the boy and the tribe as well."

Alex shook his head *"No."* Fred glared at him and with a nod indicated not to insult the shaman and to accept the gift. "What a sacred and meaningful gesture," Fred said, as mediator.

Alex pulled his hands back holding the sacred item, surprised at the shaman's beliefs and feeling way out of his depth.

Hosbayar and Fred smiled as if some treaty had been signed or some agreement between nations had been finalized. Alex held the stick, feeling the weight and examining the intricate carving.

Later after the shaman left, Fred and Alex returned outside of the yurt to talk privately.

"What was that all about?" Alex asked. All I did was sing a lullaby. I think it was as much to stem my fear as it was for Etern."

"Alex," Fred replied, his eyes excited. "You know as well as I do how these tribes utilize music to enter a trance state. Batuur says that if a warrior or an ax man had reached the boy first he would have died, since cutting the rope with an axe blow would have tightened it and strangled him. If a woman had reached the boy first he would have kicked her away in his struggles and strangled. But you reached him and hypnotized him enough to relax him with your song so you were able to free him and save his life. The shaman believes there was a two-fold reason for you to be sent here. First of all to save the boy, their magical token, if you will. And, secondly, to continue your initiation as a shaman."

Back in his office at the college, Alex looked at the stick in his hand, feeling inadequate, and more lost than ever, when at one time he'd felt so connected to everything around him. He looked back out onto the campus, feeling very far away from it, more as if he'd just stepped from the yurt, the memories were so strong. At one time, something else spoke to him, some undercurrent of the power, some trigger of imagination and mystery, miracles and curses, the infinite struggle for balance among unseen sources which tied the totality of humanity together, no matter their level of civilization. He'd witnessed power and passion; watched it stirred up by dancing, music, chanting, and, at times, only a look. He held the horse head stick in his hand, this his favorite totem, gifted him from the nomadic shaman, accompanied by Batuur's voice, *"Initiation."*

Alex recalled the last sentence Hosbayar had translated while Batuur stood over them, both focused on Hosbayar's mouth, trying to repeat the words. "The word "shaman" is the one Mongolian word to be adopted in the English language. It means "One who knows."

CHAPTER FOUR — PRIMROSE PATHS AND PRIAPUS SIGNALS

He couldn't get the ritual out of his head. But every time he and Lily tried to discuss it, they ended up eager for argument. Not daring to cross the narrow stretch of sandbar still holding them together, each of them grew silent or changed the subject, not realizing how their avoidance transformed the ritual into an even more powerful symbol.

He hoped a walk with Lily along the River Walk, with its fragrant gardens and flagstone paths beneath a canopy of trees, would bring them closer. It was sure to be one of the last summerlike days of the year. At first they were stiff and aloof, but his wife, always more comfortable with such discussions, made the first attempt. "When I met you, I was so sure I knew who I was," she told him. "And I assumed who you were. Alex, you're a storyteller. That's your gift. You're an observer and then you tell the story to the world. But you're keeping everything to yourself. You've locked yourself away from me and from your students. I don't even recognize you anymore."

Alex broke off a stem of foxglove. The small act of violence gave him satisfaction. He snapped the stalk in half and shredded the purple blossoms in his hands.

"Sometimes I wonder if you're bored with me," Lily continued, watching his hands, "because you know my story. Perhaps you feel the need to move on to the next and the next. But you feel guilty, so you won't. Instead you turn to stone. We both do. It's not your fault, but your purpose. Perhaps you'll always have to move on. I need more than that."

She looked at him, the look he feared, her head low with the shade pulled down, the light flickering somewhere in the back of her eyes. Far away, distracted, not dreamy like she could be when painting, but genuinely distracted, as if against her will. Something demanded her attention. It seemed not of this world. He usually recognized the signs it was coming beforehand. She'd peel off the label of her Coors light bottle or twist her bracelet. But today they had no beer and she wasn't wearing her bracelet— the amethyst one he'd given her, birthstones for her birthday. And he was the one with shredded bits of poisonous flower in his hands, remembering she did such a thing once...with someone else. All the years they'd been together she'd never told him what happened afterwards, after the infusions and ingestion. Even then, he'd felt like only a witness, never a participant; never allowed in, as if people of her ilk, her calling, saw something deficient in him which allowed him to come only so far.

Alex felt the anger rising at the back of his spine. "That sounds like a cop-out. Maybe it's you who are bored with me," he said, avoiding the real issue, as he always had. "You want someone who creates the stories, not someone like me who just writes them down." They stopped. They squared off and blocked the path of a family with a baby carriage.

She stepped aside, her face flame red, her eyes burning, as she let the couple and their baby pass. "People love for different reasons. For some, it's security; for others, the connection is for their growth. Sometimes the deep reasons interfere with what we think we want in life, but our soul knows. I still believe the connection between you and me is important, even if you don't. You knew what I believed when you married me. You had a choice then."

"But there's something other than that, something you want from me— as if to make me change," Alex said, feeling trapped. He sprinkled the foxglove pieces at her feet…a curse or supplication…he wasn't sure.

"Yes, I do want something out of you…but not change. Rather, I want the core of the man I met and married, the man who trusted his instincts, who followed his curiosities, who saw beyond the surface of life. I miss the man who was fully alive in his skin, in his discoveries of the world, both outside and inside. "

"You wanted a magus, a magic man, something beyond everyday life!" He yelled at her, his voice fierce in accusation. He stifled the urge to hurt her in some way.

"Yes. I did and I met him seven years ago. But he's not in front of me now. Now I look at a person I don't even recognize." She stepped back onto the path and, before he knew her intentions, she turned and raced toward the stairs leading to Main Street.

"Wait." He grabbed her arm, jerking her around more violently than he intended. Fingerprint bruises immediately formed on her fair skin. "Something happened to you at the ritual. It all got worse then." He was desperate, the anger drained away.

"Alex," she said, her teeth clenched. "Yes, the ritual was spiritual, transformative for me. It reinvigorated me to approach my work again, to find some sense of passion in my life…some purpose. I found it to be life-enhancing. But I'm afraid you found it be frightening. I don't know. You won't talk about it."

"Okay. It did disturb me. There was something negative and threatening about it. But it told me there's more to life than what we have." Alex stepped up his pace, unaware of his agitation.

"What you and I have?" Her voice was high-pitched now.

"No…no. I didn't mean it that way." He shook his head in frustration, not finding the right words to describe his level of disillusionment.

"What Americans have, what type of lives we have. The threat, the danger is right around the corner, but we're all too spoiled and lazy to see it."

"And that's the most valid way you've spoken about your disillusionment up until now. We each have our own interpretation of life's events. Instead of letting your lack of faith in society infect our relationship, why don't you do something about it?" She spit the words at him as a direct challenge. Then she quickened her pace and headed toward the stairs to Main Street.

He caught up with her. She turned on him, the way he had on her. "You can't deny me my right to take the experience as a way of opening up," she said. "And I can't negate your right to see it open up something in you. Perhaps you have to look below the surface of things and see what's wrong. Maybe I need a different way." She stepped up her pace. "Either way, it was life-altering and if we're going to make it, we've got to each allow the other our own way of interpreting it and acting upon it, if we need to."

"What does that mean?" He tried to keep up, fearing the worst.

"I don't know yet." She walked even faster through the arts district towards her end of town. "Sometimes we have to stay in that place of confusion until the answer reveals itself or our subconscious figures it out." She stopped, her breathing heavy. She'd almost been running away from him. She turned and looked in the window of an antiques store, obviously trying to control her emotions.

He wanted to reach out and grab her, but couldn't make himself do it, either because of resentment or fear...which, he wasn't sure. She stared into the dim window with its dusty clutter of antique glassware and old printing equipment. She wouldn't look at him. Then he saw what had captured her attention. It was a stature of some indeterminate tarnished metal and age, a Greek or Roman god, his arms out, his hands held shoulder-high, palms out. A look of corrupt mischief creased his face. He wore nothing but an out-of-proportion erect phallus.

"*Priapus*," she solemnly pronounced the word. "Son of Dionysius. Passion."

When she turned away from the window, the color had drained out of her face, her eyes as naked in their pain as he'd seen them in months. In an eye-blink, the cold look returned.

"I've got to go," she said, as if the past moments hadn't transpired. She looked at her cell phone and checked the time. "I'm late for my meeting with Diane at her gallery regarding my show."

CHAPTER FIVE — TO SNAG A SHAMAN

Alex leaned back in his chair and waved at Laney as he entered Dougal's. They frequented the Irish pub near campus because the beer wasn't cheap and the food was not fried. The Irish pub was one of the few places they could meet without being surrounded by students.

Laney had been oddly distant during their recent phone calls. He'd drop a quixotic sentence or two and then say he had to ring off, claiming he had some pressing duty to fulfill.

Finally Alex arranged for Laney to meet him. "Look, Laney, despite what you think of my reaction to the trip, what would it take to arrange a meeting with the shaman in person, maybe to interview him?"

"I'll try," Laney suspended a forkful of shepherd's pie. "But shamans, by nature, are shy and illusive." He was even more irritatingly cryptic than usual. "It took me two years to arrange a meeting with him and then at least six months before he would open up. And it was all arranged via a complex circuitous route."

"Okay, I understand it's difficult," Alex said, "and you know I'm not one of the people who uses the "who-you-know" method, but I do know you're one of the most respected researchers in this field. You're the next Zora Nicole Huston." Alex knew he was putting the pressure on just after Laney had been published in one of the most prestigious anthropological journals. "You know I'm not just paying lip service. People respect you. Your papers set the standard in the field, honest and meticulous without caving in to socio-political trends of black culture or Haitian politics. But I think I have a different angle here. You focus on the grand scale, the big picture, the whole backdrop of how voudou culture develops. All I want to do is interview one man— the more one-on-one approach. Not journalistic, but more interpersonal. You know, from my past work in Mongolia, it's one of the few approaches I'm good at."

"Don't be putting yourself down, Alex; you've made your point. Okay, give me some time," Laney conceded. The more reserved man smiled. Even on campus, the word with the students was that if Professor Laney smiled, you'd earned more than a good grade or internship. "I know the powerful impact such an experience can have," the infuriatingly cautious man continued."I've got to get through this next lecture tour, so how about I call you about a month from now."

Alex sighed. He knew how determined Laney was, so he might as well trust him and have patience. People often misconstrued the black man's physical presentation. They saw the brawn and size, more fitting for a linebacker than an academic. But once they displayed the guts to take on the hematite gaze hidden behind wire-rimmed glasses, they never doubted the vast intelligence residing there. Alex often wondered if Laney were an initiate himself, as Zora had become. Perhaps Laney's penchant for white suits was more than affectation.

Six weeks went by before Alex saw Laney on campus. But it was still the same story. "Haven't heard back, yet. He's on the move. When I know, you'll know." Then he'd change the subject.

As far as his research, Alex knew it was going nowhere. He couldn't get the ceremony out of his head. He couldn't write. He taught by rote. He dreamt about the unnerving scream and the lullaby and how it made him feel.

Months passed. Both Lily and Alex were changed.

"I don't know how to talk to you anymore," Lily said one night, exasperated. She was on the verge of tears. "You've put up these huge walls and won't talk to me or tell me what's wrong and I've no choice but to speculate."

"I don't know," he said as they sat on a side porch, his book open but unread on his lap. Her sketchpad was covered with architectural drawings and figure studies, another testament to her determination and his lack of anything resembling even a goal, let alone a process. "Nothing gives me any enjoyment anymore," he said flat and unrepentant, the acceptance of his ennui an easy passive-aggressive method of giving up. "My work is floundering. It just all seems for nothing." He felt as if even his answer wasn't good enough.

"Alex, we're like survivors of a tragedy who can't bear to speak about the horrors we've seen. Except there's been no tragedy, no horrors," her voice was pleading as she deftly removed his whiskey glass from the patio table. "Do you want out, and don't know how to say it? Is that it?" Have you met someone else?"

"No, I don't want out." He didn't mean to sound so angry, but the fact she might not trust him made him defensive, closed. He didn't take his eyes off the glass and wondered about the evolution of power, of control. "I haven't met anyone else," he said, too frustrated to be compassionate.

"Then what the hell is it?" she asked her voice rising, nearly hysterical, crying now.

He pulled back further. How easy it was to shut down. So much easier than dealing with the tension that threatened to eat up the room, eat up the small slivers left of his psyche.

She, for the moment, refused to let it lie. "Well, do you want to bother working on this relationship?" She asked, deadly calm, in a voice colder than he'd ever heard her use. "Do you think there's anything left to salvage?"

When he couldn't answer her, because he had no answers, not even the right questions, she left and went to her studio in the West End. At that moment he didn't care.

But on other nights, bad nights, the lonely nights when she stayed at her studio painting all night, Alex sunk into further despair and self-loathing. He should have learned something from that night with the shaman, but he didn't. Except how his life had no meaning and he didn't know where to turn next.

In painfully obvious counterpoint, Lily did. Her work blossomed: potent images, full and vibrantly alive and frightening, all at the same time. He envied, maybe even resented, her ability to produce, to feel the release in her work. She left the ritual inspired. He left it constricted.

He'd spent months rewriting his book, editing hunched over the computer until muscle spasms attacked his back. The doctors warned he had torn ligaments and would need surgery if they didn't heal. They spoke of internal bleeding and months of recovery. He blocked it out, refusing to believe. *How could I have torn ligaments sitting in a computer chair?*

It was way too hot for September. The atmosphere on campus didn't help Alex's mood any as he watched students playing toss football on the quad or picnicking as if it were spring. The Indian summer made him feel deprived, not revived. All it did was make him go over the ritual in his mind yet again; the night by which he measured both his days and nights, all of them falling short.

Before he even reached the house, he sensed the situation would come to a head. Lily's car was in the driveway, three hours earlier than she usually returned from the studio. She knew he liked the afternoons to himself. When he walked in, she was nowhere in sight. But out in the courtyard, she'd set the table with the Tuscany-tinted china reserved for special occasions.

He hardly touched the chipotle soup and homemade bread. They exchanged the same rote everyday talk during the meal. To Alex, everything had the same bland taste. He filled his wine glass again, hoping he could wash the miasma away, even if it took a second bottle of wine. Every day felt the same. He was cardboard, a hulk of a person, and, in some large measure, he blamed her.

She leaned on the table across from him, then grabbed his hands and looked firmly into his eyes, locking on target, for the first time in months.

"What's going on with you?" Her mood undisguised this time, sad, weary.

Alex looked away. He couldn't think of the words. He didn't know how to talk to her, this woman who knew more about him than anyone in the world, this woman who knew the deep-down real Alex like no one else. The only person he could stand to be with on this useless planet. He couldn't look her in the eyes or tell her what was going on. Fear held him back. Fear that maybe, if he said it out loud, it would be true, that he was having a nervous breakdown, a crisis of confidence, and a loss of faith in everything he'd worked for and believed in. That he was a fake, a nobody with aspirations towards grandeur, a guy who didn't have a clue as to who he was or what he was meant to do.

"Do you think drinking and pain pills are the answer?" Her face was a hard mask, without a trace of the compassion. "You haven't been alive since we got back." Lily went on, wishing she knew the means to summon the Alex she first met. She needed to see somebody home in those rare blue eyes, like a mountain lake willing to reflect whatever was around it, sap green or cloud gray, and even, at times, flashes of fire, sunset, when he was enraged. He'd always been the one too engaged in life, too involved emotionally. Anyone could read it, even when he didn't want to share, as if his eyes would defy his physical being and refuse to be anything but real.

"I don't know. I'm obsessed," Alex said, making an attempt. "I need to have answers and I can't find them. My life seems useless. All this study, all this work, and I've nothing to show for it. No grants to continue. My book proposals have been rejected more times than I can count. I find my classes routine; the students bore me, as I'm sure I bore them." He wriggled his hands free from under hers, feeling inadequate to provide her with answers, let alone love. "I feel like I'm drying up into dust here, while things are going on in the world I need to know about. I need to be in the field, not sitting in libraries."

"Follow your gut, then," she said simply. "If you have to get out into the field, do it. Forget tenure; put your book aside for a while. Maybe everything you've been doing here is the preliminary work. We both changed that night. You know it and I know it. And maybe the change will be harmful to our relationship. But whatever it started, we need to explore it. If we don't we'll resent each other. I don't want that to happen. We can't stop each other from changing. My work's internal. I have to explore my inner world. Yours is external. Follow it. Perhaps we'll survive whatever needs to come next and be the stronger for it. If not, then at least we know we didn't hold each other back from what we need to do to feel alive. I can't go on seeing you suffer and become a shade of who you are or need to be."

"I don't know what to do," Alex was unable to keep the self-pity out of his voice. "I wish I had the answers."

"Perhaps there aren't any answers and only the questions are important."

She looked away, off into the garden as if it could offer answers. The candlelight flickered on one side of her face and put the other in shadow. She looked older, tired. He could see the wrinkles around her eyes. *Have I done this to her?*

"All I know is that I refuse to continue to watch you flogging yourself this way. I won't watch you become addicted to alcohol and Loratabs." She pushed her plate away, rough, angry. He wondered if she'd pick it up and throw it. She'd told him she'd been known to break dishes in the past. But he watched as she clenched her fingers to keep them from moving, as she sublimated the anger.

"Are you saying we're over?" Alex was appalled, in shock. She was his rock, his support team. He panicked at the thought of losing her; unaware he'd already thrown her away. "Are you going to throw seven years of our lives away because of one night?" He asked, turning the blame again on her.

"It wasn't one night. It's been building for a year or more." She seemed to relish the fact she now looked down to him. But then he remembered something he'd taught her once. How when speaking, to make the statements more powerful to stand up, even if on the phone, in order to speak from your diaphragm. Automatically, the words had more effect.

"You feel trapped and I feel solitary," she continued. "Perhaps we need this to save our relationship. Right now, at this point in time, there's nothing to work on." She left the room. The view of her back was one of the most final gestures Alex had ever witnessed. He photographed it in his mind. Her hair swept up from her neck; her shoulder blades, angular, tense; her walk graceful, easy; her dancer's walk. As if it was a simple act, turning her back on their marriage and walking away. A ceremony that was meant to bring them closer together now drove them apart. And Alex, in his drugged up ignorance, wanted to blame that walk on her, not wanting to face how he had snuck away like a thief, using drugs and alcohol to dull the pain as he pulled away from her in fear and jealousy, never realizing how final it could be.

CHAPTER SIX — THE SEED OF A PLAN

The next morning, Alex accosted Laney in the hallway of the Humanities Building, again. Maybe public supplication would help. At this point, Alex didn't mind resorting to whatever shameless methods he'd have to employ.

"What have you heard about the shaman?" He asked, not even bothering with a hello.

"I'm beginning to feel less like a friend and more like a dealer," Laney said, his voice serious, but his eyes kind.

"Is it so obvious I'm that obsessed?"

"Alex, I'm not the only one on campus who's noticed— how shall I put it— your distractibility for the past few months. Not that it's all that unusual, but we're used to seeing it in our students, not in our professors. But maybe I can ease the stress a bit, and recommend a leave of absence. You might even want to consider a sabbatical."

"What are you saying?" Alex could barely get the words out; his heart was beating off-kilter for the first time in months.

"It's arranged," he said. "Meet him at the corner of Chartres and Decatur on Oct. 20th, 8:30 p.m. He'll be there." He said this all with a straight face, as if the corner he mentioned was down the block, not two thousand miles away.

"This soon? In New Orleans?" Alex asked in disbelief.

"That's where you'll find him."

"But I thought we were way out in the wilder parts of Louisiana, in Cajun country. The ride to the ceremony took hours." Alex said.

"Does it matter? Would the affect on you have been any different, no matter where you were?" Laney asked.

"I have no idea. I don't know what to think," Alex said.

"Well, then just accept the fact that you'll never know where it was, because it is not necessary to know." He looked sternly into Alex's eyes, like a father teaching a child a most important lesson. "Do you only care about facts, or are you interested in what happened to you on a deeper level? Do not confuse the two."

"I mean, I was just curious." Alex badgered him, knowing he should shut up but not able to stop.

"Don't you understand? What you experienced is highly individual and highly personal. Some believe it's an experience to make or break the spirit. Find yourself or lose yourself, growth and salvation, denial and stagnation. As with every important moment in life, we must balance on the head of paradox. You may discover the location is immaterial. And, if you can't see that, then you won't see anything." Laney eyed Alex with a look that warned, *"I am done with you now. Learn it or forever be quiet."*

Alex looked back at him, hardly recognizing his friend. He was exhausted by the exchange. He suddenly felt so far out of his depth he doubted not only his ambitions but also his deeply held beliefs. The professor, who'd been slowly dying these past four months, was finally depleted, perhaps defeated. But inside, a small insidious voice was elated.

CHAPTER SEVEN — YOU WANNA BE A ROCK STAR?

Alex went to New Orleans to revive the human in himself.

He cancelled important lectures, endured the wrath of trustees and administration, and buggered off to New Orleans like a teenager gone wild. Lily, perhaps Laney, who was mysteriously unavailable, he considered the only ones who understood. In a last-ditch effort to save his marriage from a slow death by long distance, he asked if she'd go with him. "I have my work; I can't." He replayed the scenario as he leaned back in the airport limo watching the shattered shell of New Orleans speed by. "Somewhere deep down you know how important it is to me." She'd been calm, almost surreal in her acceptance of what he saw as the first step to the last step. In the private language they learned separately last night, he knew her work did not mean her painting, but rather the deep self-awareness search she'd chosen.

While she'd been left with inspiration, calm, and purpose, he was stuck with burning questions. He still hadn't figured out how to quell the anthropologist, the researcher, or the inquisitor. He wondered what he'd pay for that mistake.

He'd pawned his computer to buy the airline ticket. It would be more than unfair to drain their limited savings account. He wouldn't need the laptop for a while anyway. The thing had destroyed his back. There'd been nothing else of value. The books could only appeal to academics and would take too long to sell on E-bay, bringing only a fraction of their worth.

He leaned back in the seat as they drove through the modern New Orleans…or what was left of it after Hurricane Katrina. His welcome was a gauntlet of twin rows of huge metal sign holders— the glass and neon gone, the metal twisted into weird symbols, a horrific debauchery with the row of palm trees now stripped away. Several miles of hotels, apartment buildings, restaurants, wealthy subdivisions, stood empty with all the windows gone—blanked-out eyes staring in the void, curtains flapping in the breeze. An entire mall was decimated, left in a U-shape of rubble. Three-story million-dollar homes tilted. Cars and people were oddly non-existent. The damage was the work of the wind, not just the water. Only a powerful eruptive force could have twisted the signs of the Marriot and Hilton.

Alex was relieved to find the 1870 Banana Courtyard open. In the lost city of New Orleans, Raefaella, who manned the front desk of the quaint hotel, informed him Bad Jacqui's was the bar where everyone went for refuge, mental health, commiseration, and bizarre Katrina jokes. He unpacked quickly and headed out into the Quarter, which at least could boast people on the streets. On the way to the bar, Alex was amazed to see refrigerator after refrigerator standing on the sidewalks, the new symbol of New Orleans, similar to cities such as Chicago which boasted cows, Athens, Georgia with the bulldogs, or Hendersonville, North Carolina with the bears. Only, instead of animal statues painted in bright colors, every refrigerator was decorated with the same obscure reference: *Voudou 5 Here Today*.

At Bad Jacqui's, it was business as usual, despite the chaos and teeming darkness surrounding the Quarter. He checked his cell phone for about the fifth time in the last half an hour, 8:15 p.m. and it was Oct. 20th, 2005.

At exactly 8:30 p.m. the man from the ritual walked in surrounded by a group of young men. He was dressed casually in black jeans, T-shirt, black leather jacket. The wooden stick was noticeably missing. He shrugged his shoulders, high-fived his friends, and then sauntered over to Alex's table.

"I recommend the rum," he said, sliding into a chair opposite Alex as if they were old drinking buddies. The voice of the ritual was gone. He was the image of a young, slovenly slacker, reminding Alex of students who didn't give a damn and cared only about clubbing, playing music, or spending all their spare time on video games. In contrast to everything else, he had the angular face of someone used to self-denial, but his eyes, whiskey brown, were the eyes of a sensualist who missed nothing. Alex didn't trust the way his mouth turned up at the edges, as if he was silently laughing, as if he knew the punch line to a joke he refused to reveal. His closed-off, dark eyes didn't match his mouth.

A young waitress with a red Mohawk came over, winked at the newcomer, ignoring Alex. "The usual?" She asked in an accent more New York than southern. While Alex had been ensconced in the mid-south, the Bible belt of the country, he'd forgotten how isolated and traditional his life had become, despite being married to an artist and living in the fringe world such a lifestyle offered. Even so, he had to force himself not to stare at the waitress. When had he become so entrenched in normalcy?

He felt as if he'd walked into some carney movie, *The Red Dwarf* or *Fur*. These people and this town were so far away from his routine at Whitten he felt notably out of place. When had he changed? He remembered the days when he was the rabble-rouser, granted more subtle than anything he witnessed here, but he'd been more wily then and determined. There were times when a well-planted sentence spoken over a round of beers had stirred up a rebellion that stretched further than a college campus. Was he now so unconsciously ruled by the conservative structure of his city, his environment that he viewed everything strange and unusual as an infringement on his security?

"You know my every want and need," the young man said, interrupting the Alex's self-doubts as he put three gold coins on the table, his eyes intent on the anthropologist. "Just double it for my friend, here."

This was not the audience with a shaman, but a drink with a street kid. Alex watched as his hopes were dashed by a gesture. His unlikely subject nodded to a poster on the wall.

"I have less than an hour until my band goes on." The arrogant man's emphasis implied his garage band meant everything. A loud heavy song, a track by Soundgarden or Godsmack infiltrated the bar noise as Alex examined the poster. Sure enough, there his shaman was relegated to the stage as a cocky lead singer fronting a band of kids dressed in black, hands stuffed in his pockets, with a sarcastic tilt to his mouth, daring anyone to judge him. His face was partially hidden by his dreads, revealing one confrontational eye.

"You play here?" Alex asked in disbelief.

"Yeah, look man, everybody's gotta make a living." He leaned over the table close to Alex's face, invading his personal space, and said very quietly. "Besides, it ain't like folks leave crops at my door, ya know. The old days are gone. A man's gotta eat. Gotta adapt, gotta find a way. I found it here." He shrugged his shoulders again.

"But heavy metal? In a dive?"

"Not everyone's a seeker like you."

At first Alex thought the man was taunting him, but his expression shifted in a moment too rapid for Alex to comprehend. He aged ten years while his face transfigured into a complex map of cynicism, intelligence, and desperation. "Yeah, man, well, whatcha wanna know?" he asked, abrupt, demanding.

Alex examined the man's expression to see if he was making fun of him. There was no evidence he was. After all, this street punk had no idea the turmoil he'd caused since their last meeting. But still, Alex felt as he was being punked by Ashton Kutcher, even as he wrote off the idea immediately. This scheme was too grandiose, too expensive to launch for a no-name small college professor.

The waitress brought them their drinks, flashed a big smile, and placed two glasses, an amber bottle and a large ceramic bowl in front of them.

"Hot peppers soaked and floating in rum," she said. "Enjoy."

The black-haired man fished into the bowl and pulled out a pepper, swallowing it like a sardine. This time his eyes smiled, before his mouth cracked into a huge grin.

He turned back to Alex. "Don't forget," he said "about the *sham* in *shaman*." The smile vanished. In that one quarter angle turn of his face, he transformed from the flirtatious wanna be rock star to the eerily self-contained creature witnessed in the warehouse. In addition, he wore a look of collusion so complete it could not have been faked. Alex felt as if he'd been made privy to the truth of him and knew instantaneously that no one else in the room, perhaps in that city, or the city it had once been, had known the truth. Alex was suddenly aware of what an opportunity this meeting was and, instead of looking at him as the rocker kid, he offered him the respect he was due.

"How did you learn what you know?" Alex began the interview not knowing how to pose all the questions racing through his mind.

"The grace of the gods," the man said, looking away for the first time, lost for a moment in his own reverie. Then he snapped back. "They gifted me with a harsh teacher," he said. "I did what I had to. And then one day it was all there, like a gift."

"Why me? Why are you talking to me?" Alex asked.

"Because you're the first one who wanted to know," he said. He obviously preferred simple statements. Alex wondered if they were understatements.

"Why would you reveal yourself, if you have this whole other life?" Alex asked sweeping the room with his hand, wondering where the question had come from.

"If you don't tell the truth, you suffer eternal damnation," the shaman said in a conspiratorial tone, then softly sang, "If you tell the truth...you are ostracized...penalized...crucified." He sang it like Trent Reznor on a Nine Inch Nails song, only with a bad joke attached. "Catch 22," he said, suddenly dead serious. "Everyone has a choice. This one is mine." His mobile face became a hard rock, the glint in his eye disappeared, and Alex was looking at a statue. Chill bumps ran up his spine. In just that simple line the shaman returned, quietly, to his table, a demigod doing a lap dance on Alex's psyche. He sat helpless until he found the strength to pull back in awe and fear. He'd encountered something so far outside his realm of reality he wondered, again, if he'd been drugged. Alex knew his reaction was way out of line to his actions. But he felt as if he were in the presence of something so much more vast than anything he'd known before; as if someone or something else inhabited the young man's body. The singer was indeed transformed. His eyes, his voice, his manner. Alex was either in conversation with a brilliant schizophrenic or something he knew existed in history but didn't want to believe. Alex thought of the voice of the Bene Gezzarits of *Dune*. Fiction, it was, yet here he witnessed it in reality. For the first time in months, he was drug-free and had taken only a few sips of the strong rum, but this experience was as bizarre as any trip.

It was to become more bizarre.

"You wanna know about *voudou*, about Shamanism? Is that it?" The question was a challenge, with a bite in his words, hot like cayenne at the bottom of the bowl, or the quick snap of a lizard's jaw. The shaman's eyes burned Alex. Or was it just the reflection of the neon lights on the deep brown of his enlarged pupils, a lost brown, the color of the old leather of a bomber jacket, beaten up but not beaten down? This would not be a normal interview. Every word was thrown out like a gauntlet and Alex felt the shiver of the words "no quarter" at the back of his skull.

"Well, let me tell you. It's the experience of the unlimited, not your passive Zen-centered bullshit, not the hallucination of LSD, mescaline or psycillicybin, not the push of ecstasy or the pull of your soul in the cavity of the woman you love. It's more guttural and at the same time more elevated. Words can't describe it. And it's useless for me to try. It's paradox to the 10th degree all snarling at each other in your solar plexus, the wolf and lion eating each other in the alembic."

His words came all in a rush, like a waterfall after a storm, a friction of elements, water scraping against rock into a canyon so deep, the primeval crash echoed miles away. "While your spirit soars high," he continued, breathless, leaning over the table but not focusing on Alex, his eyes diverted to some other view, "above the universe and your mind follows the threads of a million thoughts all at once, you experience four dimensions, five. You're the cipher in the midst of every quantum physics equation and the kernel of truth in every convoluted philosophical statement."

The shaman was lost to himself, hungry like a junkie, or someone who'd just thrown overboard the most valuable thing in his life and was hanging over the side of the boat trying to retrieve it.

Then he suddenly sat up. His head twitched, a nervous twitch, painful to watch, and he said, "Well, I digress. Let's start at the beginning." His face changed, perky and alert, almost feminine. This new attitude reminded Alex of his fourth grade elementary school teacher.

The man stood, as if reminding himself how standing allowed the voice more power. "Let me introduce myself to you. I'm Jacob Laguerre, and I'm here today to teach you basic *Voudou*, *Voudou* 101, *Voudou* for Dummy's." For a moment, Alex thought the shaman was making fun of him as a teacher, but the serious challenge in Jacob's voice said differently. "The *lwa* are spirits," Jacob continued. "Not gods, but ancestors who've gone before us."

Alex had the weird thought, I'm in for a lecture. All that's missing is the chalkboard. He'd have laughed, the shift was so comical, but he realized he was the buffoon in this particular farce. He wriggled in his seat and considered leaving, but an exit would be graceless, with the sound of him shifting his chair, let alone the awkward exit lines he'd have to enunciate in a loud voice in order to be heard over the conversational hum of the bar. He wondered how the other patrons hadn't taken notice. Were they in, on the joke? Or were they just used to his ranting?

Alex had to admit he was hooked. The guy was the penultimate showman. He knew how to reel them in, no matter what his stage, and Alex wanted to hear what Jacob had to say. Deep in his gut, he knew these were things he must know. Jacob had the secrets, and he had to discover the key that would turn every lock in his twisted psyche.

"When the dead enter the afterlife, the *Ginen*," Jacob spread his arms wide to indicate a world out there somewhere, "they take on huge spiritual stature. They each have their own qualities, their own powers, their own motives, and they operate without any rules within those parameters. But they must use men to communicate. So during ritual, the priest or priestess or shaman will open the gates to the *Ginen*, the home of the *Geude*, the spirits, and invite them in. It's an exacting ritual, drawing *veveres*, the symbolic patterns which invoke the attention of the spirits, ancestors and gods, in dust on the ground, chanting, drumming. The shaman must open himself to the spirits, be their vessel. It's often a difficult experience, in any culture, this journey to the world of spirit. If you combined looking in the eyes of the only person you ever loved after a long absence, being moved by the music that carves up your heart, being stunned by the painting that slaps you across the face, standing on a cliff at the top of the world, the best orgasm you ever had, the most dire sinking feeling of doom you've ever experienced… all these rolled into one…then you might just begin to touch the sensation with your little finger. The rush is so huge, you're lifted to a place wider, broader, more expansive than anything on this planet; you're one with all, and all is within you. It's a rush you can't ask for or duplicate. Once you've had it, you're addicted. You spend the rest of your life trying to recreate it. It's a paradoxical gift, a serendipitous event. The more you look, the more it denies you…until one day it's just part of you, your everyday existence."

The shaman leaned forward over the table, dipping his fingers into the bowl of rum, retrieving two peppers and holding one out to Alex. A dare or offering? Alex wasn't sure. "Let me tell you, Alex, I've tasted every pleasure you can think of and many you could not. Exalted or dirty, flesh or chemical, aesthetic or hedonistic. I traveled the world seeking them out. And none can touch what happens in the embrace of the *lwa*. Nothing. I challenge you to find it and offer it to me. You'll spend the rest of your life searching. And the thirst for it will never be slaked."

There was nothing to say; nothing that could be said. Alec delicately tested the heat of the pepper on the end of his tongue. He dissected it in small bites, allowing the essence to wash over his tongue, as it annihilated any memory of peppers or rum, just as the shaman was annihilating any past or pat philosophies.

"That's why I perform in places like this." Jacob said with a shrug. "It's a little needle in the arm, a tiny fix of methadone to counteract the real drug, a momentary relief compared to what happens during the ritual. But without it, I'm a piece of parchment, brittle and broken, lying in the dust waiting for oblivion. Waiting for the next boot to grind me into the earth so I can forget I ever tasted nirvana, Elysium, heaven, whatever you want to name it. But when you've been there, all you want to do is get back there. Everything else is but a shadow flickering in your peripheral vision. Nothing else is real."

Alex shifted in his chair, accepted the beer offered from the waitress who obviously knew the effect of the peppers. She also handed him a glass of water, which Alex decided against. No more playing safe.

"I love the cello," the younger man said out of the blue, his voice nonchalant, a tangent running amok as if playing a game of free-association or *guess-what-comes-next*. He tilted his head, looked at Alex slyly. "On the TV nature shows, ever notice how the crocodile always gets the cello?"

Alex thought of Nicholas Urfe in the thrall of Conchis at Villa Bouranai on Phraxos, Jimmy Page in the thrall of Alistair Crowley, Carlos Castanada in the thrall of Don Juan Matus. What the hell could come next?

"What you release from within you will set you free. What you do not release from within, will destroy you," Jacob said, so quietly, as if to himself, Alex almost didn't catch it. Before Alex could ask him to repeat it again, his demeanor completely changed.

"It's been real. But gotta boogie, man." He stood up and tipped his hat, a gesture Alex would have read as mockery, except immediately following, he nodded his head. Without a doubt, it was an act of silent, secret agreement. In fact, one of reverence, deference, like a soldier to his general, an actor to his director. He left Alex no other way to read it.

"It's show time." The shaman/rocker/punk winked, for an instant all three, until he knocked back his drink and walked away.

"Coitus interruptus," the 'tween school joke reverberated in his head, as distorted as the guitar's sound check. But nothing could have been more apt.

Alex debated what to do. The waitress appeared at his side as if on cue.

"Show doesn't start until 11:00, but since you're a friend of the band, you can hang around." She set a glass in front of him. "Jake sent this over."

"Jake?"

"The singer, Jake Laguerre. He's really good. *Chiseled Effigies*, they're one of the favorite bands here. I think they'll make it big time, don't you?"

Alex took a deep swig of his drink. "Big time. Yeah, the big time may not be quite big enough."

CHAPTER EIGHT — THE SEED GERMINATES

Lily and Laney sat at the metal high top table in the Moroccan luxury of Earshot on Coffee Street in downtown Greenville, South Carolina. The place was packed: goths and poets lounged on the cushions; teenagers with headsets created their own CD's. Some of the regulars, musicians, and music collectors gathered at the bar or sifted through the CD's in the shop adjoining the bar/coffee shop, decked out like a hookah dream. Alice's caterpillar would have been pleased.

Lily tried to relax, focus on the sanctuary this place usually offered her. She sipped her wine and listened to 10 Years on the sound system. She and Laney watched the foot traffic on the darkened street. The gas lamps flickered. Late night walkers appeared as wraiths in the reflection of the window against the dark woods and sultry colors of the interior.

Laney looked up when a shadow approached their table over Lily's shoulder. He nodded to his friend as he took the third seat. Lily traced the open metalwork of the table with her hand. She did not look up.

"I haven't heard from Alex in three weeks," she said.

"He'll be all right." Laney spoke softly. "Try not to worry."

"I've moved out of the house," she said. The newcomer took her wandering hand and stroked the shaking fingers. "You've done the right thing."

"I'm having second thoughts." She tried to pull her hand back. "I have to go. I have a big exhibit to get ready for next week."

"I'll be there," the late arrival said, his dark head bowed for a moment. His eyes caught hers, even as wary as they were. "The gods couldn't keep me away," he said.

"You are the gods, Jacob," she said dryly.

"As you are," he said. He let her hand go.

CHAPTER NINE — TALES OF THE UNDERGROUND

Alex went back to Bad Jacqui's the next afternoon. The red-headed waitress offered a welcoming smile, followed by a little a smirk, as if she had the inside scoop on either him, the situation, or something else she'd only reveal in time.

"I know this place is weird, but if you hang in there, it'll get to you," she said, as if pretending, negating the nonverbal exchange.

What is this, the town of secrets and innuendo? He wondered.

"So you gonna hang around awhile?"

"Looks like it."

"You want what you drank last night?"

"No, just a beer today," he said. "Wait a second, how about some of that gumbo?" He smiled at her and fidgeted in his seat, feeling like a kid or an overzealous fan. "By the way," he asked, fumbling with a napkin, "is Jake's band gonna play again tonight?" He couldn't meet her eyes, as if he were asking a personal question. He felt a fool, fully aware his actions were out of proportion to events. He obviously had too much at stake, but he'd come too far to lose touch now.

"Naw, they're back on the road. They never stay anywhere too long. We never know where they're headin' next." She nodded her head in the vague direction of the door, indicating anywhere in New Orleans. "They live in that old school bus excuse for a tour bus. But they'll be back in a month or so. They usually let us know a week ahead of time. You know, so we can make a poster or put it on the website. Before Katrina they drew a huge crowd. But things change, ya know?" She shrugged her shoulders.

When he didn't answer, she went on talking. There was no one else in the bar.

"It's an acoustic act tonight. You'll like the gumbo. Jacqui's one mean Cajun cook."

Until he tasted the food, he didn't realize how hungry he was. He'd been in his head so much lately, food had become something he forced to keep his body moving. But the gumbo was good, hot and spicy with great chunks of andouille. The shrimp tender, not chewy. As he looked up to wipe dribbles of soup off his chin, he noticed the waitress had taken the seat across from him at his table.

"Do you mind?" She asked, obviously enjoying watching him devour his food. "I need a break. There won't be any business for a while."

"Sure, that'd be fine," he said.

"'Sides, if you're going to be a regular, we might as well get to know each other. New Orleans may be a big city, but right now it's operating like a small town. My name's Mavis." She held out her hand.

"Alex," he said as he shook her hand, thinking maybe he could find out more about Jake. He didn't want to explain his fascination to her. Hell, he couldn't explain it to himself. He'd like to chalk it up to curiosity or as part of his job, but he knew it ran deeper than that. Jake was charismatic and mysterious and unlike anyone else he'd ever known.

"So, how long's Jake been playing here? Does he come from New Orleans?" He tried to sound blasé.

She shrugged her shoulders. "Dunno. We all think he came from New Orleans. Nobody knows for sure. He sure knows a lot of people here. He doesn't talk about his past much." She broke off a hunk of bread, and dipped it into his gumbo, then popped it into her mouth. She chewed fast, swallowed hard, and then smiled a brief apologetic smile. "Oops, sorry about that. I'm on automatic. My friends and I have lived sort of hand to mouth. We ended up sharing meals, even before Katrina. One person would order the gumbo or the red beans and rice or a po boy and we'd all dig in. Whoever had money at the moment knew they'd be covered next time they were broke."

Alex waved her apology away. "Don't worry. I did it, too, all through college, although we ate Ramen noodles and pizza. Help yourself. Now, you were telling me about Jake."

"Well, he actually did live here for a while. That's when he lived with Cate." She took a swig of his beer. "I'll bring you another one. Soup's spicy."

"Was that his girlfriend? He doesn't seem to have many friends."

"No, not many friends, but he does have a lot of acquaintances. He doesn't let people in close, ya know? But he and Cate, they were inseparable. Everyone knew them." She tilted her head sideways, thinking back. "God they were something together. He's so tall and she was this petite girl, but smart and strong. She was the real backbone of that couple, if you ask me. Jacob and Hecate, everybody called them. Because she would tempt you right into the Underground. Even here in New Orleans, they were larger than life. Characters, you know, people willing to be out there."

Alex felt like a voyeur, but he was fascinated. He hadn't thought about Jacob with a girlfriend, not like a person with a normal life at all. "How did they meet?"

"We don't know. One day, they just came to town together. She was a dancer. And, boy, could she dance. You wouldn't see them here in the Quarter, but in these little back alley bars. He'd play drums and she'd dance and they brought the house down. The audience would be standing in the street, trying to get in, ya know?"

Mavis took another swig of his beer. "It was wild," she continued. He looked just the way he does now, just as he always did— but she always looked different. Dramatic, ya know, gorgeous outfits, native dress and all from Morocco or India or Africa, you never knew what she'd wear next but they'd always be beautiful and dramatic. Stuff you couldn't buy here. She and Jake had traveled a lot. France, I think, 'cause they both spoke a French with a different accent from the French here; smatterings of a couple of other languages, not sure from where. But they weren't Euro-trash, snooty or cosmopolitan or anything, more like Roms, like gypsies. I know Cate said she went to Egypt or Turkey, someplace in the Middle East, before Desert Storm. That's where we figured she learned her dance moves," Mavis stopped talking and looked at the table top as if she had forgotten it existed. "Oh, my, look, I've eaten all your bread and most of your gumbo. Hold on a sec. Let me get another setup."

When she set the food in front of him, he couldn't wait. "How'd you meet Jake?" He asked before digging into the food again. He could see how people never left New Orleans. They obviously put something addictive in the food.

"They just walked into the Tombs and booked themselves a gig." She looked at the bread, but leaned back in her chair. "That first night was a little quiet, but the second night, wow. We couldn't believe it. I was a waitress here even back then, and I never saw anything like it. It's like the grapevine stretched all the way into Baton Rouge and all these people, not tourists, but locals, came in and got swept up into it all. Jake and Cate were eerie, mysterious. And besides alcohol, there's nothing N'awlins folks love better than secrets and mysteries."

"What happened to Cate? Where is she now?" It was getting dark outside. The bar was starting to fill up inside. He knew he didn't have much more time to pump her.

"Nobody knows." Mavis said. "One day, they left town, went away on a tour or something. The next time he came back, maybe a year later, he was singing, instead of playing drums. He never talked about her after that. We'd ask and he'd just say, "She had her own walk to do." Like he knew she was happy doing what she needed to do. And then he'd clam up...you know Jake, make a joke or sing a song. But he'd totally divert the conversation. It's too bad, 'cause we all liked her. But then you can't ever predict anything with Jake."

CHAPTER TEN — REFRIGERATOR TOWN

"Hey, buddy, this is Jake, tomorrow's the ninth day of your trip, ain't it?" Alex was taken off guard. The voice on the telephone didn't sound like the man he'd spoken with before. "The three within the three within the three," Jake continued cryptically.

"Yeah. Hey, Jake, where are you?" Alex wondered what he meant.

"Well, I'm nowhere anyone would want to find me. But I'll be back in New Orleans tomorrow," Jake informed him. "Wanted to know if you'd be interested in another little, let us say, event?"

Alex felt the hair on the back of his neck stand up, an uncomfortable sensation, the awareness that he was walking into a trap and couldn't stop himself. "You mean like where I first saw you?" Alex asked, making sure Jake was alluding to the ritual.

"Yeah, but this time, it's not my gig. I thought that since you're doing all this in the name of research, you might want to witness a variety."

"Sure, what time?" Alex reached for a pad of paper and pencil, hoping he'd have some time to get his wits together.

"Well, let's say I just pick you up at your flophouse 'bout 0 dark 30? How's that grab ya, man? I promise, you won't be disappointed," Jacob taunted.

"Yeah, great. Thanks for thinking of me." Alex felt a mixture of excitement and panic. Sweat was running down his back as he thought of another ritual, a different one. And tomorrow, he realized in a rare lucid moment, was Halloween, All Soul's Eve, Samhain.

"But, Jake, listen. You think sometime, you and I could talk, just talk? I've got a few more questions."

"Sure, boyo, we'll talk on the way," he said as if they were drinking buddies planning a pub crawl, not shaman and seeker. "It's just gonna be you and me, babe," the man called Jake continued. He sang in a dwindling voice as he hung up the phone, "I got you, babe."

***

Jake, in fact, showed up at the time he said he would. Alex expected to see the notorious school/tour bus, but there was nothing on the deserted street.

"We can walk to this one," Jake said, sauntering ahead, still sporting the crumpled top hat and the long painted coat.

As they approached Decatur Street, Alex could see a parade had stopped in the street and a crowd surrounded the activities going on just ahead.

When they were close enough, Jake politely pushed Alex through the garishly costumed celebrators. In the center of the gathering was a display like nothing he'd ever seen. Great dancing circles of live flame slashed the night sky. It twisted and shifted in a gyroscope of fire. He felt as if he was doing acid or mushrooms. His eyes could barely register the flame dancing like a dervish, defying the night, the despair, the destruction.

Then the circles and ellipses slowed. The fire fell to two parallel flames dangling in the darkness. He could now see the person behind the visions, a girl, not more than seventeen or eighteen. She wore the heavy make up and dark Cabaret bob popular even at Whitten. But instead of matching black clothes, she was dressed in a Greek citron. White gauze fell in pleats from one shoulder, gathered beneath her breasts by a thick gold cord allowing the pleats to fall in a column around her legs. She looked statuesque and fragile. When she swung the chains again, arcs of fire danced in the sky, circled around the fragile fabric, obliterating the tiny woman. Fire flowed in powerful driving circles, angry and vitriolic, mesmerizing and changeable. All the while, superimposed on the image, he saw the visions of the shaman's red ribbons during the lullaby. But this was no lullaby. It was a triumph of power over the forces of nature. This fragile girl in her highly flammable costume took a dangerous natural element and bent it to her will.

Most of the witnesses standing around were silent. But off and on he would hear an "Ah," or "Oh, no," when the streaming fire came close to the column standing so serenely in the midst of the flame's wild ride. A time or two a serious "Fuck" erupted from the guy next to him.

He looked over at Jacob who appeared just as mesmerized. As if sensing the observation, Jacob turned, the top hat cocked a bit to the side. "This is just the beginning." His eyebrows rose in a mischievous arch, a vaudeville parody. As if on cue, two large black men and a black woman appeared as if from nowhere, dancing with bared legs, gyrating in sympathy with the flames. Alex noticed the drums, different from those he'd heard with Jacob, deeper, bottom of the gut booms. As he followed the sound he watched as a large drum circle gathered on the sidewalk. All sorts of people played all types of drums, jimbays, doumbeks, large stand-up wooden African drums, half the size of a man. Hippie kids with dreads, death metal kids, black men in Middle Eastern garb, and two white women joined the dancers and drummers.

The sounds gathered and swept wilder than hurricane winds through the air. Jake bumped into Alex, jumping and head banging at his side, caught up in the building drama. The dancers broke out in sweats and moved in awkward steps, side-stepping the flying fire, challenging it.

A few of the dancers shook strange bones and with great sweeping gestures narrated a story he couldn't read. He'd never learned the freedom of such expression. But he didn't need the language to understand the power. Strange cries erupted from their mouths needing no interpretation. Patterns and diagrams were drawn on the ground, elaborate curlicues of complex designs in red.

"Vever," Jacob explained with a deep reverence Alex hadn't heard from him before. "Voudou incantations."

Then more people joined the dance, many in odd costumes which could have been summoned from the past, the future, nightmares. Alex saw the deer god, Herne; a sad Mary; a many-armed Kali; Voudou spirits along with Greek goddesses; *Dies le Muertos* skeletons dancing with Anubis. He found such confrontations and collaborations disconcerting. Time languished and then rushed by, serving no purpose. Alex entranced again, felt transported and at the same time humbled, fully aware of his ignorance. When the dancers wound down, Jacob gently grabbed Alex's arm, "Time to go, boyo, everything in moderation. You can overdose on this stuff."

Alex and Jacob wove their way down the streets of the Quarter, arm over each others' shoulder, like drunken frat boys. Sure, they were drunk. You couldn't drink gallons of Tequila from a coffin and not be drunk.

"So, how'd ya like it?" Jacob asked. "A little bit o' magic in Refrigerator Town."

"What was that?" Alex turned and looked back at the figures, some still cavorting against firelight. "Was every shaman, medicine man, seer, priestess, god and goddess on earth gathered on Decatur Street? Out in public like that?" Alex asked, still not believing everything he'd witnessed.

"Where else would you have a gathering of like minds on All Souls Night but than a lost city? The only people left or who came back are the ones who already know all this stuff. Who the hell do you think is running this place? George Dubbya? This city needs a healing and it ain't coming from the gov'ment. Maybe it's our turn now, Alex. Maybe it's finally our turn."

Jake stopped dead in the street. "Got a joke for ya, old Alex," he said, slurring his words.

"Sure, let's have it," Alex said, bleary himself.

"What if Jesus was an artist?"

"Don't know. What if Jesus were an artist?"

"He'd draw bigger crowds." Jake said and then laughed a rare uproarious laugh, struck by his own joke or the Tequila buzz.

Just as suddenly, he stopped, threw his head back and started singing, bright and bell-toned, a song filled with anguish and remorse and mourning. The notes rang out in a ripple so vibrant on the smoky night it seemed they could light the whole broken city with the polished brass notes of its pain.

Alex thought of the string theories and how vibrations might run the universe and he knew that in this moment Jacob's voice was running the universe, or at least this corner of the universe, and he thought such sounds, such emotion cast in words would have to drift over this entire country, damned by its own greed and apathy as if this voice, this voice to the gods could change the course of history.

But how could one physical human body hold all the breadth and depth of humanity? Alex wondered.

Jacob suddenly stopped singing. "'Cause I'm jacked into the universal mind," he said, reading Alex's. "Bound, wound, jacked and fucked. And let me tell ya, Alex, my friend, it's a bitch."

Jacob dropped to the ground, folded like Brandon Lee getting shot, dropped in a slow motion move, so slow, like a puppet's strings frayed by a cello bow, until he sat on the littered sidewalk, legs straight out in front of him. He bawled, in a shameless excursion into self-pity, dropped his head into his hands and sobbed, great hulking aching sobs which threatened to rip his insides out, crack his ribs and tear all the muscles in his shoulders so that, in fact, he could be just human once more.

Alex saw one physical body couldn't hold all this, recognized the anguish of being too aware, wallowing in his own sense of futility and he sank to the ground as well, wondering what on this chaotic planet they could do.

CHAPTER ELEVEN — WINE AND DRUMS

The trio of cellists played dark brown songs, adaptations of Metallica and the Cure. Ellen Stockton looked around her gallery with the pleasure of the sensualist. "Just the setting I wanted to create," she said, "threat and doom and the anger of the gods."

She slipped three one hundred dollar bills into the upturned hat that passed as a tip jar. "Just to get it started." She winked. "Keep it dark and threatening, now won't you, luvs?" She requested of the band, who looked more like rock stars than symphony musicians.

With a broad toothy smile, the fifty-five year old entrepreneur turned to greet the next rush of people coming in, uttering slightly condescending remarks as many of her naysayers crowded through the doors. She made her way through those who had overflowed into the hallway, greeting city political enemies, art collectors, artists, and envious gallery owners from all over the area. Already she knew the show was a success, thanks to the crowds, perhaps the largest she'd witnessed this year at an opening. *Yes*, she thought to herself, *I made a good choice.* Setting the conventional cultural scene of Greenville on its ear was one of her favorite pastimes. This show would uphold her reputation in that quarter.

Ellen grabbed a glass of Riesling as a waiter walked by and handed it to Dora Marston, arts editor for the Courier Citizen. "So glad you could make it, Dora. Here, why don't I see if I can sneak you in? Isn't this wonderful?" The zealous and highly confident curator said looking Dora straight in the eye, challenging her. "I knew Lily Hampton's work would draw a crowd. Now, would you like to see what they're all buzzing about?" She asked as she peeled away the layers of gauze drapery which hung in solemn columns in front of the entrance.

"The Cavern, my dear," she said, her arm indicating the way, gatekeeper to a sight she hoped would be spoken of for months to come, especially when Dora's review was released. This was just the kind of controversial show Dora loved to write about.

Ellen surveyed the room again with her highly critical eye, knowing the elitist tastes of her clientele. She had a high standard for her shows. Everything must be perfect.

The banquet tables shimmered with the reflection of many candles on Dupioni silk imported from India. "The autumn effect" she'd demanded from the caterers. "I want it to be fit as an altar to Hades." The caterers had looked at her, the question in their eyes never making it to their lips. They raised their eyebrows to each other as if to say, *just another weirdo art opening.* Then they hustled to refill platters.

In obvious contrast, Lily was a wreck. Once again she watched the entrance hoping for the impossible… Alex. When Ellen approached her with another glass of wine, Lily accepted, knowing she shouldn't, wanting to be clear, but she was unable to stop her hands from shaking. She wished she could hide in the stockroom.

"Calm down," Ellen said. "It's not like you're on trial or anything."

"I feel as if I am." Lily felt as if something might snap. Her confidence had fled hours ago and her restraint was not far behind.

"Picasso," Ellen said, punctuating his name with a stern finger in Lily's face, "was accused of aiding in the theft of the *Mona Lisa* from the Louvre. Artists are supposed to lead dangerous lives." She patted Lily on the arm.

"And Picasso also broke down sobbing in front of the judge at the enquiry." Lily turned to Ellen with a grim smile on her face.

"*Touché.* That he did." Ellen winked. "There's my girl, liven up. But it all was a rather dramatic event, wasn't it? "In fact," she added, scanning the room again, like a junkie looking for the dealer, " if there isn't some sort of scene here tonight, I'll be thoroughly disappointed."

"So, now you want to up the pressure?" Lily's eyebrows went up.

"Yes, indeed," Ellen said. "I always want to be in charge of the next storm on the horizon; one step ahead of everyone else and too loud and dangerous to be ignored. The reason I chose you for this show was to get the exact reaction we're getting." Ellen wore a smug grin on her face. "I want the works in my gallery to wake people up. My patrons should walk away disturbed, unsettled, hopefully with a neatly wrapped canvas under their arm. If they want comfy paintings, they can go to a print shop and buy overpriced Thomas Kincaids. Art should change people's perspective, challenge their assumptions, make them think."

"When I'm in the studio, I feel the same way," Lily admitted. "But now that I'm here, being judged, I feel as if I have no skin, just raw nerve endings."

"Well, put them to good use in the studio tomorrow. We'll need some new paintings to replace the ones we sell tonight," Ellen said greedily, without a hint of compassion. "Now, let's see, who else hasn't met the artist?" Ellen walked away, flashing a wicked smile, obviously enjoying Lily's discomfort.

Lily leaned against the wall. She might just impale the next person who came up to her, pointing to one of her paintings and asking, "What does that mean?"

"Whatever you want," she'd said over and over, through clenched teeth.

But then the atmosphere shifted gears. People started arriving in waves. The doorway filled with the faces of people she hadn't seen in years. She couldn't help but smile. She hugged Clarke and Nina, who she hadn't seen since her stint as a teacher. Hugs were held longer than normal and, for once, she could pretend it was just a party, instead of stringing herself out on a wire, her skin hanging in shreds.

In the middle of the mayhem, a small hush slowed the ebb and flow of conversation, as if a director had stepped in and the camera was panning the gallery in half time. She knew she was hypersensitive, but it seemed the entire room full of people felt the surge of power which anticipated his appearance. She was sure of it.

In Jacob strode, dressed in full regalia, purple top hat, long, flowing black coat, and this time he wore a long purple/green silk scarf that floated as he walked. Even his accessories obey his need for drama, Lily thought. People stared at him in this get-up, as confused by his sunglasses with one lens removed as they were about Lily's paintings.

Lily wasn't sure whether to be relieved or upset. "Good *Guede*," she said under her breath. "What absolute audacity."

Once aware all eyes were on him, Jacob turned to his entourage: a tall black man dressed in the garb of the dessert, bearing a huge drum, followed by Jacob's twin brother, Perry, physically unlike Jacob, but who moved with the same slick grace. At the sight of him, Lily knew she was no longer in control of her evening. Events were rushing too fast. Memory upon memory crowded her mind, of them as teenagers in Haiti, in the temple, of rituals in New Orleans. She sucked in her breath and smiled at the arrogance of them both, scene stealers, drama mongers. The scenario continued and the onlookers leaned forward waiting to see who came next. A smaller white street-kid, blond dreadlocks to his waist, toting another big drum, and between them a buxom black-haired woman, dressed in black swirling skirts and veils adorned with hip belts and necklaces of coins that jangled with every step.

Lily hoped they didn't enact a ritual in the midst of the gallery. She sank back against the wall, drained her glass, but couldn't summon the courage to smile as Jacob flashed her an overenthusiastic grin implying, *"let's see what I can get away with."*

He waved his hand in a gesture suitable before a royal court and the drummers began playing. The oddly dressed woman, to the amazement and then encouragement of all, began moving through the crowd with long confident strides in a combination of Middle Eastern folk dance and American Tribal styles. Along with the crowd, Lily stood just as much in awe watching hip circles and graceful undulations deftly executed in time to the beat drummers were playing. Jacob looked at Lily with a sly look on his face, then whipped off his hat and dipped in a deep bow, brandishing his arm in the triple spiral salute rivaling that of Kashmir, in homage or in warning, she couldn't tell. His scarf dragged the floor as if to say, *deeper than this, I shall take you.*

"For m'lady," he said dramatically. "A gift from the East." And with that he stepped aside and the dancer took full stage in the midst of the gallery, twirling and parting the crowd as she moved through the viewers, her skirts fanning out in a huge rapacious circle, eating up the air, her uncensored sensuous moves heating the night.

A Beledi, Lily thought. *Curse him, he knows me too well.*

It had been years but the music brought it back...another place, another time, when she danced to this very tune, with Perry as a drummer among many, instead of the Tarique tribal drummers she remembered from Morocco, gathered around a huge fire upon the shore of a lake beneath a sky of lapis lazuli. And one young man, a very young Jacob, piled wood on the fire to make the blaze so high it seemed to torch the cobalt sky.

On that night she'd danced to this *Beledi*, the tassels at her hips swinging slowly, the veil twirling about her in a play of hide and seek. That night changed her whole life.

How could he do this? But she was already hypnotized and the beat took her away as he knew it would and soon she was dancing, too, the old moves on the tip of her muscles as if she had never stopped dancing. There in her embroidered silk cocktail dress, not the garb of the desert, she danced anyway, heady on wine and drums.

She forgot it all then, Alex and Jacob and her nerves and even her friends. She only felt the beat as it raced her own heartbeat and the luxurious sensation of muscles creating art with lines as fluid as any she would ever be able to paint. She was lost in the moment, as she was when she painted, At odd moments she would see the people milling about, some with surprised looks on their faces, some put off, and then those who soon joined her, grabbing a spare drum or dancing alongside her.

She was flushed when she stopped, and embarrassed. But her friends were delighted with the spontaneity of loosing their facades as well. Even though some of the more dowdy patrons left, some were still gathered in the gallery, chatting in small groups.

Ellen flashed a conspiratorial smile to Jacob, then, raising her eyebrows, indicated Dora in the corner scribbling away in a notebook.

Lily wore her smile a moment too long. In seconds the façade returned. In her world, she knew, nothing was given without a sacrifice. She wondered if she was willing to pay the price.

CHAPTER TWELVE — DEBRIEFING

After the show, Lily lit a single candle and curled up on the sofa. She pulled herself into a ball. *How had all come to this?* She'd made a mistake, perhaps an irreversible one.

Before he'd left, this would have been the time when she and Alex would do a debriefing and analyze the results of the show: what worked, what didn't? How to make it better next time? They would laugh at the overheard comments or speak affectionately of old friends they hadn't seen in a while. But instead, she'd spent much of the night looking at the door, hoping Alex would walk through and surprise her, as if he'd remembered the date, realized how important it was to her. She'd encouraged him to leave, even as she'd wanted him to stay.

Those nights six months ago seemed years past. She'd let him down after he'd supported her, but now she felt let down. Had she always been so caught up in her own ambitions? Did she help him at all during his time of doubts and transition? Now he was gone and she realized how much she'd leaned on him, when all the time she felt him draining her. How could any couple maintain a balance when both people were still just half people, half alive?

Keys turned in the door. Jake walked in.

"Commiserating or recuperating?" he asked her. He said it if it were a joke, but she knew differently. He took off his coat and threw it on the chair along with his hat. "It was a good show." He sat on the edge of the couch.

"It was a disaster."

"What did you expect, praise and adoration?" His tone was severe. "You can't get in someone's face in this town, not the way you did. You can't disturb their nice safe worlds and locked-down psyches and expect them to thank you for it."

"Tell the truth and be crucified," she recited.

"You did your job. You tried to wake them up. And the ones who were ready, they'll be altered. The others aren't worth worrying about. You can only offer a signpost. *Blue pill or red pill.* You're not meant to know if you made a difference."

"I drank too much and looked like an idiot."

"What? How can you think that?" Jacob was genuine this time. She knew it. "You danced beautifully. You gave the Greenville art scene, the intelligentsia, the critics, and the literati a night they'll never forget."

"I never should have danced."

"And Ishtar never should have been born to beckon us all to our deep selves. You think this was all about art? All about educating a city built on the balance of their bank accounts? These idiots will never figure it out. Only art will outlive and out-value them all."

He bent over. Dark dreads obscured his face, as he slowly removed his boots, still caked with the mud of New Orleans. He turned to her, the glint of one black eye glaring at her, something lizard-like, reptilian in the wetness of it. "We have to keep at it, no matter the cost to ourselves. The sleepers must awaken." He removed his boots, wormed his way in behind her. She leaned back into him, surprised at how natural it felt after all this time.

He drew close to her and whispered in her ear. "You are Ishtar, Persephone, Hecate." He made the skin on her back crawl. "You're skilled in Middle Eastern dance for a reason. Any tool we have to alter their perceptions, any skill we summon to shift, we must use it, weapon or a wand, to alert, teach them how to rip the veil of Maya. You're smothered here. You've forgotten who you are. You've a responsibility. It's about time you faced it."

"You know, when I was a little girl," she said, "at the all-girl Catholic schools they taught us God could see you every minute everywhere. He could see if you did something bad, but he was also always there to protect you."

"But one day…," Jake said in a sing-song voice, as if he was telling a fairy tale.

"I found out he wasn't there to protect me. God as an absentee landlord, like in *The Devil's Advocate*; or an abandoning father."

"And then…," Jake continued as if he already knew the story, "the little girl found out that wasn't true as well."

Lily nodded. "And now come to find out the gods are just like everybody else…only there when you need something."

"Bingo," he whispered.

"Well, what is it this time?" She demanded.

"As you've guessed, you must wait, while our Hecate down-under holds the torch for our victim…I mean hero. *When the levee beaks, there ain't no place to go-o-o-o,*" Jacob sang a Robert Plant imitation.

"So I'm back to hanging by the wrists, is it? Seems to me you have quite a sadistic attitude about this whole affair."

He smiled recalling one of her most disturbing charcoals. "Have you forgotten, Lily, it's your sister who has put you in this position, not I. Don't threaten the messenger —he may not return with word of your release."

Then he put his arm protectively around her and held her. "Seven years is a long time," he said.

She didn't answer, assaulted by doubts, too many memories, too many struggles. "Do you remember one time years ago you confessed you were in love with innocence?"

"Rings a bell, my tormentor," he said.

"Well, you can't learn it back by osmosis. It's not as simple as transferring money by writing a check. It's a one-off," she warned.

"So, how does it feel to vanquish the vanquisher?"

"What was that you said about waking people up?"

He didn't answer but buried his head in her back, wormed his hand under her side to cup one breast, as if it were a handhold and she the only cliff-face he'd ever learned to cling to.

"Innocence. And now that's why you've fallen in love with Alex, too...that day at the ritual," she realized as she turned their comfortable tourniquet.

"Not unexpected," he said pulling her so close she couldn't breathe, only feel his breath on her neck.

"Nothing is the way I expected," she said quietly.

"Is Persephone having doubts?"

"If I am, are you to be my Orpheus?"

"Perhaps, or Bacchus...," he traced the line of her cheek, "to lead you to pleasurable diversions." He tilted her head so he could see her eyes. "Or shall I revert back to your favorite, *Thanatos*? Shall we dance that danger dance again?"

He held her eyes for a long time, longer than was comfortable, searching for answers she couldn't provide. Then he closed his, breaking the game, and sang. *"Love is not lost, but it's nailed to my cross and crucified all I've held onto,"*

She recognized the lines from a song by 10 Years.

She was exhausted and curled up, trying not to sleep but needing it. Jacob, jealous of even sleep, leaned into her. His whisper, at just the right decibel, as if testing her theory of sound, circled through the whorls of her ear and sprinted up her spine. *"Remember me."*

When she woke up, he was gone. A spring of rosemary was left on her pillow.

CHAPTER THIRTEEN — THE CALL OF THE PIT

Alex found himself at Bad Jacqui's again. He was hoping to see Mavis. For some reason it comforted him and, as usual, he was on the lookout for word of when Jake might return.

When he entered the dark room, it was, once again empty. *Good, maybe Mavis and I can talk.*

He claimed the same table, hoping to establish himself as a regular. Maybe it was time he learned the menu and didn't just order the first dish which came to mind. He looked up at the shuffle of feet on the gritty floor and peered through the dim interior, lit only by striations of light from between the shutters. He couldn't hide the shock on his face. Not Mavis, but an older, tough-looking brunette stared at him.

"How can I help you?" She demanded as if were a home invader, not a patron. She held a glass of water in her hand.

"Uh…is Mavis here today?" He looked around the bar.

"Naw, it's her day off. She's cleaning up her studio," the waitress didn't place the water on the table.

"Studio?" He asked. For some odd reason he'd assumed Mavis was always here.

"Well, how do you know Mavis but not know she's an artist?" The waitress didn't bother to disguise her disgust.

An artist, Alex thought, ashamed at his narcissism. He'd never thought about her life…how she lived in this mess. It had never occurred to him to ask. He felt like an inconsiderate idiot. The waitress obviously thought so, too.

"No, I didn't know she was an artist. I just got here a few weeks ago. I know Jake," he said, feeling even lamer than before.

"What are you…construction worker, electrician, EMS?" The woman interrogated him, shifting her weight from one foot to the other, like an antsy prize-fighter. The water glass in her hand could have been a weapon for the look on her face, all stern eyes and severe haircut.

"No, actually, I'm an anthropologist," was all he could think to say.

"What, are you down here to study the local inhabitants and the new cultural pastime? You like watching us hauling our lives to the gutter? Is that what you're studying, Mr. Research Anthropologist?"

"No, umm, I mean no. I was studying voudou culture before all this happened, before Katrina. I just got caught in the middle," he stammered.

"Look, I don't have to serve anybody I don't wanna in my joint, ya know." She plucked the menu out of his hands and tucked it under her arm. "And I'm not sure I wanna serve somebody down here snooping around about sociological this or anthropological that when they got two strong shoulders and two good hands. Instead of sitting here drinking my liquor, why don't you haul your ass down to Mavis' place and help her salvage what little she has left. That's the kinda hands-on work you sissies need to be doin' to know what's happened to a culture like nowhere else in the world. Ya know? The one that almost got wiped out? Did you ever think you could do more for a species by saving it than by writing about it?"

Bad Jacqui—he assumed this was Bad Jacqui—let the sarcasm drip thick as the whiskey he was craving. But everything she said was right. He'd been so caught up in his own obsessions he'd never considered what Mavis went through during Katrina. He realized he'd been using the poor girl, maybe using this whole town, this whole situation to get what he thought was the secret story. He felt like some sleazy reporter from the National Inquirer.

"You know, you're right," he said, hanging his head. Deciding against it, he looked her straight in the eye. "I've been a real jerk. There's no excuse. I don't blame you for not wanting to serve me. I deserve everything you said. Do you think Mavis would really accept my help?"

"That poor girl would appreciate it." Jacqui sat down, raked her hands through her hair. "She's been through a lot. We all have. This is an entire town full of zombies trying to make some sense of it all. Mavis sat in her attic for three days, all alone, sweltering. Luckily she's been poor for so long she's a hoarder, ya know? Had lots of canned food in the house. But she was too stubborn to leave, which I think in the long run was a blessing, because those who found a way out may never get back. And she loves it here. She'd suffocate anywhere else." Jacqui had tears in her eyes.

Alex didn't know what to say.

"If you go help that girl, I'll let you back in here." She pulled out a business card and scribbled on the back of it, then slid it across the table. "This is her address, Jefferson Parish. It's not too hard to find."

CHAPTER FOURTEEN — THE NETHERWORLD

As Alex navigated the debris-cluttered sidewalks, the army of refrigerators, the sludge and mire, he recalled something his favorite professor had once told him.

"Be prepared, as an anthropologist you will encounter things bigger and more absurd than you've ever imagined existed on this earth. You'll meet powers stronger than any explainable force. You'll be tempted, challenged, possibly destroyed. You'll meet the gods, angels, and devils who will surely take you to hell. It's part of your job. Don't flinch or worry, just know that many have gone before you looking for the answers."

Surely he was now in Hell. Nothing he'd ever seen in movies, on TV, or read about prepared him for this. The Catholic flames of Hell were clean and purging compared to this slow rot, this slow death. Nuclear radiation was quicker, Pompeii's ash cleaner, an earthquake neater.

The devils had certainly come here, opened a fissure in the bowl of the earth and poured all the toxins man had devised on one city, one example. Noah had it good compared to these people. Horror writers couldn't imagine such a mix of gore and disgust. It looked as if the gods had abandoned this stretch of earth, this once rich bottom land, and allowed all of man's sins to be visited on these poor people.

He thought about the houses further on, in the Ninth Ward. Here it was November, two months later and 6,600 people were reported missing, one thousand of them children. People would come home after all this time away. They'd find their grandmothers, brothers, nieces, and nephews dead and rotting in their destroyed houses.

His feet kicked up brown dust as he walked. Every house was ravaged by the wind and waters. Garish red Xs scrawled by the searchers informed the rescue and retrieval workers what the next procedure would be. The top portion showing the date the house was searched, the left the abbreviation of the search team, the right if there were answers to yells or knockings. The bottom was the grim total: the number of dead or alive. Of all the bizarre signs, the row of red marks were so much like the red *vevers*, but told a different tale, enforcing the feeling of desolation.

The mountains of goods at the roadside only enhanced the hopelessness.

People's entire lives, books with their pages desecrated, a baby's Christening gown soiled, chairs and couches that reeked of chemicals and gasoline and damp, children's toys, shoes, sewing machines, Dell computers, family photos, each had a story to tell. But was anyone strong enough to listen?

Alex felt as if he were witness to the end of the world, which, for many, it was. He didn't know how Mavis could walk home through this every day and not want to slit her wrists.

All the grass was covered in muck, all the bushes stripped away, or were browning out, huddled against twisted fences and mangled wrought iron. The magnolias were dying, many trees had been uprooted and lay at awkward angles to the earth, as if unwilling to fall and die in the muck. In weird sarcastic contrast, like a bad joke, all the crepe myrtles were blooming, a garish, Mardi Gras pink…a retort…a closed fist in his gut that said, yeah, it's horrible, but it's not all dead, not yet.

When he found her house, he saw Mavis pulling huge canvases out through the crooked doorway. The whole house tilted like a Bourbon Street drunk. However, the pile in front of her house was different from the others on the street…canvas after canvas covered with oil slicks, who knew what chemicals. Streaks of color showed through, glimpses into lost worlds.

***

She noticed him looking into the front room. Guitars, Peavey and Marshall amps were strewn among the wreckage.

"Clay's stuff. He…er…was my boyfriend," she explained as she nodded to the jumble of instruments, amps, and wires. "He told me to do what I wanted with it. He didn't have much, just his musical equipment, but I don't have the heart to throw it out. She hung her head and spoke quietly. "He says he's not coming back. He's on tour in Europe and said he can't bear to see New Orleans like this. He said there's nothing to come back to. He's gonna take the insurance money and start over somewhere else." She looked as if she might cry, but instead turned on her heel and went into what he guessed was her studio.

Alex didn't know what to say.

She yanked more canvas off the walls. Each wore the telltale stripe halfway up, the bathtub ring circling everything in this cursed place. She laid the painting on the table, grabbed a box cutter, and harshly sliced the stiff fabric off the frame. Then with a deft hand skilled from practice, slit the painting down the middle over the watermark.

"Maybe I can do it over if I have this half to go by," she said, as she rolled it up and tossed in into a plastic tub.

"What can I do to help?" He asked, not knowing where to start. He wanted to reach out and touch her shoulder, but was afraid one gesture could collapse the will power she'd summoned to tackle such work.

For hours they dragged furniture, easels, and books to the curb. They swept up tube after tube of oil paint into an old wheelbarrow and dumped them all on the pile. She stacked canvases higher than her head.

"If it wouldn't pollute the whole place, I'd just burn them all." She tossed another one on the heap. "Have a true sacrifice, instead of just letting them rot on the curb." She looked at him for a moment, the red hair spiking in its own corona, her eyes backlit by held in tears. "My life in the gutter; I guess my mom was right all along."

She turned and headed back up the rickety stairs. Her shoulders were dejected, but she kept moving. "I just keep putting one foot in front of the other." She picked up a hammer and pried a piece sheetrock off the wall. "That's the only way I get through each day. I put one foot in front of the other."

After they'd gutted one wall, he grabbed her hands. "Come on, let's get cleaned up. I'm starving and I need you to show me someplace we can go grab something to eat, have a drink, take a break. I don't know about you, but I'm exhausted."

He could see it in her eyes: the exhaustion, the despair creeping in at the edges, the desperate look in her eyes, the grim set of her mouth. She looked off-kilter, almost broken like a doll dragged around by a three year old. As if she'd just fall apart, limbs separating from torso if he held her too hard.

She looked at him, a long dark look, anger bubbling, as if he'd interrupted something in which he had no business meddling. Just as quickly, her look altered, her eyes shifted to the side, like a spooked animal. It was just a glint, lightening quick...fear, terror. Her shoulders sagged and she said in a small voice, "Yeah, I am tired. I guess there's always tomorrow."

He could see she wanted it done, finished, that part of her life erased: Clay and her studio and the droppings of Katrina. But he knew she couldn't go on. She'd drop if she kept it up like this. She was running on raw nervous energy. She'd just collapse if she didn't rest.

"A break will do us some good." He led her upstairs so she could change. "You'll see. It will give us a fresh perspective on things. A change of pace. That's what we need. Let's go someplace different. Not Bad Jacqui's, but someplace else, just for a couple of hours."

"Okay, maybe you're right," she said.

He didn't know why he felt the freedom, but he followed her up the stairs. What he saw stopped him short to the point he took a step backward. While most of the room was normal in sharp contrast to the chaos down below, the walls were not normal. Every inch was covered with painted vignettes: a storyboard of anguish, a tale of terror. She'd painted what she saw during Katrina. His stomach jolted at the stark images painted in vivid reds and blacks and purples. Wind battered a shotgun house; one house was blown apart. Children's heads peaked just above the roofline as their mother struggled to grab a passing rowboat. Bodies floated while helicopters hovered high and distant. And then there were the images she'd painted of herself: her Mohawked head poking above the tiles of her roof, the axe in her dropped hand, standing in her attic exhausted and confused, the roof still intact; her sitting in the dark, cross-legged, one candle in front of her, a stack of letters on her knee; painting the walls looking like a frantic teacher at a blackboard in no man's land. The figures were distraught; the rough brushstrokes spoke of haste and fear and a great agitation.

"It was the only way I could stay here," she said simply, becoming suddenly demure. "Do you mind waiting downstairs while I get dressed?"

***

Walking through New Orleans at night unsettled Alex. He looked over to Mavis. She looked numb. The city which had boasted 1.2 million was now a town of 75,000. Many still had no electricity and whole sections were lost in the blackness. Here and there he'd spot one dot of brave light way off in the distance in some wasteland of a parish, a light from a generator, he guessed. Wind rushed up from the Gulf, and from the shadows he could hear the creak and yawn of timber like on a boat, except it was houses, all the crooked houses tilting on all the broken streets.

Mavis was jumpy and seemed to be reading his thoughts. "Eerie isn't it? Like we're the only people left on earth. Although, right now, New Orleans is safer than it has ever been. All the criminals bailed."

Once they were seated at a back table at Flannagan's, he noticed her relax to a small degree.

"How do you do it? How do you smile at people and wait on customers at Bad Jacqui's? I had no idea you were dealing with all of this," Alex asked her, viewing her as more than the punky girl he'd met the first week he was here.

"When I walk through that door, I just pretend Katrina never happened." She picked up a hunk of bread and broke it into pieces. "I pretend everything is the same and my life is normal—well, as normal as it was, because it feels normal there. That's how I stay sane. Jacqui helped me a lot. When I realized the water wasn't going down, I started to swim out." She looked at him a haunted look in her eyes.

"By yourself?" he asked, incredulous.

"Yeah, everyone was gone by then. I grabbed a plank of wood and took off. It was weird. The water was warm, warm as bath water, but it had the consistency of tomato soup. I mean, it had weight and I had to use pressure to swim against it. Plus it was colored with all these weird swirls in red and purple. On one hand, I wanted to make paint repeat those colors, on the other I was terrified as to what chemicals did make those colors." She stopped to take a long swig. "It's one thing to paint canvases with tubes that hold lead and arsenic; it's another to swim in it."

"How far did you have to go?" Alex asked.

"Luckily, not too far. Good thing, too, because I was really grossed out. Two guys on an airboat came by and picked me up and dropped me off on dry land so I could walk to Jacqui's. She and Doreen put me up in their place above the bar. Then the National Guard put up the barbed wire and roadblocks so I couldn't get back into my neighborhood for a few weeks."

"You were probably better off not going back right away." Alex offered.

"Yeah, maybe, I don't know. It actually feels pretty sane there. You just keep going, y'know? There are enough people here who believe we can make it through this. "

"But you have to get away, sometime." he said. "Already you're relaxing a bit, and once you can start painting again, won't that help?"

"I guess so. It's always been better than therapy. And it gives me a rush. " A small smile tugged at the edges of her mouth. "I lose all sense of time when I paint. I can stand for eight hours painting and not realize any time has gone by at all. I get lost, but it's a good lost."

"I sort of know what you mean," he said. "My wife back home, Lily, she's an artist, too. She's the same way. She goes to some trance place and makes it all happen."

"I can't wait until things are back to normal—well, the New Orleans' version of normal. When the tourists come back and people return home," she said wistfully. "I used to sell my paintings at Jackson Square. It's so easy in New Orleans. It's a real artist's town, like Paris. You apply for a license, and if you're early enough you get a spot in Jackson Square. And even though my stuff's not the usual jazz or Mardi Gras or architectural motifs, there's enough of the dark, funky people, like the Anne Rice and the Poppy Z. Brite fans who go for my gothic stuff. When I first started doing it, I felt weird. But I figured if Modigliani and his buddies could sell their stuff on the streets of Montparnasse, then I was in damn good company."

Now he wished Lily were here. He suddenly realized how much he missed her. The odd way she had of looking at things, her unique perspective and calming grace. "You'd like Lily if you met her," he said to Mavis. "You'd get along. Your work even favors each other's. You're very talented, from what I could see. You need to keep it up. Don't give up."

"Clay gave up."

"Yeah, he did. And one day, he'll be sorry." Alex said. "Now what about Jake? You two seem close. Did he abandon you, too?"

"Jake? No?" She looked shocked. "He's got a mission." She waved her arm. "Bigger than this, bigger than Katrina and New Orleans...certainly bigger than me." She turned her head away.

Alex wondered what their story was. Were they ex-lovers, or best friends? He had a hunch it was more complicated. The feeling of something not right nagged at him. Did Jake collect disciples, in a cult way? Because if that was the case, then Alex had to take a good long hard look at himself.

"Sometimes I think Jake does run away." Mavis rearranged the items on the table, the glasses, ashtray, the silverware and small plates. "The way he's always disappearing." Alex realized she was creating the red X he'd seen on all the houses. "Isn't that what you've done?" She asked him, a sly look on her face.

"Well, I came here to do research...but, um, yeah, in the end, I guess you're right. I did run away in one way or another." He fingered the rim of his glass, did not look up. He couldn't look at her anymore. "Maybe more than anyone can know."

After dinner, she took him to Z'otz and they listened to music by a band she really liked, A Particularly Vicious Rumor. It wasn't long before they stumbled out onto the street, needing to get home before the curfew. For a few hours, they forgot reality along with everyone else in the bar, all shell-shocked but, maybe, in slow recovery.

Alex looked around, amazed at the strength of these crazy people. Maybe it was this craziness which allowed them to prevail over the crud, the endless FEMA paperwork, the government lies, undependability of banks, mail, gasoline, food, electricity, water, patience, and futures.

He was ashamed of his own lack of coping, the way he was falling apart, too, what with the estrangement of Lily, the strangeness of Jake, and now the strange ties he felt to Mavis.

When he walked her home, they were silent, lost in their own thoughts. At her house, he lingered on the steps, not knowing the protocol for disasters or how to say something which could help. "Stay with me tonight," Mavis said slowly, her eyes hidden in the shadows of the club so he couldn't read her meaning.

A rivulet of emotions…fear, anxiety, hope, snaked up his spine, gave him a twinge in his side. He took a step back, not knowing what to do; ready to bolt, ready to say "yes."

"I can't. I have a wife, Lily. She's someone I really care about," he said softly, not wanting to hurt Mavis' feelings.

"No, no. You misunderstand. It's not like that." She put her face in her hands. "God, it's not that at all." She looked up at him, tears in her eyes. "It's just…I've felt so alone, so incredibly alone. Doreen and Jacqui have done all they can, but this is like nothing anyone could ever imagine. Your life is ripped out from underneath you and there's no manual, no roadmap about how to get back on track. When I'm not at the bar, all I can think about are those three days in the attic, not knowing if Clay was dead or alive, not knowing if I would make it. Not knowing what happened to all the people I love here."

"Okay," he said, without thinking. She looked ready to collapse at his feet, her fragility obvious now despite the punky façade.

"C'mon, you can finish telling me inside." As he led her over the threshold, he silently put Lily to the back of his mind, knowing she'd agree. They sat at Mavis's kitschy 60's plastic table. All of the upholstered furniture had already been hauled off.

"Okay, if you feel like it, but I don't want to pry." He pushed a coffee mug in her direction, the steam a tiny reminder of normalcy. "I'd really like to understand. What was it like here?"

She looked around the kitchen as if she didn't remember getting here. Then she wrapped her hands around the mug, took a sip and closed her eyes. "Well, the first night, it was very dark. You couldn't even see lights reflected off the water. There weren't any lights. I heard people yelling, kids crying, calling for their Mama. And then it would stop and I didn't know if they drowned or went to sleep or what. You just knew they were scared. I tried to sleep but I couldn't. It was wet and cold and the water kept coming higher. And I thought it was just us, just our neighborhood. I had no idea it was the whole city. I remember seeing the helicopters and watching them take people away." She stopped, looked off into the distance as if she were witnessing it all again. "At first, I tried to hack my way out of the roof, but I couldn't. I gave up. I hid. I was too afraid to leave. I have nothing else but here. This is where I've been my whole life. On the first couple nights when I'd hear people on their roofs, I knew I wasn't alone. We'd yell back at each other and tell them how many we were and how we were doing and who to tell they were alive when we got out.

"When I looked outside there were houses pulled off their foundations, out in the street, smashed against other houses. It looked worse than a war." Alex could hardly see her face through the gloom; only one side of it was lit by a candle on the nearby bar. Her forehead was creased with worry lines.

"But then, the third night everyone was gone and I was so alone and the helicopters and boats didn't come anymore and I thought I'd die alone, so utterly alone," she confessed, her eyes lost, her frantic voice raspy, the words catching in her throat. "I thought about my life and how no one had ever really known who I was. Not one person on this planet knew the real Mavis. Clay was on the road too much to learn about me, and the other guys I dated were too immature or too selfish. I never had much of a family to speak of. I didn't want to leave without anyone knowing who I was, that I had existed, that I spent time here— no matter how short. You've no idea what it's like to look at your imminent death and feel helpless to fix all the things you should have while you had time." She took a deep breath, leaned back in her chair so her face was now totally in shadows. She took a large gulp of the drink in front of her.

"That's when I started painting on the walls. Art's the only way I let anyone know me," she said, introspective now, more as if she were reminding herself. Then she looked up, directly at him, forcing him to look back. "I rip open my soul and pour it out in paint." Her voice was defiant. "But by the second or third day, I didn't have any more canvas, so I just started using the walls to tell about my last days here, what it was like, because I thought it was just us, just our neighborhood. I had no idea the water could take away a whole entire city."

"And I knew how the cavemen felt. Why they did the paintings, because each of us sees a unique portion of this planet, one little corner, one little neighborhood full of hopes and dreams and pains and losses. And I wanted someone to finally know me, to know I existed. I didn't want to die and just be forgotten, wiped away like a bug, as if my existence never mattered." Her face was fierce, challenging him to know her. She laid the task at his feet, not gently like a request to the anthropologist in him, but as human to human, desperate, grabbing him like a drowning person in quicksand struggling in the last desperate throes, desperate to be rescued.

He'd be inhuman if he didn't take it.

"I'll stay," he said quiet but sure. He'd meant to be reassuring, but he was firmer, a man with the insight of the desperate, as if she were still in danger of dying and this was a last chance to vindicate himself, maybe begin to make up for his litany of past insensitive failures.

"I died that night, you know," She said almost reading his mind. "I think I really did die of heartbreak."

He got up from his chair and took her hands to pull her slowly to her feet. She was lighter than he expected, barely there. He led her to the bed, peeled back the covers, and helped her lie down. He took off her slippers, covered her. When he lay down beside her, she was tense and shivering. He pulled her close beneath the blankets, like an adult comforting a freezing, frightened child, and held her close, her head beneath his chin on his chest, her shallow breaths tickling his shirt. Her hair smelled like lily-of-the-valley, a fresh, natural smell, the first good smell he'd experienced since he arrived in New Orleans. He wanted to thank her for this small gift in the midst of all that was brown and ugly.

"Sometimes I think I still might die," she half-whispered. "I don't know if I can do this anymore. It's too hard. It's all too horrible. There's nothing left to hang onto."

Everything he thought to say sounded like platitudes. Nothing hopeful could answer such tragedy. But he had to reply.

"You've got to keep trying," he said. "You've got to prove all the naysayers wrong. You've been given this gift, your art. You were kept alive to be the messenger. Only because you went through it can you let people know what happened here. The people of Pompeii didn't have a choice. They didn't have time. You had a choice and you decided to survive. You had a choice and you decided to stay. You have a way to touch people more than words," he said in a tone harsher than he'd ever used, even with the most rambunctious student.

He wondered how much of his words, his anger and fear, was really aimed at himself.

CHAPTER FIFTEEN — ICE AND THE BROKEN TREE

For weeks after the opening, Lily wondered if she could recover from the cyclic depression and malaise. It was her way, she knew, a huge outburst of creative activity, a big event or a finished piece, and then a residual depression that threatened her enthusiasm and confidence.

She knew work was the only way out. So, she painted; badly at first. She brushed on the last bit of phthalo blue mixed with a hint of lamp black. The night sky was a sharp contrast to the parchment colors of the muslin wrappings on her figure, half dancing, half flying, maybe falling. It was a figure released to the energy of its body, oblivious to its surroundings. She'd finally felt as if she'd captured the image from her mind after days of scraping off paint and redoing, often ruining what may have been her best attempt. But now she was relieved. This was better than all previous tries. The slightly obscure, hazy image, as if photographed through silk or smoke, perfectly conveyed the feelings she needed to release.

She heard a knocking, no, a banging on the studio door. Relentless, almost angry, she almost didn't answer it, but it was so insistent she knew the visitor wouldn't leave. She hoped it wasn't Jacob. She wasn't up to his games at the moment.

But before she could get reach the door, she realized the knocking was a strange banging at the transom window. The transom flung open in a loud scarping of metal on metal. A huge black flurry of air, wingsound and aggression flew into the room towards her. It was a black crow, huge and threatening. Without thinking, she picked up a wooden stick and began beating it. There was no time to plan, only impulse and reaction. *We have too much of this.*

There was a crack and a strange give from the bird beneath the tension of the stick. Immediately she came to her senses. Appalled at her actions, her hand slackened and the stick fell. She expected the crow to be dead, her violence had been so intense, but instead it hobbled at her feet, one wing broken. She kneeled to try and gather it up and instead of pecking at her, its eyes pleaded with her. In an instant thought, she realized it was a messenger. *Why would she try and kill the messenger?* And now, with the window open, it was cold. The bird thrashed about on the floor, and then a swell of noise from its wings, a harsh scratching, and then a thumping.

She put down the stick…again.

The thumping escalated, like drums or rolling and crashing thunder. Suddenly she was sitting up in her cot in the studio. The cold almost paralyzed her, but as she began to move, she realized she was soaked, sitting in a lake of water, colder than the Atlantic off the coast of Maine. She heard creaking, a strange harsh eruption of sound and a rain of ice crashed down on her. She ducked and covered her head as pieces larger than ice cubes fell through the roof along with pine needles and leaves, pine cones and brittle branches.

She jumped from the bed shocked to see a tree impaling her ceiling. She remembered now...the weather reports, storm warnings. *An ice storm. My gods, a tree through my roof.* In the same second, she remembered the dream of the crow ,and it was indeed a dream, but then the cold shock of the water and the crashing sound, beating sound, the three wicked looking curved branches. It must have been the hemlock which fell. The hemlock she and Alex sat under in the spring, her table set with candles. A meal of sweet and savory foods set upon linens she'd embroidered years ago. She reached for the light switch but the power was off. With every step, her bare feet crunched on ice particles, as painful as burning coals. Her nightgown was soaked through. She couldn't stop her shivering or her teeth from chattering.

After she crawled beneath a particular low hanging branch, she found her clothes and thanked the gods she'd changed near her easel. At least her jeans and sweatshirt were only damp and not soaked through.

As she dug beneath the table for her shoes, she heard another strange sound, a small squealing cry of pain. There was a candle on the table, but where the hell had she put the matches? Her hands were covered with the oil paints left over from last night and she cursed herself for not having paid attention to the weather reports, not gathering candles, matches, and batteries. *The last time I lit the candles, Jacob had been here. Where did I put them?* Finally she found them, but they were soaked through. The squealing continued.

As she plunged on hands and knees through the studio, crawling in the ice, ducking beneath branches, a new cascade of debris and sleet burst through the roof. She followed the sound and soon was close enough to see a small live thing flopping about on the floor. She scooped it up in her hands and realized it was a small bird, a Carolina wren. The poor thing was shaking. This was too much...the wren and the crow from her dream. She rocked on her heels until her back came to rest on the wall. What had happened to her world?

When had the edges from dream to reality blurred? How could they have crossed over like this? The dream... the cold, the crashing and now this...two birds. Was this another dream? If so, I need to wake up and wake up now. Even as she tried to wrap her brain around what was happening, the little bird in her hands became still. The pitiful noise ringing in her ears stopped as the wings fell open in a fan. It was then she felt the warmth…the warmth of tears falling down her face. *Alex, what have we done?*

It was then she realized it was the beginning of the end.

CHAPTER SIXTEEN — ESCAPE FROM ST. JOHN'S ISLAND

Jacob loathed the trip, this highway back to no way.

He was alone again, as he always was the weekend before Christmas. He hadn't been sure he'd make the trip this year, but in the end, he found a way, got the cash for gas, took a hiatus from gigs and the temple, and entered the current twilight zone...for a change, not one of his own making.

He must face the reverse of the linear, the backwards path to the time before time. But, as he'd learned from Lily, life was not always linear, and if he wanted to keep in touch with what was important, he needed to follow the cyclic path, the way of the moon and the spiral which led to the center.

After he'd turned off of Folly Island Road, he gritted his teeth and unclenched his knuckles from the steering wheel. His tires crunched over the seashell driveway to the ramshackle ranch where he'd partially grown up. The green asbestos siding had faded to blend into the trees, Spanish moss, and overgrown shrubs. He had to suck in his breath to stuff his memories.

His mother didn't greet him at the door. He never expected it on a Saturday. So he called out her name and entered bearing a small stack of gifts.

The Christmas tree was lying recumbent and contorted in its usual position of submission on the floor where the cats had mauled it. She'd decided never to get rid of the plastic monstrosity. She claimed it was the one thing that kept the cats off the table at turkey time, although he couldn't remember the last time anyone had cooked a turkey in this house. His mom had erected the tree every year as if it might be her last. She'd fret over the sadist's jigsaw puzzle of limp limbs and broken plastic ornaments. It wouldn't be five minutes before the tree lay battered and exhausted on the floor...the way Jacob always felt the minute he walked into the small room choked with too many nautical trinkets.

He found her as usual on a weekend; curled up in her bed, too bitter to change her life, slave to her depression and her nowhere job at the Department of Motor Vehicles. She never got over the fact that America wasn't the land of instant opportunity, where she'd be blessed once she stepped onto American shores. She'd literally believed the line about the streets paved with gold. Jacob still couldn't figure out why she stayed in St. John's Island, a place of bridges and oceans, just one more reminder of the day which tore everything apart.

He'd taken her to the emergency room once, demanding she see a shrink. But she refused, saying in her clipped Haitian accent how people shouldn't talk about their private lives, hang their wash out on the line for everyone else to see. After that he didn't try anymore.

"Mom, it's Jacob. It's two o'clock. You wanna go get turkey dinner?"

She stirred a little. He knew if he made a lot of noise getting the coffee going, she'd pull herself out of her stupor. She could always wake herself up for a meal which didn't consist of seafood. He set the steaming black coffee on the nightstand and settled in for a chapter or two while she stumbled around, took a shower, put on makeup.

"What kind of occult crap are you reading now?" She hissed as she came into the living room and pulled on her coat.

"More of the same, Mom."

"Well, you know you'll suffer for it," she said. "Just like your grandmother and your brother."

"Already am, Mom. Just trying to get it over with ahead of time." He closed the book. He'd learned a long time ago not go into discussion over Maman Simone, the only real Maman he felt he'd ever known. And his twin brother, Perry, that was a whole different argument. One of the more obvious triggers of her insanity, at least that's what she claimed, but the whole downward spiral of their family had actually been initiated long before.

"Stop sassing me back and let's get going before the place gets packed." The place she was talking about was on Folly's Island. Most of the island was shut down. But the Conch always stayed open, just for the year-rounders, the regulars who had nowhere to go. He'd rather take her someplace nicer in Charleston, but she hadn't gone near the port city since his dad had died, although it was less than ten minutes up the road. He'd made his peace with the place years ago. There wasn't a place near the ocean he couldn't love.

"Mom, it's never packed this week. There's no one in town. The roads are deserted," he reminded her. "Even the Christmas lights aren't turned on." So now he was back to his grin-and-bear-it self, as he listened to her go on about how she just wanted to be dead and why couldn't she have died first.

All through the meal she ate with urgency and the determination to devour every bite. She never asked about his life or what he did or how he fared. And he didn't volunteer information. This was a duty he would never forget or forgive. And so he looked out the window. She would curse his dad for spending his pay on everyone in the Sea Urchin Café. And then rage on about Faraday Steel and how they had killed her husband on that bridge, as if they had cut the rope themselves; how they gypped her out of the insurance money, saying her husband had been drinking on the job. He watched as she downed cup after cup of strong hot coffee and then finally, when she exhausted the litany of abuses, he drove her home. When they reached the house, she said she was too depressed for any more company and so he left, the presents unopened but his Christmas duty finally over and— halleluiah— the gods lived after all.

Now he was free to head to the fun family celebration...the always-crazy reunion with his Uncle Max.

CHAPTER SEVENTEEN — RESCUE AT THE CRAZY DOLPHIN

Jacob was on the road again. In fifty minutes at seventy miles per hour, he finally reached the point where he could release the ball of nails in his gut. He expelled a huge blast of air through his nostrils and his mouth when he reached the Crazy Dolphin, Highway 501. It was the first welcome and last vestige of the plastic life of Myrtle Beach, a popular stop for tacky tourist crap, and for a moment he was a bit nostalgic. The nostalgia was driven away by the memory of the rapid cycling of shame, refuge, and release. The emotions ravaged him, just as they did back then, as if the years had never passed. The day, years ago, at this same place, where his uncle had held no quarter; the place where he'd made one of the pivotal decisions of his life.

Jacob pulled into the parking lot and just sat in the car, remembering how, all those years ago, his Uncle had pulled into the Crazy Dolphin for road cokes and Doritos. Once he'd stopped the car on the noisy gravel, he had turned slowly to Jacob in the back seat.

"You sure you want to go with me? You sure you want to leave?" His uncle had asked. Jacob was thirteen. His uncle's small dark eyes had held neither compassion nor judgment— only an offering from one outsider to another.

And, at first, Jacob didn't want to go. He felt too guilty for leaving his mom. He didn't dare picture her reaction to his running off with the one person she thought of as a bigger loser than his dad. Uncle Max, the "procurement specialist," the guy who lived all over the world, just one step out of prison. But Jacob swallowed the lump in his throat, knowing he and his uncle had something in common now. He shook his head, *yes*. After the stunts he'd pulled, not just shoplifting, but plotting to blow up the high school, he knew it was juvenile detention or worse. He couldn't turn down a ticket out of the mess he'd made of his life. Maybe that was the first time he'd decided to run, instead of face the consequences.

"This is your one way ride to the future," Max had told him. "No going back, the last time I rescue you."

And Jacob figured if he didn't snatch it, he'd be lost.

And so they drove on the last fifteen minutes to his Uncle's home in Myrtle Beach. Later on he'd realize that he'd gauge everything by the fake sham and glitter of the tacky beach shops. He'd hike in the Blue Ridge Mountains and see a waterfall and think how it looked just like the waterfall lights back home— as if the mountains were an altered copy of the cheesy light box, not the other way around. Maybe that's why he loved New Orleans. It was a huge treasure chest of cheap trinkets and gaudy façades. And that was a world he already knew how to navigate. He'd learned it at Myrtle Beach as soon as he was tall enough to snatch a sand dollar off the counter at Surfside T-Shirts and run the gauntlet of tanned legs back to his hidey-hole behind his uncle's shop. It wasn't much to graduate from that to cigarettes and CDs on the Grand Strand to the wallets of drunken frat boys on Bourbon Street.

Now, he couldn't understand why anyone would live anywhere other than New Orleans, in all the bland cardboard towns where every street seemed chalked over with a pall of cigarette smoke.

His uncle taught him well. "The way of the wise," Max would say, mimicking Mr. Miyagi, and then he'd laugh his harsh smoker's laugh. "Wise-guy, that is. Don't ever let them see who you are, boyo. Show them what they want to see and the world will open up like an oyster at Casamento's."

CHAPTER EIGHTEEN — YULE

It was as if her studio were painted in lamp black, the most rebellious of all the pigments. It smeared every time she touched it, gathered everything into itself and altered to its own needs, the one paint which refused to behave, to be sublimated. The black diffused light, ate it, twisted it. The lack of light even sucked more darkness from the ceiling, gathered its implosive nature into her shivering hands—heavy as a real entity, converging, a reverse spotlight of black, a focus of nothingness. She sat with the non-weight of the dead bird in her cold hands.

Get up, get up. But her legs refused to react to that *purgatorio* of black, craving surrender in the escape of its nothingness.

Give up, give up, it seduced.

Okay, get a grip, she told herself, still not knowing what to do. Her mind couldn't shift from dream to reality. Was she dreaming still? But one index finger stroked a slight hint of ochre brown, as absent-mindedly as she'd stroke her cat and told her this was no dream. An insistent but barely audible inner voice warned her, *get up!* Her legs were numb, her finger tips tingling, a sort of welcome pain, the foreplay to the numbness she viewed as exit. She remembered how when she was first brought to Chateau Burgogne, during an unexpected snowfall, she'd gone outside to play. When she'd lain down in the feathersoft snow to make a snow angel, she didn't get up, just didn't get up. She'd watched the sun and thought, as she grew numb, she'd be able to fly, an angel with access to the other side of the sun, where her father went after he died.

But then the tingling had reminded her of how the Keeper of the Swans had found her. They'd carried her into the house. How painful it had been for each inch of her to wake up again. She hated them for weeks for finding her before she could fly.

Now, in the house, the adult in her submerged the child. She forced herself to get up. With reverence, she forced herself to lay the bird on the edge of her bed, a relatively dry edge, thinking all the while of the crow and her regrettable violence.

She found her boots and coat, wet but serviceable. With numb fingers, she pulled on the boots and looked around the studio. *All this,* she wondered...*did it really mean anything after all?* She banished the thought, gathering up her canvases to pile them high on top of the table, the file cabinet, anywhere she could find space away from the floor and the three crescent shaped holes in her roof.

Then without a look back she grabbed her car keys. Many of the streets were blocked with trees and power lines. After three U-turns, she headed towards the house she and had Alex had shared. The house she'd abandoned not two weeks after he left.

Ice still fell as she drove. The roads were crunchy with crusted packets of ice bits. Branches crashed in sparkled fervor, as if to rival the diamond waterfalls of South African jewelers. The windshield wipers struggled in vain against the deluge of falling debris, but the car, heater intact, kept plowing through the mess, as if its existence depended on it. She drove focusing her attention to navigate the unrecognizable war zone, once familiar streets. A transformer exploded in arcs of green light. Her right foot floored the gas, her heart pounding more with excitement than fear of the storm. What she feared the most was what she'd find in the house. Was her dream really a dream?

When she finally reached their street, she saw many branches were down and more still falling. The power was out, but it appeared tree limbs hadn't landed on the house. She left the car on the street, fearing the oak which hung over the driveway. She slipped on the ice, all the way to the door. She'd made this trip so many times, absent- mindedly, laden down with groceries. But now, every step took superhuman effort as her feet slid backwards down the gentle slope. The driveway contrived to keep her away. She felt as if she were on a conveyor belt in reverse; with each step the house receded into the mist. Twice she fell on the treacherous cement, once hard on her tailbone, jarring her teeth, knocking the wind out of her. She was refused access. Her rights had been revoked by nature itself.

She crawled the rest of the way, her back a knot of raging pain. She had the strange feeling that if she didn't make it now, she'd never walk into this house again.

She pulled herself up on the iron railing they'd had made for the house by Ryan Cunningham from New Orleans. She sucked in her breath, wondering what she'd find.

Even once inside, it didn't feel like their house. Cold seeped in through the sixty-year-old windows. Everything felt damp and slick. She considered going upstairs but her back probably couldn't take the stairs. She wondered what kind of damage you could do to a pelvic bone. She went to the closet where Alex kept the flashlight and matches and began the ritual of re-entry. In the light of the oil lamps, the familiar furniture took on a stature not its own. She remembered Alex packing, her watching in cool detachment, while he struggled with the decision.

The dream came back, too real, the look in the eyes of the crow she'd injured; the pain she had caused, too much to bear.

There was nothing; no Alex, no crow, only an open window and the lingering agitation and remorse, aftermath of a dream.

CHAPTER NINETEEN — RETURN TO MYRTLE BEACH

Each year, this stretch of the beach on King's Highway was empty. Everyone vacated the area, even the residents, for a location more conducive to the image of Christmas. The restaurants were closed, the shops abandoned, the roller coaster stationary, dark, devoid of its neon lights.

The coastal smells, the ocean and cotton candy, brought back a flood of memories. Back when he'd first moved in with his uncle, he thought living near the boardwalk was living the high life: crashing the Dunes, a crappy flophouse of a hotel where the bands kicked in the walls, tore out the air conditioners, and pulled up the carpets. His uncle didn't seem to notice Jacob's truancy while he made acquaintance with almost every drug, and the even better highs of being on stage at Dante's Inferno. The experiences there marked his transition from a creepy kid to a full-fledged freak.

Jacob tried to repress the flood of blurred pasts— all the lost days and wild nights— but he had to admit, he came by it honestly. The smell of stale beer was mixed with the fond memories of his father, uncle, and the rest of the Arcadians who bred their doomed dreams in the dark cave of the Breakers social club. There was no denying he loved the dankest dark places better than the sunny torture of the beach. Even though the sea was in his gut, summers were a curse, and he lived like a vampire for years before vampires were trendy. A little scrawny mulatto kid who could still blister under a South Carolina sun. So, he told himself he did it all for survival— bailed from the real world, because Myrtle Beach was as far away from any real world as you can get; nothing but plastic pleasure in a bottle of coconut oil and the ever-present sight of too-tanned ass cheeks and silicone tits. Was it any wonder his ideal woman was pale and flat-chested with dark circles beneath her eyes and illusive thighs hidden beneath long skirts?

The memories resurfaced: the way he rambled around all night, getting drunk when he was thirteen, trying to pretend his boardwalk shoplifting buddies were family, because he'd deserted his mom, or maybe she'd deserted him first, lost to her depression.

He wound his way to his uncle's ramshackle place away from the midway. The structure was originally a cement block garage, but his uncle had added on lean-tos and aluminum sheds as rooms, the boats and motor parts always taking precedence over living quarters.

The mixed blend of oil, fish and shrimp kicked Jacob fifteen years back, even more dramatically than the triggers of road signs and familiar landmarks of plastic dolphins and monster-sized miniature golf creatures. Perhaps Max hadn't been the best role model, his uncle's hero being Jean LaFitte. But he knew Max loved him. The proof was especially pronounced when he'd show off his most prized possession: a six-page pamphlet, sleeved in plastic like a comic book, but printed in the 1700's railing against Lafitte's blockade of Charleston. His uncle had paid $40.00 for it, a lot of money at that time. Books were as much his uncle's passions as boats.

When his uncle opened the door, dressed in his usual of black band T-shirt and Wrangler jeans, Jacob was greeted with the ever present aroma of cat piss and propane.

"Let's go grab a steak at Chuck's," his uncle offered, as soon as they'd dispensed with the pleasantries. The humble place was more welcoming than his mom's, even though it only boasted a chipped ceramic Christmas tree perched atop a beat up barrel. His uncle tried. Jacob noticed the sole wrapped present and knew it was for him. He could tell it was a book. Mac's presents were always books, but only something his uncle thought Jacob needed to read: philosophy, metaphysics, art. Jacob never could tell. The single package brought the fact home: Max had no one else now.

Jacob hoped Chuck's wouldn't be open. He hated the place. But even before they had gone halfway down the deserted sidewalk, he could see their open sign.

"This place is a curse." Jacob laughed, as they walked in. "I wished I'd burned it down, when I had the chance."

"Yeah, but it's still standing, despite your efforts," Max said, sliding into a booth. "If you'd succeed, I'd be visiting you in jail, instead of you coming to the Redneck Riviera."

The restaurant was a taxidermist's dream. A full grown bull greeted the guests, even more disgusting in a gaudy halo of twinkle lights. The bench seats were upholstered with cowhide and over every formica-topped table was suspended the head of some large animal with his mouth wide open and teeth exposed: boars, coyotes, even a rhino. The steaks, as if unfamiliar with their origins, were bad cuts full of gristle and fat. The side dishes were cooked to baby food stage. But it was family holiday tradition.

As they sat across the table sharing a pitcher of beer, Jacob noticed how much older his uncle looked. More cross-hair lines filled the creases around his eyes and the under eye pouches were deeper. But one thing pleased Jacob. The creases around Max's mouth were the opposite of his mother's. Hers went down, his went up. Jacob wondered how his father would look now, if he'd lived to this age. He was a year or two younger than Max, and when they were young they favored each other. Would his father have aged so rapidly? Would his mouth turn up or down?

"I'm going back to sea," Max didn't look up. He sliced his steak into tiny chunks, separating the gristle from the red meat. He might have looked like a redneck down at the shop, but he'd been taught, like everyone else who had privateered on a Laguerre ship, to eat with finesse and polished manners. On land Laguerre's seamen had to charm the gentry, often in foreign countries, where actions spoke louder than bad translations.

Jacob realized Max's meticulous attention to his meal was to avoid an obvious question. If Max was at sea, how would Jacob spend his future Christmas holidays? Neither of them ever said it out loud, but at Christmas, this time together meant a lot to both of them.

When Jacob didn't say anything, Max blundered on. "You know how long it's been? Not the old racket, I've been offered a berth on *der schwarze Geist.*"

"What the hell is that, a German U-boat?" Jacob finally re-entered the conversation, as he watched Max's hands.

"*The Black Ghost*, in English. It's a German ship, all right, but not a U-boat, nothing so mundane." Max looked up, his face animated as if Jacob had offered him a reprieve by not trying to talk him out of his plans. "It's a tall ship, and you know what's even cooler?"

"No, you tell me, Uncle Max." Jacob smiled. It was good to see Max so excited again, even though Jacob had mixed feelings regarding Max's age coupled with a return to the high seas, and, yeah, he had to admit it, the hole in his life Max's absence would carve when he left.

"The entire ship is made out of concrete!" Max leaned back in the booth and took a long swig of beer, slapping his glass down on the table in triumph. He looked pleased as all get out. He nodded his head and smirked. "So, finally, I've trumped a Magus, stumped a shaman!" Max leaned forward. He slid the pitcher over to Jacob. "You never did hear of a ship made out of concrete, did ya?"

Jacob was intrigued. Before him sat the old scallywag uncle once again. The man who could take almost anything on, as long as the first step started with *A*, as Max would say, "*A for adventure!*"

Max went on; knowing he'd hooked his nephew. "Old buddy of mine, he's got a berth on this tall ship, built in Germany the '40's, believe it or not, during the Second World War when steel was hard to come by. And she's a beauty, 100-footer or more, a little beat up, needs paint and some repairs, but they're putting her back to sea as one of those fancy training vessels for spoiled, fucked-up kids, you know, runaways from good upscale families who never had time for them, kids who went into drugs and shit trying to get attention. And they want tough old birds like me to train these kids, train them hard. A rich man's Outward Bound, sailing out of Portugal of all places, open sea, mostly port to port, but some hardcore training. It'll be one of the easiest gigs yet. After all, I cut my teeth on bringing you up, boyo! And I'm not gonna meet up with no *voudou* shamans on a ship like this." Max whipped out a photograph he'd printed from the web. It had been played with in Photoshop, but Jacob could still make out the original ship beneath the airbrushed photo manipulations. *The Black Ghost* boasted three masts; a schooner, not a brigantine. He was envious.

"Concrete?"

"Yeah, don't you remember when I told you all about them?" Max reminded him. "Guess you were still a kid then. They've been making concrete ships since the late 1800's, when steel wasn't available. And, yep, I know you want to ask how concrete ships float. Well, they do…and they don't rot and they could take cannonball fire. Now, the U-boats made in World War Two, that's a different story. Most of them were sunk by subs, most of them are at the bottom of the sea. But America, Germany, other countries built them, even the American army had concrete ships. This is one of the last ships of its kind still sailing. This is a later version, made with ferro-concrete built for merchant sailing near the end of the war. Germany didn't want to accept the realization that they were out of the international trading business until late in the game. Then *The Black Ghost* was docked. On the inside, she looks brand new, they tell me." Max raised an eyebrow in a question mark. "Why don't you join me, boyo? They need experienced seamen. Let you get back to a normal life."

"I wouldn't call working on a ghost ship a normal life, Uncle Max." Jacob said through a mouthful of mashed potatoes. "You won't be home for months."

"Yeah, I'm sorry, kid. We won't have Christmas like we do," Max confessed. "But this may be the last time, and the occasional odd job on a shrimp boat's not cuttin' it for this ramblin' man, ya know?"

"Yeah, I know." Jacob admitted. "But right now, I feel like I've got something else to do also."

"What, Jacob? I know you. A mission?" Max's eyes crinkled but Jacob couldn't tell if it meant worry or amusement.

"I just haven't decided how yet." Jacob looked off into the distance. It was time to get back to work.

CHAPTER TWENTY — SHAMANS, MYSTICS AND WITCHES, OH MY

As Jacob drove the nearly deserted South Carolina highways away from the coast, miles of palmettos, reedy stalks and runty scrub bushes dotting the sandy flats, he exhaled a deep breath. Eventually the low country marshes and sandy shoulders morphed into red clay. The pines and maple of the South Carolina Piedmont flashed by, then shifted into the endless stretch of deforested roadside in Georgia, punctuated by the manic exclamation point of Atlanta, leading to the smell of smoke and the iron-clad windows of Birmingham. More endless highway, but soon armadillo road kill littered the roadside, replacing possum and raccoon. He was more than halfway there and couldn't help but think about Lily, the shotgun shuttered house where he'd dubbed her Cate, short for Hecate, and all the memories it sheltered.

In the wind whistling through the open window it was as if he could hear her voice, hushed and reverent, his mind conjuring distinct words which sent him back to their life in New Orleans years ago. A memory he'd forgotten, as if someone else had provided the cue, enjoying a cruel joke.

Behind their little shotgun house, he and Lily stood over the huge slab of rock which formed a table in the courtyard. The area was enclosed by overgrowth of camellia and jasmine. Here they'd explored the meaning of personal ritual. He'd come to it from a world where alcohol was god and life was one big gamble until all went black. She'd come to it from the opposite view, based upon a calendar cohesive with nature, an intuitive litany for gods and saints, solstices, and holy days.

The small things they did might have seemed silly to others, but she had a way of bringing the sacred to the mundane in counterpoint to his Mercurial methods of *dancin' and trancin'* to summon the power he knew stretched further than he could imagine.

He loved her serene offerings, turning the most insignificant things into items of magic and wonder. After gathering the herbs and woods of the season, the fruits of her hikes, persimmons and raspberries, she constructed simple pantheistic shrines to whichever gods she was most enamored with—or feared—at the moment. Lizards and rare tiny red spiders were left to run on the altar. Ishtar, Mary, Pluto, Hades, Saturnus, Athena— culture, religion, or system didn't matter.

It was all a counterbalance to his manic methods of dance and song; his frantic Dionysian Mercurius/Hermes need to force them to notice, to listen, perhaps obey. If Loki needed placating, he appeased him with his dervish methods of trance, possessed by energies he could never explain.

When it was time to draw upon the wisdom of the past, she paid homage to the old gods. She'd complete *Dies Le Muertos* paintings or create an altar for All Soul's Day. He required the active approach: a *voudou* dance of passion unleashed in physical movement or a complicated *vever* drawn to Baron Semedi, the *voudou* Lord of the Dead. He sought the high of the trance while she sought the depths the pit had to offer.

There were times he envied her quiet confidence. But at other times, her willingness to walk into the abyss frightened him. He would wake in the pre-dawn hours to find her gone. Off to consult Saturn and Hades, lost deep in the dark empty places, relishing the feeling of cold rock, obsidian, flint. He would hear the repetitive motions of rock on rock as unnamable things were placed in a marble basin and patiently ground to dust.

"We're reminding ourselves to re-remember, that's all," she said, standing up on her toes, moving his dreads aside and slipping her voice into the channels of his ear. Her whisper gave him a twitch in the side, raised the hair on the back of his neck.

Early in their relationship, in France where they met, where they wandered The Burgogne Vineyard, where'd she lived when they first met, she confessed Herne had lead Jacob to her. It had been a golden fall day, the leaves not yet fallen. They watched the gleaners picking the last of the grapes. It was too warm for fall, but the deep afternoon shadows hinted at winter. "Herne and the silver branch," she explained, "hemlock and hawthorn branches, bound together with white ribbons, decorated with silver charms, snake and crescent, cross and spiral, and many tiny bells twinkling, chiming in the firelight. That's how I brought you to me," she admitted. "Day after day, I added more silver bits, charms, things I found at the side of the road, not always real silver…but silver in sound. This tool uses the magic of sound." She'd given it a shake. The charms danced catching the sunlight, turning it silver. The tinkling had reminded him of goat bells at a great distance.

"Sound summons at a distance, whereas smell summons over time. You know how sometimes a smell hits you and suddenly rushes you back to a childhood kitchen, full of tastes and memories? Sound does that as well, although in our crazy world, we block it out. People who love music know it. But many of us choose not to hear. It makes life complicated as the sound crosses out of our three dimensions, even beyond four or five or six." She shook the branch again, grinning a challenge. "Do you hear it?"

"Of course," Jacob answered, lying back on the woven blanket on one elbow, watching her, happy to have met a girl as crazy as he was.

"Now this time go over that hill, where you can't see me, and listen," she pointed.

"I'm too comfortable," he said. "I like watching you."

"Perhaps it's time you stepped out of your comfort zone. Even as outlandish as you are, we each have our own boundaries. If you want to know me better, perhaps you might like to learn what my boundaries are," she taunted.

So he agreed. He'd walked over the hill and sat down. He resisted the attempt to watch her, but instead followed her directions and counted out in his head, his lips moving, one Mississippi, two Mississippi. Around the number thirteen he felt it, as opposed to hearing it. There was a physical sensation, a shiver. The type of feeling explained away by the old saying, *"someone just walked on my grave."* However, instead of a cold chill running amok on his body, he experienced a warm stream soothing him from the inside out, a sensation akin to cupping his hands around a cup of hot chicory coffee. He counted again as he walked back, just as a test. At eighteen he felt it again.

"Thirteen and eighteen," she'd yelled before he was within easy speaking distance. "Did you feel it?" As he'd walked towards her, he couldn't miss the smug look on her face and the strange light on her face, making her eyes liquid and changeable, as if lit from behind. He'd actually looked around— the light was so strange— to see where the reflection originated; from water, her mirror, even the wine bottle. But the stream and their nearby blanket were in shadow.

"I felt something. How did you do it? Is there a trick?" He looked at her strangely, not knowing what to believe.

"Why would I need to trick you? I already know how to make this sound. Perhaps you need to learn how to listen."

"But I didn't listen. I didn't hear anything. I felt something."

"Perhaps we don't listen with just our ears. And I didn't just ask 'hear' on the count of thirteen; I asked that you continue counting and walk towards me and that you'd 'hear' it again on the count of eighteen...just to prove my point." Her face was serious now, disturbing. It was no longer a game.

The experience unnerved him; he, of all people, who knew strange and mysterious energies were at large in the world. This was a magic he didn't know of. It was too personal, too powerful. He felt out of control. "But you didn't summon me in particular,. How could you have? You didn't know of my existence."

"No, I didn't. But whatever you want to call it, the universal mind of Jung, the random access cultural memory, the knowledge of angels, if we avoid using these tools for our egos, but rather for our higher selves, we find our requests are answered in ways beyond our expectations." She shook the branch again. This time the sound did send chills up his back.

"I summoned my next teacher," she explained. "That's who I asked for with this silver branch. But now it has become more personal, more connected to just you, your higher you."

"And so what type of magic is this, what system?" He asked, trying to relate it to his training and the influence of the *lwa* or the *legba*.

"There isn't any system, only the concepts we summon to make it easier for us to visualize, as they did in the past with the various mythologies and rituals. I believe it's an energy all around us. Quantum physics now proves it. Scientists are discovering a wide world of quantum events where Luke Skywalker's "force" is no longer fiction. But beyond anything else…whether reality or magical reality, it's what we make it. And that is very personal." Lily sat back down on the blanket and patted the spot beside her, as if sensing how much her words disturbed him. He thought of the "magic" as out there…the realm of the *lwa* and he was just a vessel.

"Are you saying we each have a choice in how we use this so-called 'force'?"

"Of course." She looked shocked. "Don't you believe in free will?"

He shook his head, looking at the ground. He didn't know. He liked action, not ruminating on things he couldn't control, such as how Baron Semedi would use his body. Her idea that it was personal made him uncomfortable.

After their talk, he tried to learn to let himself go, allow his ego to be washed away as the energies flooded through him, transmuted and enlarged. Lily had been right. The strength of it grew and those who could sense such things found him. They reinforced it and demanded it. But he had difficulty in keeping his ego out of the way. To him it was all combined. The more he attempted to give up control, the more uncontrollable he became.

She retreated for guidance. Her path was marked by a descent, a call to isolation and an escape from the raging chaos he could fling around him in a bouquet of whips. Yet she became the anchor holding him to the center of all things, sacrificing herself in the process. He watched her descent, as she looked back from a place without light, breath, or sound. He knew no way of reaching her there.

Sometimes he'd look into her eyes and see the void looking back. She'd look into his and see the light of trickery and the wild excitement of willful mayhem. He coiled the energy; she sublimated it. Like two magnetic poles once drawn to each other through un-seeable sparks, they now repelled each other. The coiled jack-in-the-box spring in his gut sent him off to unknown futures while she burrowed into the universal past.

As he drove through Mississippi and then into Louisiana, he struggled to replace the memories in that hidden box he'd carved in his heart years ago. He needed to be in the here and now when he reached his destination. He knew he was getting close. A blue heron told him so, as it flew too low, a slow motion exit from a more secretive marsh. It dipped its wings, coiled its S-snaked neck and assessed him with one eye. Jacob sang over and over, "This is necessary. This is necessary," thanking Tool for the mantra he needed in order to follow through on what he had to do.

CHAPTER TWENTY-ONE — THE INVITATION

Jan 12th, 2006, 11:00 a.m. CST, George W. Bush, President of the United States of America, met with small business owners at a Round Table Discussion at the New Orleans Metropolitan Convention and Visitors Center to discuss the impact of Hurricane Katrina. Members of Congress and community leaders were present, including Ray Nagin, Mayor of New Orleans, who was positioned to the left of the President.

Jacob, nattily dressed in a pale celery corduroy sports coat, his brown hair pulled back in a ponytail, sat in what he considered the cheap seats. Only sixteen people were invited to actually sit at the gathering for small business owners. Most of them were politicians. The real small business owners, from places like Mick's Barber Shop, The Magazine Street Bar and Launderette, Blast Records, Crunchy's Metal Fabricators, Bad Jacqui's, Wendy's Used Book Store, and Smitty's Po Boys were relegated to a realm of silence. *So much for group participation.*

Jacob nodded at some of his neighbors. They all nodded their approval. They didn't know how he got in, but they knew why he was there.

President Bush spoke, looking towards the front seats. "We've done a lot and there's a lot more to do, but there's a certain optimism and hope that's coming. I hope you feel that."

Jacob watched as Bush smiled his crooked smirk into the TV cameras. Jacob leaned over to Crunchy. "There's the got-ya-by-the-balls-again grin," Jacob whispered.

Crunchy looked at his friend, but just shrugged his shoulders.

As Bush continued, speaking of how the city of New Orleans was dramatically changed from his previous visit and he was here now to assess the damage, Jacob couldn't stop the running commentary in his head. Lies, *Wag the Dog* style, putting a positive spin on what was still an ongoing disaster.

Jacob examined the faces of his friends, even as he attempted to stifle his outrage bubbling just beneath the surface. It looked as if the small business owners wondered why they'd come.

"One way to make sure that the private sector leads the recovery for New Orleans," Bush said, mispronouncing New Orleans, "is to make sure the tax laws encourage investment. And I want to thank the members of Congress for passing the GO Zone legislation which encourages investment. And that will be helpful for the folks here."

"Yeah, right," Jacob said, loud enough for those close by to hear him. "As if they're going to invest in broken buildings and lost businesses.

What are you talking about? Casinos buying up the land? Investments aren't gonna help the small businesses." Jacob turned noisily towards his friend. "You got anybody wanting to invest in your record company, Mick?"

"Cool it, Jake, let him talk. Maybe somethin' will come of it." Mick sunk down in his seat.

"Don't hold your breath," Jacob said.

"We're aware of the issues here," The President continued. "I'm looking forward to hearing more from you all about how we can continue to work together." Secret Servicemen closed in around him.

"You're oblivious," Jacob heckled.

The President stood to leave.

"What? Are you leaving?" Jacob asked in shock. In moments he was out of his chair. Mick laid a hand on his arm.

Jacob shook it off. "But he hasn't let you talk! He hasn't heard anyone yet." Jacob positioned himself to move. He turned, just as a Secret Service man grabbed his arm, slapping a firm hand on his shoulder.

"Just quiet down, kid," The Secret Service man said. "You don't want us to escort you out, do you?"

Bush nodded in the direction of the Mayor of New Orleans. Nagin's face was blank. "I know you're beginning to welcome citizens from all around the country here to New Orleans," Bush droned on. "And for folks around the country who are looking for a great place to have a convention, or a great place to visit, I'd suggest coming here to the great..."

"But this is bullshit," Jacob yelled. "You can't be talking about the same city. Just take a minute and listen to the stories of these hard-working people." The Secret Service man dragged Jacob down the aisle. "They're American citizens." Jacob yelled, trying to fling the guy off.

Instead, he found a tougher grip applied to his other arm. In an instant, Jacob's arms were pinched back. "Let me go. I'm the voice of the people. I'm just trying to get him to listen to the real folks. The people here who are suffering. "

"Look, we don't want any trouble," a deep threat of a voice said from behind him. "You don't want any trouble." The suits dragged Jacob toward the doors. "Call your Congressman," suggested the shorter man. "Take it from me, that's your best bet. Otherwise you're wasting your breath."

"But...," Jacob struggled, but they were in control.

"Look, kid," the taller, much broader man said, "We know it's been rough. But save yourself a lot of heartache. You don't want to get arrested. You don't want us questioning you for two hours, digging up every scrap of information from your past, making your life more of a hell than it already is. Walk away while you still can."

Mick and Crunchy showed up on the sidewalk. "Come on, man, let him go." Mick said. "We'll take him home." Jacob snarled at Mick, gave one last pissed-off shrug. The guards let him go and pushed him towards his friends.

"C'mon, Jake, chill out. You can't win with these guys." Mick led Jacob up the street.

"Yeah," Crunchy said, patting Jacob on the back, prodding him. "There's still a lot we can do our own way. Let's go to Bad Jacqui's. We'll come up with a plan over a beer. "

"Okay, okay, I'll go." Jacob turned and stared at the Secret Service men. "But you know it's all a scam— a huge scam— and someone's gonna pay one day," he yelled.

Crunchy and Mick took the place of the Secret Service guards, flanking each side to escort Jacob to the Bad Jacqui's, hoping he wouldn't bolt.

***

It was three or four a.m., Jacob figured, after he'd left the bar, bitter bile still bubbling in his throat, rage coursing to his fingertips. He never even finished his beer. As he drove the deserted darkened streets, he knew he had to attack the apathy head-on. He would purge the fouled air of New Orleans, offer up a message to those who felt betrayed.

An hour later, in a deserted parking lot dockside, somewhere in the industrial, rotted-out Westwego area of New Orleans, Jacob launched the first phase of vindication in time with the first rays of another desperate day in the most desperate city in America. "Okay, Spin Doctor, let's see how you like this version of the recovered New Orleans," he hissed as he methodically loaded the school bus down with his precious cargo.

CHAPTER TWENTY-TWO — THE ACCOMPLICE

Thursday, January 12th 9:45, p.m., Jacob and Alex stood in the center of the two-thirds of New Orleans that was still in black…the drowned out parishes, the lost city.

A million questions raced through Alex's head, but the look on Jacob's face deterred him. He'd seen Jacob in a limited number of odd situations, but Alex knew Jacob was illusive when it came to his emotions. Tonight, they flittered across his angular face as fast as cloud shadows racing over the devastated streets. For the moment, right now he wore a look of absolute power and determination, a Bruce Willis, Anthony Hopkins, Clint Eastwood, not-to-be-fucked-with look.

"The City that Care Forgot," Jacob quoted.

"Mavis said the locals hate that title," Alex said, wondering where the hell they were headed in the pitch black. He'd assumed this midnight jaunt was another ritual Jacob would allow him to witness, but they were alone. There wasn't a soul, not a sound, just a hollow darkness, rife with the smells of leftover lives, slowly decaying, and an obstacle course of unrecognizable household goods.

"Yeah, she's right. A moniker like that can create a future. They should have butchered the guy who came up with it," Jacob yelled back over his shoulder to Alex, who was lagging behind, ragged breaths interfering with his progress, shards of metal and wood hampering every step.

"I can't forgive the people who've already forgotten," Jacob didn't even sound winded. "The very people who used to love to visit New Orleans, do they give a shit now?"

He kicked something aside. Alex automatically jumped back as it rolled in his direction. Could have been anything from a ball to a bucket or a head, for all he could tell.

"They came here to party," Jacob added. "They looked for solace in the bosom of its courtyards and excitement in the bottom of a plastic hurricane glass, but now they forget all about it." Jacob stopped and turned to Alex, his eyes blazing even in the dim light.

"They've all forgotten it! Damn this "use it/lose it" society!" Jacob continued in his rant. "Now this city, this most unique city, is nothing but a living purgatory, a limbo worse than any conceived by the Catholics. Wait for FEMA, wait for Bush, and wait for your countrymen. Wait and wait and wait until the government buries you in legal papers higher than the debris dumps so they can bulldoze your neighborhoods and build their casinos and turn everything into plastic: plastic facades, plastic physiques and faces, plastic money. Forget a house of wax, let's make New Orleans plastic; then we don't have to fix the levees 'cause plastic is indestructible. The hell with *those* people. There's more where they came from." Jacob stopped to turn and stare at Alex. "That's how they think, those elitist bastards, those smug in their consumer-based lives. How *dare* they?" Alex took a step back, hardly recognizing Jacob. His lips were pulled back in a snarl and his eyes burned holes in the night, the inflamed eyes of the self-righteous.

***

Thursday, 10:00 p.m., while President Bush relaxed on Air Force One on his way back to Washington, Jacob led Alex through the rubble of France Road in the Lower Ninth Ward.

"Where are we going?" Alex tried to hide his labored breathing. "How can you even see the way?" Yet again, he wondered what the hell he was doing here. There was something eerily off key. No ritual, no people, just what appeared to be one madman.

"I'm fortunate; I've got good night vision," Jacob said in a voice which sounded perfectly normal, as if traipsing around in the dark of a destroyed city was an everyday passtime.

When Alex's eyes finally adjusted to the dark, he saw the landscape was as desolate as the set of the movie *Road Warrior*, and as bizarre as *Elmo in Grouchland*. He had thought them both funny at the time.

Jacob stopped and rummaged around in what was left of a small shed.

"Here's my baby," he said in a strange sing-song voice. "You ready to get to work? We've got a big job tonight."

"What's going on?" Alex finally had to know.

"Well, Bush has invited the rest of the country to visit New Orleans as if Katrina had never happened. I have more important guests in mind," Jacob said. "'We're gonna build a fire so big the gods will remember us again.'"

Alex recognized a bad imitation of Michael Wincott as the character Top Dollar in *The Crow*. The phrase made him shudder as he remembered what came next.

Jacob rolled a metal barrel out from inside the shed towards a huge pile of debris. All of this stuff was part of people's homes, people's pasts, Alex thought, looking up at the pile higher than a skyscraper: wallboard, furniture, washers, dryers, refrigerators.

"One hundred feet high, people will say tomorrow. This pile is a hundred feet high." Jacob turned a spigot on the drum. Alex heard liquid flowing like a stream. The smell of gasoline curled in his nostrils. Jacob inhaled deeply.

"What the hell are you doing?" Alex yelled at him. "We can't do this."

"*We,* as in the third person, plural, is incorrect." Jacob said in the tone of Alex's fourth grade English teacher. "It is *I,* first person singular. *I'm* doing this. I only need you here as witness." Jacob's voice was so solemn Alex's mind went blank, white. He couldn't even think of the right words to discourage him.

"Think of this as a random act of kindness," Jacob said, his voice thick as syrup, sweet as Grand Marnier.

Alex jumped up and down, agitated but too afraid to confront Jacob physically. "This is an act of vandalism, an act of destruction," he yelled. "This is an act against a city already destroyed." Alex tried to block Jake's way, as he fiddled with something in his jacket, but the man was deft and easily side-stepped him.

"Think of the Tower in the Tarot," Jacob's voice was cold and flat. "It all looks like destruction and calamity, when in reality the damage was already done. The self-destruct course was set in motion years, often decades, before. But there must be a cleanup, a symbolic purging of the old to make way for the new."

Jacob removed a long stick-like object from an inside pocket of his coat. Alex heard a plastic "CLICK CLICK." He recognized the object as one of those cheesy barbecue lighters from Wal-Mart. His split-brain, emotionally detached mind chastised Jacob for using the least shaman-like tool he could find. The flame lit up Jacob's face. He wore the pained expression of a parent ready to punish a child, but then that expression shifted to the assured calm of someone arriving at the end of a long road.

It didn't take long for the flames to take hold.

CHAPTER TWENTY-THREE — THE MASK

Lily, now fully aware of her surroundings, and her situation, took off her soaked clothes and rummaged through the closet. Damn, she thought, she'd already moved all of her clothes out of the house. She ended up pulling on a grey ribbed sweater she'd loved to see Alex wear, but the only pants close to fitting were his old sweatpants. They might not be fashionable, but they'd work fine if she rolled up the cuffs. She was oddly comforted by the sweater and grateful it made her feel closer to Alex. After the phone calls to utility companies and tree surgeons, she finally hunkered down to heat canned soup over the small fire she built in the fireplace. It wasn't until afterwards that she decided to call Alex.

He wasn't at his hotel room, in fact. had checked out, the front desk clerk said. Perhaps he'd call her tonight and let her know what was up.

She couldn't deter the feeling that the house no longer looked like hers. The ice storm, her physical and emotional distance, the return of Jake, and now the absence of Alex all contrived to alter the way she looked at it. It no longer felt like home but more like a museum – or was it a mausoleum, she wondered. Her eyes scanned the collection of South American and African tribal masks above the fireplace and fell on one in particular. The Guatemalan mask. In the briefest moment, it brought back an army of memories. The first time she'd met Alex had been on one of her yard sale Saturdays in a funky neighborhood in a city short on funk. As she approached the yard, the strangest man left the house, walked by and spoke to her in French. He wore a skintight diving suit. A rubber bathing cap covered a bald knobby head. Thick goggles covered his eyes. He looked exactly like the diver from one of her favorite movies, *The Big Blue*, although there were no Greek or Arctic oceans nearby. In fact, the nearest ocean was four hours away. But then the oddly-dressed man seated himself on a paper-thin Titanium bicycle and sped away down the hill. She must have transposed the images one on top of one another, like she sometimes did in her paintings. It was going to be a surrealistic day.

As she stepped into the yard, the bizarre atmosphere continued. Among the items on scattered tables were Mexican gold leaf icons, medieval statuary, and a pink mask. It was of Hispanic or Latin origin, she gathered, and had the same type of Day of the Dead skeletons she loved to paint. As she reached to pick it up a long slender hand shot out of nowhere and snatched it from beneath her hand.

"Oh, that was mine," she said quickly.

"Nine-tenths of the law," said a young man. His flashing blue eyes challenged her to confront him. His arms were full of masks.

"Well, um, I was looking at it," she replied lamely. "I paint Mexican Day of the Dead images."

"Well, first of all, it's not Mexican, it's Guatemalan. And, secondly, I seem to have it in my hands, not you." He was condescending and sarcastic. She could have slapped him.

"But how can you be so greedy?" She could feel the hackles on the back of her neck go up. She knew her face was flushed red with a sudden anger, way out of proportion to the event. "How dare you talk to me like that? You have all those others!" she yelled at him, incredulous.

"I was here first. I've been here for at least half an hour." He looked over to the woman selling the items as if for affirmation.

The woman stepped out from behind her table. "But you do have all those others," the woman said, not taking his side at all. "Can't you spare just one for this nice woman?"

"But it's exactly what I need for my class," he said, discounting her suggestion.

"Then why didn't you pick it up first?" Lily asked belligerent, feeling as if she could beat him down with the aid of her supporter.

"Well, my hands were full. I meant to get it," he said, as he was forced to juggle the masks. They seemed to take on life and began shifted in his overburdened arms. "It's so much more effective if I can show my students a variety of cultures." He almost dropped the one she wanted. His long hair fell over his face as he tried to get a grip on each fragile piece. Lily watched in smug humor as he stumbled about, trying to regain his balance. She had to restrain herself from laughing out loud when he tripped over a basket of shells. The pink mask fell to the ground.

Lily picked it up and flashed a huge *now-its-mine* grin. "See, you can't even respect it. It's only papier-mâché and you've already dropped it. You could have broken it and then what good would it be?" She took a long look at the mask, wanting it even more as she saw the detailed work of the skeleton sitting on a man's face, its butt propped on the nose, the head turned to challenge any viewers.

"I have an idea," Lily said, looking up, trying to calm her voice. "Why don't you let me buy this one and I'll loan it to you for your class. You do have all those others to have and to hold," she laughed not caring about the lame pun.

The man looked abashed. "I guess I've been a bit greedy. I just had this image of them all laid out in my classroom."

"What do you teach?" She asked, still holding the mask, seeing him soften.

"Anthropology… at Whitten University," he said.

"Oh, now I see," she said. It was a small college, but exclusive with a reputation for brilliant professors and high standards. "Will you go along with my suggestion?" She said suddenly, wanting to wrap this all up.

"Yes, I guess that could work." He looked doubtful for a moment but then eyed the stash in his hands. "Um, how would we make arrangements? I'm teaching this part of the world now. Where do you live?"

"Well, actually my studio is not even five minutes away from here. I could show you where it is after we pay this very patient lady."

"Yes, I'm very sorry," he said to the woman hosting the yard sale. "I'm not usually this ill-mannered. I don't know what came over me."

Greed, Lily thought.

"That's fine," the yard sale proprietor said as she handed him a box. "Especially since it appears you've come to a workable solution."

In the freezing bedroom, Lily picked up the mask and wondered what Alex was doing at this moment in New Orleans. She wondered if he thought about her. Their phone calls had become less frequent and were brief when they did talk. Alex promised lengthy e-mails since the phones were still so sketchy. But that didn't happen. She knew nothing worked right in New Orleans now, but she still wondered if Alex was thankful for the lack of easy communication. Lily shivered and grabbed an old coat of Alex's, one he'd worn when she'd first met him, the younger Alex, more alive, full of zeal. She hadn't seen it in a long time. She'd hated him those first few moments, but once he'd arrived at her studio he seemed to be a different person, considerate, but with a keen inquisitiveness asking her probing questions about her work.

He'd touched everything, without permission, his long elegant hands feeling the textures. She remembered how he was back then, radical and edgy and fiercely intelligent. He was not the type of man she was usually attracted to. She'd always fallen for the dark men with deep eyes she could fall into, but there was something oddly appealing about Alex. He was slender and, with his long pewter-colored hair, seemed androgynous. He was unsettling, intriguing. His pale coloring gave him the aura of some Nordic ice being, some elemental. In features he was not the blatantly passionate type she usually lusted after. But the paleness set off his drive and the way his passion boiled beneath the surface: magical, elusive.

But somewhere along the line, over the years, the passion had died down, his drive had been stifled. She remembered how he'd paraded his agility when he hung the returned mask over a doorway in her studio in what amounted to a little ceremony.

Now, these last few years had almost broken him. He was hunched over, the bookworm taking hold. It had been a long time since she'd seen the lights in his eyes dance the way they had when he'd challenged her.

That first year, when they started dating, the fiery lights were in his eyes often. In late night conversations at Dougal McGuire's pub over a table loaded with empty Guinness bottles, where he participated in sarcastic exchanges and enjoyed the camaraderie of other fringe people: writers, poets, artists, musicians, scholars. They'd drink and argue until they were kicked out somewhere near dawn and be ready to fight the establishment another day. But lately something had changed – the struggle for tenure, a crisis in confidence, she didn't know what, but Alex had lost something in the ivory tower of academia. She hoped that he was finding it in New Orleans.

CHAPTER TWENTY-FOUR — TALL TALES AND LIFE STORIES AT THE CAFÉ DU MONDE

Mavis handed Jacob the January 14th *Times Picayune*. She nodded her head and flashed a huge smile. Alex sat numb beside Jacob, hardly noticing the way the other patrons at the Café Du Monde were looking at the trio who looked too weird for early morning, even in New Orleans.

Jacob circled the article in yellow highlighter. "Geez, is that all we get?" He asked, as he grabbed another beignet, downed it with a huge swallow of chicory coffee, then a swig of rum from a flask.

"It was on the NBC News last night," Mavis said, trying to sound hopeful. "Martin Savidge of the New Orleans Bureau talked about it. It was the headlining story."

"Yeah, I heard about it. Something about adding insult to injury," Jacob said in disgust. "A cliché and, in fact, all wrong. But that's the media for you. No originality, no truth. Make a ton of assumptions, go for the cheap drama, and the idiots continue to believe the idiot box."

Jacob handed Alex the newspaper. "Here, give it to me." Alex rubbed his bloodshot eyes and speed-read the piece, skimming over the incidentals.

"Katrina Debris Ignites in 9th Ward," Alex read aloud. "A huge trash fire that began late Thursday night in a "mountain of debris" in a Lower 9th Ward scrap yard continued to smolder Friday night, a fire official said."

"Just the details," Jacob demanded. "I'm not interested in what unnamed officials and anonymous sources have to say. Just the facts."

"Let me finish, will you?" Alex shook the paper and found his place. "Flames leapt feet into the air at 3500 France Road around 11:00 p.m." Alex peaked over the edge of the paper, raised his eyebrows. "You want numbers?"

"Numbers would be satisfactory." Jacob pulled out a small notebook. "Statistics…that's what we're after." The shaman turned fire-starter leaned back, and sat with his pen poised, like a secretary, except for the fact he propped his feet on a nearby chair.

"Okay," Alex continued, "One hundred foot flames. Pile of trash, four hundred by five hundred feet. Flames leapt one hundred feet in the air. And, thank the gods, not one injury was reported. "That would have been awful if someone had been hurt."

"I'm not going to further jeopardize the people of this city." Jacob flashed Alex a disgusted look. "I did my research. I knew no one would be around."

"All right, all right. Are you interested in the rest of it or not?" Alex didn't wait for an answer. "Now, where was I?" He hunted for where he'd left off. "Okay, here it is. They had to put the fire out with cranes and a fireboat, *The Gen. Roy S. Kelley*, using water from the Industrial Canal. Now, that was resourceful of them."

Jacob finished his notes, slapped the book shut and abruptly left the table. He returned with a second Café Au Lait and a new batch of beignets. "Okay, that's over and done with. Now, onto other things. So, Alex, my boy, you ready for a little background?" Jacob stuffed his mouth and spoke through a confectioner's sugar smirk. "Get out your notebook. There'll be a test later." Jacob took a huge gulp. "What ya wanna know?"

"Umm, let's see," Alex was taken off guard but could see it wouldn't help to attempt to finish the previous conversation. He opted to pretend it never happened, even though Alex realized he might be learning the negative aspects of Jacob's tutelage. "How'd you become a shaman?"

"First off, you don't become a shaman, you just are or you aren't. You may not know it for a long time, something or someone has to remind you, to wake you up." Jacob pronounced casually as if they discussed common facts.

"Okay," Alex bit. How'd that happen?"

"Simone. Simone Villieux, she did it."

"And who was she?" Alex continued to pump.

"My grandmother," Jacob began. He leaned back in his chair, stretched his long legs, and sipped his coffee. Alex took it as a good sign and finally relaxed as he listened to Jacob.

"When I was thirteen," the shaman said, "I sort of ran away, was snatched from home in St. John's Island to go live with my uncle in Myrtle Beach. He was a small time thief and rum runner. Later we moved to New Orleans. For a while we lived a wild, reckless life. He taught me good thieving practices. I sometimes went to school, but spent most of my time picking pockets, shoplifting, maybe scoring the odd ring here and there from the antique shops on Royal Street. And then he took me back to reunite with my grandmother, Maman Simone, as everyone called her, in Haiti."

"Haiti?" Alex asked, grabbing a second beignet.

"Yeah. After that my uncle ran small boats back and forth to Haiti with illegal stuff. I guess he was a fence-combined-boat-captain. When Maman Simone saw how much influence Uncle Max had on me, she convinced him to leave the small ships and go work with her dad. Simone has a rich mulatto daddy who ran legal liquor and lots of it, and he was in need of a good seaman. And that was the one thing my uncle was better at than thievery. She cleaned Uncle Max up, dried him out, and he became captain of a pretty big transport ship. I, by association, became a mate. So all of a sudden my wild days onshore turned into hard days at sea and I learned the business."

"This sounds like a yarn to me," Alex said winking at Mavis.

"Just wait, it gets better," Jacob said, in an Eddie Izzard imitation.

"But I wasn't at sea all the time because Simone, who really ran the show by now, said I needed an education. She pulled me off board and I went to live with her in Haiti, while Uncle Max stayed onboard. That's where I began my education, and where I hooked up with my twin brother, Perry, again. We'd been separated since we were little kids."

Alex looked at Mavis. "Have you ever met Jacob's twin brother? The thought's kind of scary, two Jacob's running around."

"Yeah, I know Perry. Great guy," she winked at Jacob. "But they're nothing alike, believe me. They're as different as twin brothers can be."

"That's for sure, Mavis," Jacob said. "And good thing. Perry's a much better man than me. A saint, really. I guess I'm the sinner. You see, my mom met my dad and his brother, my Uncle Max, in New Orleans. They were in the Coast Guard out of Charleston, having grown up on St. John's Island, but they used to go to New Orleans if they had a long enough leave. We all lived for a short time in Haiti with Maman Simone while Dad was at sea, after his stint with the Coast Guard. Let's just say my mother wasn't capable of taking care of both my brother and I. So when Dad and Max decided to get jobs on land, we all moved back to South Carolina, except Perry. I don't know, we were two or three years old when we were separated. My mom took me with her and left my brother with Maman Simone. You'll probably get to meet Perry at some point. And you'll see we're twins all right, but not identical."

"What do they call it? Fraternal twins?" Alex asked. He didn't notice the look on Mavis' face.

"Yeah, but, you see, we're even out there for fraternal twins. My mom's mulatto but she looks black, and my dad was white, Arcadian, French from Canada. It seems it's rare, but it does happen, and when we were born, we were something for the newspapers, although in Haiti, you don't want it in the papers. I'm *quatrain* and I look more on the Caucasian side of mulatto and Perry looks very black, like our mom; other than that we look pretty much alike. But in Haiti, it's looked at as either a curse by the upper classes or as something so different, it's magical. My family had to protect my brother. Things were unsettled politically there at the time, well, as they are all the time, but more so. Simone's a *voudou* priestess in the *voudou* religion. They looked at Perry as being special so he was trained under Simone."

"Geez," Alex shook his head. "This sounds so bizarre, you wouldn't believe it if you'd read it in a book. I never heard about of bi-racial twins. I could see how in Haiti it would not be a good thing at all. Even if your mom didn't separate the two of you, the class structure there would have. But why did they have to protect Perry?"

"Well, that's Perry's business and not mine. That's his story to tell." Jacob stood up and stretched his back. Looked out to the where the streets were getting more crowded. "Okay, where was I?" He asked as he sat back down. "Oh, yeah, so Simone taught Perry from when he was very young. I didn't start training until I was sixteen or so, after I'd lived with Uncle Max for a while. At the *ounfo,* the temple, with her, I just took care of repairs and stuff at first, while Perry took part in the rituals. But then she started teaching me all about the *lwa,* that's the ancestors, and some of the gods. She taught me how to draw *vevers* and make herbal medicines and all about the rituals. And she figured out I was clairvoyant and so seriously started training me to become an initiate."

"But then you lived in France, too, right?" Mavis asked, as a waitress came over and refilled their cups with the steaming chicory *au lait.* She shook confectioner's sugar off the bill before adding chit marks to the total. "At least, I heard you mention it before," Mavis finished.

"Yeah, a couple years later, into the picture steps Simone's papa with his big bankroll. He says he's okay with me learning *voudou* but I also have to get a real education, so I get sent to this college in Paris to learn the import and export business."

"Wait a minute, Maman Simone's father sent you to school in Paris?" Alex asked incredulous.

"Yeah, mulattos are considered an elite class in Haiti. Maman Simone went to school in Paris, and was trained to go into the family business. But she rebelled against her dad. Not long after researching her country's history and its most prominent national religion, *Voudou,* she became a priestess and started her own temple in Port Au Prince. She didn't follow the lifestyle of the mulatto class. Look, in Haiti things are very complex. I was mulatto so I got special treatment, even as my mom lived in near-poverty in the U.S. She wasn't mulatto so she got skipped over by her grandfather. Simone tried to but she didn't have much. She lost most of it when she turned her back on all of that class stuff. I guess my grandfather thought he'd have a chance with me, since Simone had gone against him and I already knew stuff about shipping, at least the hands-on end. So you wanna hear more about Paris?" Jacob sounded a little ticked to have been interrupted.

"Yeah, go on, I'm just trying to understand." Alex motioned Jacob to continue.

"Well," Jacob took a deep breath, "this little college in Paris happened to be a weird place because kids from all over the world who couldn't speak French went there. So I hung out with kids from Germany and Norway studying architecture and kids from Lebanon and Israel studying finance and before you know it, I'm hanging out with the Vikings and the Arab Mafia and I do what any *voudou* aficionado does and I start borrowing their gods."

"One of the other anthropology professors in my department, a guy named Laney Deschenes, wrote a paper on the practice," Alex interceded, "and how it was as much a method for survival as anything else."

"Yeah, that's right. When the slaves were brought to Haiti from all different tribes in Africa and then deliberately separated, their entire culture was ripped from them. The French plantation owners tried to convert all the slaves to Catholicism and they just adopted the saints while at the same time they were housed with Africans from other tribes, and discussed each other's gods and their ancestors. Instead of god-bashing like most religions do, they said, hey, that guy is cool for healing this illness, can I borrow him and make an altar and see if he'll help me, too? Pretty soon they were adopting gods from everywhere, even from the Amerindians and the Spanish runaways who lived in hiding the mountains.

"Weren't the *verver* paintings from the Amerindians?" Mavis asked.

"That's right. They also borrowed the rattle the priest uses to invite the *lwa* to the ritual," Jacob added. "*Voudou* parishioners don't do *this my god's better than yours* deal. If they like someone's god, they learn all about him and, bingo, soon enough there he is on the altar. For example, Simone is a Reiki healer, a licensed professional counseling astrologer, has met the Dali Lama, has been on retreats with the Jesuits, has studied Jung and Joseph Campbell, and has her Masters in Social Work.

"You're kidding. The Dali Lama, a Masters in Social Work?" Alex asked, realizing that even with his research he'd held a narrow viewpoint on what *voudou* entailed.

"Yeah. Voudou is a polytheistic religion," Jacob said. "I ended up borrowing gods and methods that way, too, when I was in Paris with these kids from all over the world. I was just naturally fascinated with their religions, as well. I loved learning about it so much I transferred from import and export to comparative religion"

"How did you get from that to playing in a rock band?" Alex asked, not knowing whether to believe this stuff or not.

"I'll have to make a long story short." Jacob was thoroughly enjoying himself now. "When I was hanging out with the Arab Mafia, that's what we called them, they used to have these huge parties and these guys would start drumming and these girls would start dancing these Middle Eastern folk dances. Kind of like belly dancing in the moves but not in the costumes or suggestiveness."

""That's where he met Cate," Mavis piped in while Jacob took a breath.

The table went into a dead silence. Alex could have sworn the birds stopped chirping and the people around them stopped talking. Jake flung Mavis a look of such malice blended with horror that Alex felt as if Mavis would turn to salt or blow away in a stack of dust. He'd never seen anyone harbor such cruelty in a stare.

"Be quiet," Jacob said. His eyes were as dark as the sky last night before the fire. They were banked with the same amount of hidden fuel; a history larger than the piles of debris; kindling eager for conflagration, waiting, just waiting for the flame.

Mavis shrank into her chair, pulling her head into the collar of her blouse. "I'm sorry, Jacob," she said meekly.

Alex sat there stunned. The beignets turned into rocks in his gullet.

"Anyway," Jacob continued as if nothing had happened, "I started to learn how to drum because it was a cool way to meet chicks, and I found out I really loved it."

Alex balled his hand into a fist in his lap and battled with the urge to punch Jake in the face. He missed half of what Jake was saying.

"Hey, Alex," Jake shook his shoulder. "Are you listening? You want me to shut up?"

"No, no, go on," Alex said, un-tensing his hand. He didn't dare turn to look at Mavis. He felt like a heel but didn't have a clue what to do. He didn't want to hit Jacob, not really, but he didn't want to see Mavis mistreated, either. There must be a lot more to the story than he thought. After all, a guy has a right to his privacy. And obviously Jake was very private about his girlfriends. Alex waffled. *Maybe, something bad happened. Maybe I need to respect that.*

"At the same time," Jacob rattled on, "I was also hanging out with the Viking guys and they played death metal so they taught me how to lay down a beat to their music, too. I never really liked it and wasn't all that good, but you just had to be loud and fast. If I drank enough, I was. So I started drumming with these horrid college bands and we'd play a few parties here and there. One day our singer got sick so I took the mic and let a hanger-on drummer try out. It was a great gig and I was hooked. It took me back to my days in Myrtle Beach and when I hung out backstage at the rock bars. I loved being onstage." Jacob finished in a fake sing-song voice, trailing off like someone talking in a dream.

Alex had probably missed most of what the unpredictable jerk said in the last five minutes. He couldn't believe the guy's fluidity. How he could be malevolent one minute and turn the charm on the next. The psychological labels narcissistic, borderline, bi-polar, came to mind.

Mavis drew curlicue patterns in the confectionary sugar on the table, not looking up, barely breathing.

Jake sucked in his breath, as if he'd read Alex's mind. The arrogant rock star, not the shaman, wore his face in a hard knot, the story-teller vanished as if he'd fled down Decatur Street, as Alex wanted to do. Jake slowly slid his feet off the chair. He leaned over the table scattering white ceramic cups and sugar-laden napkins. "Hey, man," he snarled, his face very close to Alex's, his body half out of the chair, propped on his elbows, the white of his teeth inches from Alex's nose. "Hey, man, why didn't ya hit me?"

"What?" Alex pulled back.

"I saw you make a fist, back there, when I was yelling at Mavis." Jacob's voice was very low. "Why the fuck didn't you hit me?"

"I don't know," was all Alex could say. "I didn't know what to do. Things got so weird." Alex wanted to bolt. The rock in his stomach was turning to bile.

Jacob moved even closer. "I deserved it. I was an asshole, yelling at her like that. I deserved to be hit. I have no business acting like that to a good friend like Mavis."

"I wanted to hit you," Alex confessed. "But I don't know, maybe you had a reason. Maybe she was betraying a confidence or talking about stuff that's private, you know? I didn't know what the hell to do." Alex felt as if he were shriveling in his chair.

"Alex, you are a fucking coward," Jacob said leaning over the table, blocking the sky from Alex's view, invading his personal space. "You are too afraid to follow your impulses, but you're too curious to stop looking. Alex, you're a voyeur. And that's not a pretty thing to be." Jacob's eyes flashed anger, then remorse. "I'm sorry I mistook you for something else," he said quietly.

Jacob stood up, scraping the legs of the metal chair on the concrete in harsh symphony with the racket raging in Alex's mind. Jacob displayed a sly evil grin at the sound. Then his face became solemn, hurt. He turned and walked away from the table, away from the Café Du Monde, down Decatur Street, past Bella Luna restaurant and the Market into the *Vieux Carrè*. Alex watched until he could no longer see the battered top hat and threadbare coat swaying as the shaman walked. One of the most miraculous beings Alex had ever met had just turned his Doc Martin heel and abandoned him. Alex sunk his head into his hands.

CHAPTER TWENTY-FIVE — THE YAWN OF THE ABYSS AND SIGILS IN THE DUST

A week later, Alex was awakened as Mavis lifted the sheeting fabric they'd rigged as a tent to keep the mosquitoes out. He usually woke hours before her, soaked in sweat and scratching the newest bites. He didn't know how she could adapt so well. He'd get up and read Doug Cash and Chris Rose in the *Picayune Times*, brew the coffee, tidy the house and then go downstairs and launch the daily battle of Clorox against the evil villain, Mold. The whole time he did it, he wrote a comic with Cloroxman as the superhero in his head.

But this morning the coffee was already brewing. He was shocked and happily surprised to hear the shower running. Never again would he take that sound for granted. Finally, the water was running again. For nearly a week after he moved into Mavis' they had to take showers at Bad Jacqui's, eat off paper plates, flush the toilet with buckets of rainwater Mavis gathered in an old oil drum behind the house.

"What's up?" Alex asked as she exited the bathroom in a huge blue towel and puffs of steam.

"I've got to go find my friends," she said hurrying to the closet, wrapped in a terrycloth bathrobe. "Yay! The water's back on! It's a bit rusty but it works."

"What friends? Who?" He handed her a cup of coffee.

"My friends in the Ninth Ward. Lizzie and Creggie, they're friends of mine, they lived down there in a warehouse they'd turned into a loft and studio space." She said quietly to herself, "I wonder what happened to them. They came from South Carolina like you, but have lived in New Orleans a few years now. I've put it off long enough. It said in the paper yesterday that 3,200 people are missing and here it is, five months later. That's higher than the death toll of 9/11, which numbered about 2,700. We can't just ignore that. Did the country ignore the dead and missing count with 9/11? I don't think so. And besides Lizzie and Creggie, I have even more really good friends missing, regulars at Bad Jacqui's, some of Jacob friends, some people from the temple. They're still unaccounted for."

"But maybe they're holed up in Texas or Oklahoma or something," he said hopefully.

"No." She was adamant. "They're still on the missing list. I checked it yesterday on Jacqui's computer."

"Speaking of Jacob," Alex said Jacob's name for the first time since the incident at the Café Du Monde, "did you see the article on the fire in Westwego?"

"At the Budget Iron Works on Louisiana?" Mavis asked.

"Yeah." Alex rummaged through the two sets of clothes he found serviceable in this new territory. Half his clothes were useless. Khaki pants just didn't last long in the City of Sewage. "You think it was Jacob?"

"I'd bet a bottle of Jaeger on it." Mavis had already pulled on a VAST sweatshirt and duck boots. "He used to tell me stories about Bayou Signet and that whole wharf, docks and industrial area. Didn't the paper say warehouses storing boats were burned, too?"

"Yeah."

"Well, he had a vendetta against some boatmen down there, old story, slack dangerous sailors, thieves, too, if I remember correctly, slammed into their boat, almost drowned him and his Uncle Max." Mavis looked off in the distance.

"What's Jacob trying to prove?" Alex was shocked again at Jacob's behavior.

"I don't know. But with Jacob there's always a master plan." Mavis looked at Alex as if for the first time that morning.

A half an hour later, Alex was waiting for Mavis on the front step so they could leave. "What kind of get-up is that?" She asked laughing. Alex wore jeans, an old windbreaker, a pair of rubber warehouse gloves, and plastic bags duct-taped around his hiking boots. A surgical mask hung around his neck.

"This is my *go-with-Mavis-to-the-Ninth-Ward* look." Alex smiled. "What, it's not fashionable enough for you? Do I need some jewelry or something, an Armani scarf or Dior sunglasses?"

"No," Mavis said hugging him. "But I think an axe, shovel, and rake might come in handy. How do you feel about playing caveman?"

"Role-playing huh," Alex joked. "Now you've got me interested. You got a little French Maid outfit around here somewhere?"

"This is New Orleans, Alex." Mavis pushed him down the stairs and out the door. "Hold your wiener, now, southern boy. If, and I do mean if, that time ever comes, I can surely come up with something better than a French Maid outfit. This is, after all, the costume capital of the world."

As they walked through the broken streets, Alex looked around. Every day he saw it with new eyes. New shockwaves. "Remember after 911, how the bookstores were filled with books, photo essays, *Time* and *Newsweek* specials, all on 911 and the victims and the after effects?"

"Yeah? So what?" Mavis trudged along.

"Well, don't you think it weird, but the few books being written now on Katrina are buried under categories like Natural Science or whatever. Before I came down here I looked all over Barnes and Noble for books on the aftermath. They had two. And I had to ask to locate them. After 9/11 they had huge displays at the front of the store for months." Alex side-stepped a lopsided Lazy-boy.

"Well, around here they've heavily advertised books and book signings, like the one with all the refrigerator photos and the poems and stuff by local artists," Mavis said.

"Yeah, that's local, but what about national?" Alex asked. "Where the hell are the national campaigns? I'm sure the journalists and photojournalists have been down here. Is there a shutdown by the big media conglomerates, you know, like the way the photographer from CNN was threatened when he filmed dead bodies?"

"I don't know," Mavis said. "I guess living in it, I hadn't thought about it. I don't particularly want to read about it. I may in five, ten years from now, but at this point, it's all I can do to get from day to day."

"I know, I know," Alex said. "It's just that the rest of the country needs to know. I needed to know what I walked into. I could've come better prepared to help. I had no clue. What you see on the news can't give anyone the scope of it. The magnitude. They need statistics, numbers, how many homes destroyed, how many miles affected. Without those statistics, it's easy for other parts of the country to think they can send a check to the Red Cross and that should take care of it. They have no idea that the effect was comparable to five or ten nuclear bombs. This is a disaster Americans can't even imagine."

"Yeah, I don't think they can imagine it." Mavis turned to Alex. "You've no idea how much your help means to me." She turned and walked the narrow path which led through wrecked homes on one side and trash on the other. Here and there they'd see a lone person, usually a man, his family off in Texas or someplace else, working on trying to salvage what he could.

Alex wondered if talking off the top of his head was out of line. Mavis had obviously built up some kind of filter, letting only so much info in at a time in order to cope. The last thing he wanted to do was upset her fragile balance.

"Mavis, are you sure you're ready to do this? You sure you can handle it?" He hastened his step to keep up with her. She could eat up the mud-soaked pavement, even with her short legs.

"Yeah, Alex, I've got to. It's been five freakin' months. Someone's got to. We just can't let people be forgotten, abandoned."

Alex thought she might start crying. He wanted to hug her, but was afraid any small gesture would break her resolve. He had to respect her decision. At least try. The guilt could eat her up. Just as it would have if ruined him, if Bad Jacqui hadn't shown him how to help Mavis, although, unlike Mavis, he'd had nothing to lose.

He guessed they'd walked probably thirty minutes when the landscape changed. Instead of rows of houses lined up in states of disrepair and discoloration, they now reached an area where he couldn't detect where even the streets had once been. Piles of kindling, once houses, were stacked by the water. At some point, someone, the National Guard, the debris collectors, neighborhood cleanup teams, had erected makeshift barriers out of whatever they could find to keep people out of the danger zones. More and more he had to help Mavis climb over or around piles of debris. Most of the buildings were no longer standing, but instead tilted on their sides, the roofs intact but the walls collapsed. Garden sheds and garages were scattered like blocks or monopoly houses lying in the most outrageous places; one sat on a neighbor's roof, another was lodged far over their heads in a tree. Glass was everywhere, and piles of mud-caked vehicles were stacked on each other as if they were Hot Wheels abandoned by a bored kid. Some stood ass-end up against trees; others were squashed by telephone poles. Power lines were still strewn everywhere.

Alex felt as if this could have been his own neighborhood. "It's so weird," he said. "On TV, they make it sound like the neighborhoods that were destroyed were all poverty level. But this looks a lot like my neighborhood, an old mill village in Greenville, houses about sixty years old, not too small, well lived in, but not what we'd call shabby. Lily and I didn't think of ourselves as poor. Sure, an artist and a teacher don't make a helluva a lot of money, but we thought we were middle class." Alex found it difficult to look, but couldn't look away.

"Yeah, I haven't seen much TV." Mavis picked up a photo album, its cover boasting pink and purple daisies peeking through the smears. "This whole family might be dead." She tried to open it but the pages were stuck together. She shook her head and brought herself back to Alex as she dropped the book back on the ground. "What I have seen appears to be slanted," she said. "But that's New Orleans for you, at least the way it used to be. Maybe it will change now." Mavis stopped dead in her tracks. "My God, I hardly recognize this area. But this has to be around where Anton and Donna Signorelli lived. They owned the Sunrise Bakery. I loved their Italian cookies."

"I didn't know Italians lived down here." Alex said.

"Sure, there's a huge Italian population in New Orleans, but a lot moved to the suburbs. A lot of hard working people built their dreams here. I bet the bakery is gone, too. It's so weird what you take for granted. I came here dozens of times for supper but I can't remember what all the houses looked like. Just theirs. And I can't see it anywhere. I'm totally disoriented." She spun around in a circle trying to get her bearings.

"Well, let's see if we can see any house numbers and count off from there," Alex suggested. "What number was their house?"

"Nineteen. They were close to the top of the street."

"Let's see. Stay put a minute." Alex walked down the makeshift street. "Even numbers are always on the right, so they'd be on the left." *Or what was once left,* Alex thought. He peered at lots where all that remained were the front steps. He'd gone about a block before he found a house number. "Here's nine. We just have to count down eight more houses."

"They're not houses anymore," Mavis said. She looked as if all energy had drained from her.

"Here it is," Alex said, not knowing whether to sound hopeful or not. The white cottage was two-thirds demolished, not as bad as some of the lots which were just a pile of kindling, but its red roof had slid sideways, taking most of the house with it, while the porch stood intact. They could see through the entire house where portions of wall had been torn away. Ash-colored fabrics, insulation, and distorted Venetian blinds flapped from the openings. Muck-covered furnishings were unrecognizable.

Mavis stood still. Alex could see her trying not to cry. "Look," she said in a shaky voice. "Their car is gone. That must mean they evacuated."

"Do you want me to go check the house?" Alex was already climbing towards the porch. "There are no rescue worker symbols painted on the houses. They never made it to this neighborhood."

"Do you mind? It looks a little dangerous." Mavis followed.

"It's not bad," he yelled, "but you stay back. There's no sense both of us falling through the floor."

"Okay. Holler if you need help."

"It doesn't smell that bad here," Alex said hopefully, feeling morbid as he said it. "I don't see anyone. Here, let me get to the attic area."

Alex disappeared for a few minutes.

"Look out for nails," Mavis yelled, picking up a baby doll. It was filthy and undressed, but the face was only smudged in a few places, as if someone had come along and wiped its face. The eyes were glazed over and pitted, as if it was in shock from having seen too much. "I found one of Teresa's dolls. That's their three year old," Mavis said over the sound of boards being moved around.

"Nope." Alex emerged from a hollow on the back side. "There wasn't anybody here. They got out."

"Halleluiah," Mavis said in relief.

When Alex reached her, tears were running down her face. "Well, that's a good start. Where next?"

"Three houses down, Lizzie and Creggie."

More than two hours later, Alex grabbed Mavis latex covered hand. He had to convince her to go home. Her face looked sunken in and her eyes were red from holding back tears. She looked close to the breaking point. "That's four families safe," he said, steering her back the way they'd come. "I say it's time we head home and take a break. We've been almost the entire morning now. Don't you have to work tonight?"

"Just one more in this section? Please?" Mavis pleaded. "I know you're tired and I am, too, but it's not far from here, and then we'll have finished this neighborhood."

"Okay, if you insist. But then we head back."

They hadn't walked more than two blocks when Mavis stopped dead in front of him, forcing him to side-step a couple of trash cans and an upside down doghouse.

"Why are you stopping?" He wondered what the odd look on her face meant.

"Jacob's been here."

"What?" Alex didn't know what she was talking about.

"Jacob's been here. That's his *vever*." Mavis pointed to a spot on the sidewalk in front of a badly damaged house. "Oh, no, this is where Johnny and Louisa lived." She started crying.

"What's wrong?" Alex wanted to grab her and run. He had a bad feeling about the complications that could lie ahead.

"This is a *vever* to Baron Semedi," Mavis explained. "He guides those who've passed to the land of the dead, to *Ginen*."

When Alex reached her, he looked where she pointed. It was a complex pattern drawn out on the ground in red dirt or clay, a cross with small boxes around it and curlicue designs. Part of it was already obliterated.

"How can you tell what this is or that Jacob did it?"

"Each *voudoo* priest, or, I guess, in Jacob's case, shaman, has his own style, even though the patterns are the same," the exhausted girl explained. "I'd recognize Jacob's work anywhere. And besides, Baron Semedi is Jacob's *lwa*, the one spirit who connects with him, so to speak. They call it "sitting on the head." Like the spirit resides on Jacob, I guess kinda like the Catholic guardian angel sitting on your shoulder. And Baron Semedi deals with death and the otherworld. So that's Jacob's territory. Some *voudou* priests or priestesses only handle issues of love and weddings; Jacob deals with death. He must have come here looking for the dead. Johnny and Louisa were in the same temple as Jacob."

Mavis sounded close to hysteria as she climbed toward a pile of debris. Just behind it, an attic was visible. "This *vever* is a charm to Baron Semedi so he can help the dead find their way to the Haitian version of heaven or the otherworld. If the dead aren't shown how to get there, they remain trapped here in a halfway world. They can get angry and cause mischief or take revenge."

Alex ran after her, but before he could reach her, his nostrils were assaulted by the stench of death and decay. Mixed with it was a strange aroma of citrus laced with mint and herbs. "Wait, Mavis. Let me look."

Alex passed her, signaling her to stop. He crawled up over the pile, looking for an entrance, a window, anything to peek into the murky interior. Then he headed towards a section of wall which had been pulled away. As he climbed down the back side of the pile, he saw the two odd constructions in the back yard.

"Do you see anything?" she yelled from the street.

"Wait. Let me check it out. I'll be right down." When he reached the constructions he knew from the shape, they must be above-ground graves. Wood picked from the debris had been squared off to form ankle-high vaults. Two names had been painted on a top piece of wood. There were other smaller *vevers* laid out on the wood and a date, just two days previous. Alex guessed it was the burial date.

Alex wasn't sure how to break it to her. He agonized over what to say as he climbed back to her position on the make-shift street. So he just said it. "Mavis, it looks like they didn't make it." He gently took hold of her arms. "Someone, Jacob, maybe buried them. There are two graves in the backyard."

She screwed up her face, trying not to cry. He pulled her into his arms, held her while the sobs took her, hard and fast, wrenched from some deep place where she'd buried it all in the past five months.

After a while, when she calmed down, he led her home.

"Jacob must have done it," she said from the couch while he brewed tea. "If someone who practices *voudou* doesn't have the proper burial rites, their souls wander like ghosts stuck between this world and the next, not knowing where to go. The *geude*, or *gede*, Baron Semedi, whatever they call him, guides them safely to their new life. I wonder how long Jacob's been doing this."

"It had to be within the past few days," Alex guessed. "That design, that *vever*, whatever you call it would have washed away in the rain we had two days ago," he said. "The designs were pretty fresh."

"There must be hundreds that need to be buried, who need the rituals," Mavis said in a frantic voice, her hands pulling at fringe of the blanket on her lap. "There were a number of people in New Orleans who practiced some level of *voudoo*. We have to find Jacob. He can't do this alone."

The sounds and smells of the courtyard lulled Lily into a false sense of reverie, of memory. She could hear the barges plying the Mississippi even from here, two streets over. The bougainvillea was blooming, drinking in the humidity from the air, the blossoms heavy and oblivious, pregnant with vitality in sharp contrast to the grime-covered streets. Mystery. Birds betrayed the truths of the lost city, as if corruption and nature had never married. She didn't know whether to view this brief glimpse as a past never to be visited again, or as a curse. She could almost smell a hint of jasmine. Another vapor, another lie.

The air still shimmered with the weird current she always felt in New Orleans, an eerie hum beneath the surface of everyday life, born of longing and secrets, plots and bacchanals. It permeated everything here. This taste of life born on danger and wild extravagant hopes, deep sudden loses, and misplaced miracles. Nowhere else on earth was the past, the influences of thieves and charlatans, mystics and spiritualists so mixed with the very soil, evident in the vague promises hidden beneath the cloak of Spanish moss and flagrant in the lust of rampant vegetation. Most of the everyday sounds were absent: music no longer blared from Tippitina's, the strains of blues or jazz were absent from Decatur and Bourbon Streets, trucks no longer delivered cases of beer, and the clop clop of the carriage horses in front of Jackson Square no longer signaled the slow/fast pace of the Quarter. The only sound remaining was the clinking of glasses from the open-air bars.

She knew now why she'd been afraid to return. It wasn't the fear of finding a city doomed and in the throes of final destruction. It was to find out the all-pervasive passion, this wild uninhibited world of abandon, where anything could and would happen, was gone, too.

"Does Jacob know you're here?" Perry Laguerre asked her. He handed her a stem of lavender.

"No." She hid her face behind the stems, breathing in the fragrance as if it could give her answers.

"Or Alex?" Perry sat down across from her.

"No. Only Laney." Lily squirmed in the wrought iron chair, sipped the last of a double Bloody Mary.

"And is your sister-in-crime in the dark, as well?" Perry laughed, "No pun intended, dearie, I mean more dark than usual."

"Yes, I'm afraid to some degree she is." Lily idly traced the outlines of the assorted items on the table. The squares of slub-woven silk dyed with indigo, piles of herbs, bottles of oils and flower essences.

"So now, honey, are you trying to tell me our Orpheus is to be led to his doom without benefit of knowing the damsel?" Perry began mixing some of the items in a large hand-hewn wooden bowl. She couldn't tell if he was joking or not.

"You know as much as I do. It's not my choice." Lily said.

"We always have a choice," Perry said in an oddly severe moment. "You made yours by coming here."

Lily looked at Perry, a despairing look on her face. It was like looking at Jacob, a negative of Jacob: the same intense face, high cheekbones, deep-set eyes and narrow mouth. She always found it disconcerting, and one reason why she loved Perry so much. No one could believe he and Jacob were twins because of their coloring. No one could deny they were twins because of their almost identical features and height. It was a fluke, an odd throwback, and one reason Maman Simone expected so much from them both.

"I know you don't want this to happen, dearie," Perry patted her hand, "not to either one of them, but you knew the game plan. It's not as bad as you think."

Lily wanted to believe him. After all he knew Jacob better than she did. But there were things Perry and his family didn't know about Jacob, days when Jacob, wild with dreads down to his butt, set Paris and then New Orleans on fire with his passion, his unstoppable living to the fullest. He was the epicenter without even trying, because he cavorted through life without compromise. People didn't follow dopers with dreads, not in those days. But Jacob was no doper; instead, he was a walking contradiction, a challenge to the judgmental assumptions. He was an expert at eliciting outrage and then, just as quickly, allegiance. He had a gift for it. And then he'd be gone. Gone. Just gone.

"Now you've seen Jacob again, can you forgive him?" Perry read her thoughts.

"I'm not sure. Forgiveness and forgetting are too entwined." She ripped herbs into small pieces and pressed them into the silk squares. "You know as well as I do how much pain he inflicted when he left. I understand his need to do it, but his method was unnecessary…and cruel," she shook her head. "All those days of waiting, worrying."

"I know," Perry put his hand over hers, stayed it from shredding the herbs. "He hurt me and the rest of his family, too."

"Why? Why did he do it?" she blinked away the tears in her eyes, not wanting to remember the empty car overturned in the creek, the bloodstained finger trails on the window, the broken glass and shredded metal.

"He told me he just detached." Perry tied red ribbons around the packets of fabric. "Something happened to him in the crash. An ending, an awakening. It was too much for him to comprehend. He said he had to get away to think. When he walked away from that wrecked car, he was different. He said his life had to mean something now that he had a second chance."

She wondered how Perry had taken it all: the searches, the nightmare round of hospitals and morgues; the not knowing. "But did that mean he had to throw away everything in his life? Even the good?" Feelings resurfaced. She'd thought them dispelled. She was ashamed of the ache still in her voice, in her soul.

"I know your heart still feels like a gardenia left out to dry and turn brown. But I don't know if he could tell the difference anymore." Perry stared at her. "Maman Simone used to tell this old tale of a strange effect that happens to people around the time of a crisis, sometimes it's a near-death experience, but most often not. A person goes through his life, fairly unaware and then there is an impact. All of a sudden. Later they can trace it back to the exact moment, a housewife at an ironing board, a road worker at a crossroads, a musician in a car wreck. They become someone different, more complex, outside of society. Even in the 70's, Simone said there was a rehash of a very old story, with the New Age philosophy, they thought it quite possible. It's when a stronger soul from a higher plane has a mission to accomplish. They look around for a person not happy in their life, someone apathetic towards life or even with thoughts of suicide, who felt like they never belonged on this planet. And the higher soul slides into that body, takes it over, they push the original owner to the sidelines. The soul needed a vehicle. That's all our physical bodies are after all. Jacob describes it something like that."

"You mean like *Invasion of the Body Snatchers* or Anne Rice's *The Body Thief*?" Lily asked, shocked.

"Yes and no. That's horror, fiction, overly dramatized and skewed," Perry explained. "The concept is similar; the reasons and reactions are quite different, the same way novelists and filmmakers treat *voudou* in a horrific manner. This acquisitioning of a body was a good thing. It was for the benefit of the planet. The evolution of mankind needs the awareness, the influence of this higher soul. It's actually very similar to *voudou* but the spirit who takes over the person in a *voudou* ceremony is an ancestor and it's temporary. I know it all sounds a little hokey. But some people believe it. Stranger things have happened on this planet."

"Like when at rituals, when you witness possession, when the *lwa* 'rides the horse'?" Lily helped Perry stack the packets.

"Yes, but the transformation or, better yet, transference, Jacob might have gone through after the wreck is different because it's permanent. Supposedly, even friends and family of the original person can see a difference afterward. The person has more purpose, more confidence, becomes driven, obsessive. The original owner is still present, but they become more of an observer or an aide. They recall their memories from before the soul invasion, but it feels like someone else's history. They feel like a clean slate, able to start over, but now able to access the combined knowledge."

Lily leaned back in her chair, thoughts racing through her mind

"Do you really believe this stuff?" Lily's voice was unsure.

"I don't know. Some days I do... some days more than others. Jacob was a different person after that. Maybe it was the near death thing, who knows. But he's not the only one I saw it happen to. I witnessed it in people in Haiti during some of the uprisings, people who were beaten down to the point they had no self-confidence. And then they changed. Not like the people who performed rituals in the temple and who had a support system, but ordinary folks, who suddenly became determined to make things right. They acted with a courage and confidence they didn't have before. I witnessed some amazing things."

Lily looked at her hands, wondering. Purple flowers became blessings when some people believed...and she, in fact, now that she thought back on it, had witnessed healings and acts of courage by ordinary people when driven to the brink.

"Do you think this could have happened to Alex, too...at that first ceremony?" Lily saw everything in a different light now, perhaps like Jacob might view it.

"I don't know. But Jacob does." Perry looked at her hard. "Did you go along unaware of this?"

"Yes. I saw it so differently." Lily could hardly grasp it all. "When Alex stepped into the ritual and made all those predictions, said all those things, I thought it was the *lwa* speaking. He didn't seem different afterward." She looked off into the distance, trying to remember the changes after they returned from the ritual, when all of this was set in motion. All she could remember was that Alex was hardly home, he'd become what she called a *flatlander*, one dimensional, a surface skimmer unable to look deep inside.

"Could it be something happens when an individual in that cardboard frame of mind refuses to let a higher soul slip in?" Lily continued the inquiry, hoping for a way to make it all cohesive in her mind.

Perry shrugged his shoulders. "I don't know about all that. Thinking about some of this unnerves me, you know? Even when dealing with the *Lwa*. As much as I love the rituals, there's a lot of energy and power involved, and I don't mess with it. I just figure something bigger than me knows all the questions…and all the answers. I believe there's some connection throughout the universe. I only have a narrow telescope to view it all through. Now, Jacob, he's a different bird altogether. I don't know if it's recklessness, arrogance or pure faith, but Jacob…he can't seem to live without it, the ecstasy dance, I call it. And I'm not talking about the drug. I'm talking about someone who gets there naturally. Sure, Jacob uses the *vevers* and drumming and singing to get there, as shamans have done since the dawn of history, but I've seen him get there many ways and sometimes he can get there just by being a witness, like when he used to watch you dance. He's got some door in his brain that accesses places the rest of us can't go. He runs to ecstasy, allows himself, his ego, to get lost. He's so hungry to connect with the divine, the cosmos, whatever scientific dimension or spiritual being it is who orchestrates this whole shebang. By the way, Lily, do you know what Jacob has in mind?"

Her heart was racing. Her mind kept repeating *not again, not again, we've had too much of this*. "This is not all about him becoming initiated?"

"Good gods, girl. No. This is so much bigger than a place within the temple. It's beyond the temple, beyond one religion. Do you remember when Simone did Jacob's astrological natal chart and there was a Yod?"

"Yes, my mother taught me all about it. It's the configuration called the Finger of Fate, or Finger of God. It implies a special purpose in life. Jacob has one," Lily said.

"Well, Jacob had Maman Simone do Alex's chart."

"Oh no, that's right. Alex has one, too. How could I've forgotten?" Lily dropped the packets she was tying.

"Selective memory," Perry suggested, helping her wipe up the dropped flowers. When he moved, his face became diffused with alternating shadows and diamonds of light as the sun illuminated the foliage straggling over the greenhouse. His expression was hard to read. "Maybe you didn't care to think he'd end up like Jacob."

"I can't believe I forgot." Lily had to look away; he was so disconcerting, almost testing her. She stared off into the distance, trying to recall Alex's chart. She'd read it hundreds of times over the period of their marriage, but somehow the red and blue unequal triangle, made up of a sextile and two quincunx aspects, had evaded her interpretations.

"And did you just as easily put your Yod out of mind, as well?" Perry inquired, opening her hand and wrapping it around a small green bag.

"Rosemary for remembrance," he whispered. "Maybe you should wear this."

His words chilled her almost as much as when Jacob said them.

CHAPTER TWENTY-SEVEN — SEND IN THE FOOL

In a town full of beloved and accepted freaks – no, not accepted – but welcomed freaks, Jacob never minded being one of the freakiest. "Local colorful characters" they were indulgently called after the third or fourth bourbon at Christian's. But nowadays, Jacob was just a run-of-the-mill freak. They were turning up everywhere; the folks who used to half-way blend into the wallpaper of New Orleans: the garish colors, the garish flowers. In the blur of alcohol-tinted sight the residents were dressed in makeshift hot weather gear even more garish than the usual French Quarter opposition to trends. The Nola-ites, broken down, broken up, by Katrina now broke through the facades and were showing their *"true colors"* as Cindy Lauper would say.

The first couple of days out on this route, Jacob ran into what was fast becoming a city of wayward local freaks. Even the more conventional folks trotted out bizarre outfits, in defiance, just to say *we're alive and here and we don't have to pretend anymore.* Jake met them at the few local hangouts still open every day. No longer could you tell the lawyers from the former homeless, who now had found lodgings somewhere in this city of abandoned homes and buildings.

Added to this feeling of camaraderie were the bittersweet shrines made up of belongings tossed to the curbs. The odd juxtaposition of items turned into art, made either with a flair of black humor or a poignant reminder that nothing would ever be the same. Jacob waved to an artist he'd seen on these botched-levee desecrated streets in the past few weeks. Jacob spotted Rusty, who hung out Bad Jacqui's from time to time. The young black man so thin he looked like he needed a po boy and a huge platter of red beans and rice, rummaged through the debris at the gutter. Jacob stopped to speak to him as he began constructions on another shrine. "What you up to, man?" Jacob asked him as Rusty pulled a bicycle wheel from the trash heap.

"Urban Reclamation Shrines," Rusty explained, continuing his work. We gotta remind everybody who lived here, ya know?"

"I thought you had a studio," Jacob said.

"Did have." Rusty dug through the pile and pulled out a child's stuffed hippo and a beer can. "Katrina washed it away, so now I have the entire city as a studio." He cut a beer can in half with wire cutters, added a harness of wire to the cans and hung them on each side of the hippo's back, like baskets on an Andean donkey. "No more going to the dump. I can walk down here now." He put two Fisher Price kids in each of the halved cans as gently as if there were alive and stood the hippo in front of a bent screen. As he wove bits and pieces of paper and yarn through the screen," he kept talking. "Sunrise," he explained. "Kids lived here…they like colorful things and right now they're gonna want to know there's a fun way to get out of here, take off for a better adventure."

"You don't think they'll be coming back?" Jacob asked as they moved onto the next house.

"What they gonna come back to?"

Jacob, unable to come up with an answer, watched in silence as Rusty worked. This shrine was simple: a plastic trumpet stood on its bowl between two busted up stereo speakers. "Now, that one was simple. Some of them are. It just takes an eye."

"How many are you going to do?" Jacob asked.

As many as it takes." Rusty shrugged his shoulders and went back to work.

Jacob was oddly comforted by the refugee's persistent efforts to put his individual stamp on the crisis. His inspiration helped Jacob stay true to his mission. Sure, like everyone else trapped here, he contemplated bailing every day. But at least he knew there were others willing to pick up the pieces, tie up the loose ends, all the end-of-the-world clichés. Jacob adjusted his backpack, hoping he had enough supplies to last the day. He checked the number and then sauntered up the walk to the front stoop. Bingo, he thought, somebody's home in this one. He laid the backpack on the ground and pulled out his claw hammer and axe.

This one took him 20 minutes to locate. He wasn't so shocked at the sight anymore. He didn't know if that was a good or bad thing, but it made his work easier. This one had been an old woman…and old friend, Ensie Dechamp, but Jacob knew it was better not think about that again. *Detach, detach, you've got too much work to do.* Her legs were pushed up against her chest where she was backed up against a wall when a dresser had slammed into her. She probably went quickly, didn't drown, hopefully was killed by the impact. *You gotta be thankful for the small blessings.*

He immediately stuffed the ears and nose with cotton so she would no longer be bothered by the sounds of the living, although there weren't too many living in this part of the world anymore. Only the *gwo-bon-anj.* He cleared an area on the floor to lay her down, and pulled her out from behind the dresser with all the care he'd have used if she was still alive and he'd be afraid to hurt her. Once the body was prone, he tied a strip of cloth under her chin and over her head, closing her fragile jaw gently, almost all bone now. He didn't want to break it. Then he tied the knees, and finally, with much effort, the big toes together. It was his duty as a *voudoo* priest to keep another one from walking and bothering the living.

Although if he had his way, he'd let them all walk, lead the way himself straight to Washington. He clipped some of the little hair remaining, some nails from the left foot and hand. Along with a few hard-to-come-by-these-days chicken feathers, put them in a small white pot, then passed them over her head a few times. Didn't need no more *mojo,* no more black magic. He'd burn it with the others this weekend if he could find a place for the ritual.

Then he dug around in the top drawer of the dresser and found a tortoise shell barrette he saw Ensie wear often. Jacob was surprised to find the hardest part was going into the kitchen. Seeing the enamel-topped table turned on its side just about brought him to tears. He felt the need to stand it up, find the two chairs and put them in their proper place. He rummaged through the mess of utensils, sludge, and spice canisters until he found Ensie's giant wooden spoon and her huge jar of cayenne pepper. All the memories flooded back: the smells of her jambalaya wafting out over the street, the clank of silverware on pottery as his band mates ate bowl after bowl. How many times had she fed him and his friends and just about everybody else in the neighborhood? For years they tried to talk her into opening a local restaurant so they could pay her for her tireless hours in the kitchen. But she always declined with a shy smile, saying it was her gift from the *lwa* and if she didn't share it, it might go away. So they came by and replaced her back screen door or built her yet another spice cabinet. They took her to the temple when her feet swelled from diabetes or took care of her after the amputation of two toes.

He'd figured finding a younger friend would be hard. But he finally broke down at Ensie's table, had to sit on the mold-infested chair. He swiped his forearm across the table to clear a place and lay his head on the cold comfort of the enamel and cried. Diabetes and colon cancer couldn't kill her, but her own dresser did. *How's that for the luck of the draw?*

After he got her outside and gently laid her on the ground, he sprinkled some of the liquid from a Dasani bottle over the partial body/partial skeleton. He hated he couldn't do a full cleaning with the orange, lemon and mint juice, alcohol and herbal liquid. But there was so little left and so little time and so many more to be found.

Jacob dug around in his backpack and pulled out a flowered twin bed sheet. He didn't have body bags. Even if they'd been available, they just seemed wrong. Plastic trash bags were just as inhumane. Strange word, he thought. They weren't human anymore, these poor souls, but they deserved a little respect. And if dignity wasn't actually the word he'd use for the cheap multicolored, patterned sheets he'd scrounged from the recently opened, but sadly depleted, Family Dollar and Big Lots, then he hoped that as New Orleans folks, they wouldn't mind a little tacky color.

Jacob reverently placed the remains of Ensie in the sheet, and then placed the barrette, spoon and spice jar on her lap. He laid a branch of sesame on her chest, knowing that any black magician would never be able to count all the seeds by daylight and gain access to her spirit. At the last minute, he snatched the barrette back and stashed it in his pocket. He needed some of her good magic to help carry him through the rest of this nightmare.

Once he carried her outside, graves in the muck seemed a harsh thing to do, so he made a makeshift mausoleum forming a square with pieces of wood salvaged from her home. He painted Ensie's name on the largest piece of wood with house paint along with her address and any family names he could remember. He didn't know the dates of birth or death, although he figured she was in her 70's. He weighted them down with what he could find: rocks, wrought iron fencing, mostly. *Keep it natural.* As he walked away from Ensie's grave, he ran his fingers down the tortoise shell of her barrette, borrowing some of her strength and kindness.

The next day Mavis called Bad Jacquie and told her she might be late.
She woke Alex up. "You said you wanted to come, too."

"Yeah, um, yeah." he said in a voice still heavy from REM sleep. He
rubbed his eyes. "Just let me get dressed."

"I hope we can find him. Alex pulled on some clothes. "Is there any
coffee?"

"Yeah. I put it in a thermos," Mavis, said a little impatient. "I'd like to
get started."

"Sure thing, yeah. Now where did I leave the shovel?"

Once they were on their way, Mavis charged ahead as if she had
energy left over from yesterday. Alex didn't know where she found it.

"I wish we had a car. This would make life so much easier."

"Yeah, I guess you're right," Alex said, realizing how long it had been
since he'd even though about a car. "We could cover a lot more ground
looking for him, but then we might miss him, too."

"Yeah, maybe."

Once on their way, Alex noticed she was headed in a different
direction. "What's up this time?"

"I know a shortcut," Mavis said.

When they reached a crowded intersection, crowded not with traffic
or people but with sofas, lightening rods, stoves, mattresses, and the odd
table or two, Mavis turned a hard right, making her way through a
breach as if she were an invading army of one.

Alex didn't mind square-dancing with the furniture, but he could use
a little warning. He was carrying all the equipment and could barely see
from beneath the bill of his Willy Wonka ball cap, which had slid down
over his eyes.

"Where are we going, again, my leader?" He called.

And then she stopped dead. He crashed into her, nearly knocking
them both over onto a pile of vile looking refrigerator contents.

"What the fu...?"

"Wha..?"

He turned to look where she was looking while reaching for the rake
and followed her eyes to a gaudy sequined outfit impaled on the side of a
total-loss shotgun house. "What's that?"

"It's an Indian costume from the Mardi Gras *krewes*." Mavis said in a
hushed voice as if it was sacred.

"What are they doing?" Alex asked as he noticed another one, tacked
up spread eagled further up the street.

"I remember reading about this, "Mavis said, "in the column Chris Rose writes for *The Times Picayune*. But I completely forgot about it until now. An Indian lived in that house."

"I don't get it," Alex said, remembering the bit he'd seen about the *Krewes* on the news during previous Mardi Gras events. The colorful outfits were in such stark contrast to the brown-tinged gloom of the surrounding landscape. "What do you think?"

"I have no idea. Those costumes are very expensive to make – in the thousands. They often make a new one every year. It's so weird. But that's New Orleans for you. You see weird stuff all the time and, unlike other towns, you never find a true answer. Sure, you'll meet the French Quarter news barkers and they'll give you their opinion or maybe the word on the street, and then you'll stop into some little rinky dinky bar and the locals will have a whole different explanation. New Orleans is a town for drama queens and story tellers. I don't care if it's the legal counsel from Southern Trust Bank or the lady that sells Po Boys at the Eight O'Clock Corner Groceria, everybody's gonna have their own highly original, highly imaginative take on things. You couldn't survive in this town without it."

Alex noticed Mavis stiffen up, her back more rigid, less hunched than yesterday as they pushed on through the desolation of the 4th world country yet again. Was that good or bad? He couldn't tell. He wondered why he was back here trudging through a world where Caitlin Kiernan's characters would be preyed upon. And he wasn't looking forward to another confrontation with Jacob, even if they did find him. And if they didn't? Alex would do anything for Mavis. Despite her show of strength, he could see the waif in her. But this Jacob thing, this obsession…was it getting the better of both of them? He had to broach the subject they'd avoided all week, even if it did upset the delicate balance in this very strange relationship.

"Okay, I'm just gonna come out with it. What's the deal with you and Jacob?" There, he said it.

"What do you mean?" she asked quietly.

He had to pick up his pace to continue the conversation. "Look, I know you're good friends and all, but that day he got mad at you in the Café du Monde, what the hell was that all about?"

"It's complicated. He wasn't mad at me," she said simply. "He was mad at himself and took it out on me." She marched forward, picking up the pace, as if distance could end the conversation.

"Huh?"

"I brought up a subject that I know is taboo for him. Jacob's very private. I already told you too much." The words had the impact of her pulling a zipper over her mouth.

"But why did he get so mad?" Alex had to catch up to match her step.

"'Cause he blew it and he knows he blew it," she admitted.

Mavis stopped and examined Alex with a stern downward scrunch of her brow. Alex squirmed under her predatory birdlike scrutiny. "If and when we see him again, if you have the guts, you can ask him about it. But until then, I can't say any more." The authority was out of character, yet undeniable.

"Well, wait a minute, Mavis. What about all this fire-starting stuff?" Alex probed her, seeing Jacob in a whole new light. "What about that deal at the press conference when he went all berserk? He could have ended up in prison for years a la Squeaky Fromm. Maybe he's just a small time hoodlum. Good talker, but maybe just a French fry short of a Happy Meal."

"Wait a minute...," Mavis began.

"No, let's look at this clearly. You know Jacob is not the most stable person on the planet," Alex continued, "and a lot of people who like to start fires are one step away from being schizophrenic. My roommate in college studied psychology and he used to talk about this stuff. And in addition to that, people who are charmers, you know, who can get anybody to follow them, brandishing their wit and smile, while their real lives are in a mess, that's criteria for Borderline or Anti-social Personality Disorder."

"Borderline? Anti-social?" Mavis asked, her voice still guarded.

"Yeah, Borderline Personality Disorder." Alex repeated. "Borderline because it's one step away from being psychotic, schizo. Their brain is unhinged somehow, by a trauma in childhood or adolescence, and they lose it. But they have this incredible gift to charm folks. They often don't have much of a conscience. And the Anti-Social Disorder folks don't have a conscience at all."

"What the hell are you trying to say, Alex?" Her voice dropped a register to the level of threat. "You don't think Jacob has a conscience? You think he's just a charming manipulator?" Her face was red. The veins in her forehead stood out and Alex was afraid she might turn on her heel and leave him in this no man's land.

"Well, geez, Mavis. Let's look at some of the recent activities. He sets two fires, sneaks into a presidential press conference, lives on a school bus pre-Katrina, not post, doesn't have a job, and he can charm anybody into believing just about anything. Don't get me wrong. Jacob is the most fascinating person I've ever met. But I don't see where he's on a big mission. There isn't any evidence to back that up."

"Okay," Mavis said, warming to the argument as if she'd done it before. "Well, and let's take a look at Jesus. He spent most of his time lounging around urban centers, a la a homeless person, giving speeches and preaching to his friends, or wandering the countryside looking for sinners. Buddha. Had no job, sat under a tree. St. Francis of Assisi gave all his stuff away, quit working in his family business, lived in poverty, and talked to animals. Were they any saner?"

"Mavis...."

"Let me finish. And what about the work he's doing burying the dead? Something that no one else has done in five months?" She was on a roll. The look in her eyes said *back off.*

But Alex couldn't stop himself, even though he wanted to. He didn't want to fight with Mavis and the tools were getting heavy. But he was driven by fear. Fear of what might happen to both of them if they remained caught up in Jacob's wake. "It's probably illegal." He waved his one free arm to make his point. "Granted, he has good intentions, but..." The more Alex discussed the whole deal, the more he was convinced Jacob was out of his mind, headed for trouble, big trouble, dragging him and Mavis with him. "But I'm sure it's illegal. I'm sure the coroner's office would be having a fit if they knew."

"Alex," she said exasperated. "Do you think the question of legal or illegal even matters in this no man's land? Had you ever considered, that like Jacob," she jabbed a finger at him, "you might have a life purpose, a mission, and that's why you're here?" With that, she spun on her heel and charged off. He had the distinct feeling she viewed him as a monster.

Perry, after a fastidious assessment of the floral arrangement, added another lily to the spray of white roses trailing green ivy. He stood back to examine his design in balance and form. *Yes, the single lily was just the right touch of drama.* He added a sprig of rosemary.

"Remember me," a Shakespearean stage voice said over this shoulder.

Perry jumped, not an unusual reaction when it came to his brother. "Rosemary is for remembrance," Perry joked in a falsetto. "Yes, it is, Ophelia. And so it is that you remember me."

Jacob walked into the room so full of flowers he felt dwarfed. "And Hamlet is indeed grateful." Jacob took off his top hat and executed a deep bow before his twin. It had been a long time, but the face, so similar to his, looked less stressed. Perry was one of the few people who seemed to have weathered Katrina. Jacob wondered how two people who looked so much alike, except for the color of their skin, related to the world so differently. Not that Perry was laid back, but he didn't act as if he had to fight the whole world.

Perry came forward and hugged him, a bundle of rosemary still in hand. They could see eye to eye. "So, my dear, how fare thee?"

"None too well." Jacob said, sagging a bit. "And to be honest, I'm here for a favor."

"Anything for my brother," Perry said warmly. "I see you've been a busy man of late."

Jacob raised an eyebrow. "Word getting 'round?"

"You could say that." Perry smiled. "Whenever you're in town, things start hoppin', but I have to say, Katrina trumped even you."

"How did you manage?" Jacob felt guilty. He hadn't been to see his brother since he'd returned, but Jacob knew Perry forgave him for his long absences.

"The physical temple was destroyed and there's a lot of work to do. But we have a strong core of volunteers. We lost a lot of folks, you know." Perry's face grew dim. "But it's my job now to help the living to hang in there. I keep reminding them how the family and friends they've lost wouldn't want to see them suffering. It's a hard test for everyone, but I have to say, your mission has had the strongest effect." Perry motioned Jacob to a pair of wicker chairs.

"My mission?" Jacob tried to look as if he didn't know what he meant. He looked away as he sat down.

"You forget we're more like a small village despite being New Orleans. As soon as I heard about the burials, I could see your stamp all over it. We're grateful. I'll do anything I can to help. What do you need?"

"I want to keep you out of it. The last thing we need is you and the temple hauled into the chaos, just in case it gets into legalities. But I could use some space." Jacob held his hands open on his lap, aware it was a supplication of a man at wit's end. "A room for an altar and the courtyard if you can spare it; you're about the only one I know who came through."

"Sure thing. We'll find a place for you."

"But it looks like you're busy."

"Yes, dearie, we are." Perry changed his tone, went back into joking mode. Jacob recognized the move. Perry utilized it every time Jacob wanted him in the background. Jacob wasn't sure whether Perry used the façade to avoid a confrontation, or to sidestep a sticky situation. Unlike most twins, they couldn't finish each other's sentences or read each other's minds. Sometimes he felt as if they were opposites.

"Despite all, and I do mean all, of the weddings being cancelled, we're as busy as we've ever been. Perry indicated a calendar with most of the dates crossed out and notes scribbled all over the margins. "Not that I wanted to expand my funeral business. You know how all that dark stuff is not my cup o' tea. Give me a girlie in a wedding dress who wants thousands, just thousands of flowers, and you know what a happy man I am. But all these crosses and urns. Not much room for creativity." His expression went from pout to mournful. "But, poor souls, they deserve a good send-off."

"Are you the only florist left around here?" Jacob asked fingering a stalk of freesia.

"Well, there's a couple here, near the French Quarter, but there's more opening back up in midtown and uptown now that the kids are back in school. A lot of folks came back to New Orleans for the school season, when nothing else could bring them here. I'm not a big fan of kiddos, but if they bring back their folks, more power to them."

"How are you getting all these flowers?" Jacob took another heady sniff, silently agreeing to Perry's approach.

"You wouldn't believe it." Perry said in his put-on-for-the-public drama queen style. "My old friend, Jerry Meadows. He's a floral distributor. He moved to Atlanta, where his wife's from. Well, now he's down here, helping his son's family get back on their feet. Helping out here. His son has a lunch wagon – fries, burgers, all that – and they feed the rescue and cleanup workers over in St. Bernard Parish. Twice a week Jerry makes a run all the way back to the Atlanta to see his wife and while he's home, he hits the flower market and brings me back a truckload." Perry touched his brother on the arm and winked. "Don't tell anyone. They're a little old, but he's got good refrigeration and, thank the *lwa*, so do I. Some anonymous donor left us a generator." Perry raised his eyebrows, the non-verbal question obvious. "I think it was that lawyer from around the corner, the one with the to-die-for carriage house behind his puce mansion. Talk on the streets is he's been leaving stuff all over the area on people's doorsteps, coolers full of food, air conditioners, cases of imported top of the line wine. Maybe Katrina made him see the light."

Jacob smiled, remembering the lawyer Perry mentioned. He was a tall, rather serious man, always impeccable dressed, but not a hint of his sexual orientation. He was bright, though, and when Jacob and Perry had gone off one night after a few drinks, walking the streets neighboring the quarter, they'd located his house. It had been late but the lights were on and it was easier to peer into the interior.

"Well, look at this place," Perry had exclaimed with glee. "Either our man, Warren, is a decorator or he's hired a gay design firm. What style. I could live here, if it wouldn't mean cohabitating with a man of the courts. Might as well date an actor and have a helluva a lot more fun. The two occupations are the same, if you ask me."

Jacob sighed. Despite Perry's shyness, he always did have an eye on the lookout for available partners. Jacob wondered why things had never worked out.

Perry misinterpreted Jacob's look of concern. "Oh, I didn't forget you. Sorry. You know how I ramble. Back to your needs. I'll call Jerry. Without him I'd be out of business. Just tell me what you need and Jerry will bring it on Wednesday."

"Thanks. I'll make a list." Jacob thought this might work after all. He was glad to be with his brother again. He'd never known anyone so accepting and kind.

"And if you want me to make the potions," Perry swept his hand towards the courtyard that would serve as the *peristil*, "just give me the recipes. His voice changed entirely. A different man stood in his place, formal and serious, even a bit severe. This man, even Jacob held in awe. "I'll help you all I can," Perry continued, "but you must know up front. I'm not into the *geddes*. You know my *lwa* is Ezeli Freda, love, and all she entails. So you'll have to teach me the ways of the Baron."

"Perry, you might not realize this, but one day you'll be as powerful as Maman Simone," Jacob insisted. "Everyone seems to see it but you. It scares me sometimes. You get this look in your eye." Jacob nodded in the direction of a beautifully appointed altar. "I agree it might be helpful to call upon Ezeli, too. After all, this browned-out town could use a touch of color. But I have to say, at least with Baron Semedi, we know the rules, we know where we stand. Ezeli is so fickle."

"She may be fickle, but you have to admit, she spreads love all across the board. Who else do you know could love a gay black florist with, let us say, gender genitalia issues?" Perry asked, as if she were a physical presence waiting right up the street. Jacob wondered if that was how Perry viewed her. "Such paradox is right up her alley," Perry continued. "And, yes, your Baron is a heavy-handed master. But I believe paradox is a greater teacher than fear."

CHAPTER THIRTY — MISPLACED MISANTHROPY

Mavis and Alex cross-hatched the streets of the Ninth Ward for three and a half hours. There was no sign of Jacob. Alex felt the whole time as if he were on another planet or in another reality….and not one of his own choosing. They trudged through street after street of the 90,000 mile junkyard. No sign of that telltale top hat anywhere.

"Look, maybe he took a day off. It doesn't look like he's here or been here. We've seen no *vevers*, no sign." Alex didn't want to mention the graves. "And it didn't rain last night. What do you think about heading to Bad Jacqui's and ask her if he's shown up there? Shaman or no shaman, he's gotta eat sometime."

***

On the third day they found him. Alex no longer carried the accoutrements of shovel, rake, and axe. He told Mavis he'd run back and get them if they found Jacob. It only slowed down their efforts.

Jacob was up on a roof looking very much like one of the *guedes* in a Scully Elly Katrina shrine. Alex had considered bidding on one on E-Bay. But that was before he moved here. He no longer had time to surf the web, even if you could find it.

"Jacob." Mavis cupped her hands over her mouth and yelled up to him. "We've been looking all over for you."

"Yeah? What the hell for?"

"I found Johnny and Louisa," Alex explained. "We came to help you."

"Oh…okay. Wait. Let me come down." Jacob gingerly navigated the broken rooftop, setting off a landslide of shingles.

Jacob rubbed his hand on the shirt tied around his waist. He didn't look pleased to see them. "Help me? Do you have any idea what I'm doing?"

"You're finding the folks no one bothered to find and burying them." Mavis shuffled from one foot to the other, wondering why Jacob was so defensive.

"This isn't simply an act of burial. Mavis, you should know this more than most people. I'd like to say I'd be high-minded enough to do this for the dignity of the people who lived and died in these houses. But you know it's so much more than that, don't you? Have you any idea what's happening because there have been no burial rituals? Without the *desounen* and the *kanari*, the *met tet*, the soul, can't be released."

Mavis realized she must have had a quizzical look on her face. She knew a little about rituals, but funerals weren't her favorites. She considered asking what they all meant, but there just wasn't time.

"Without these ceremonies all these souls are lost," Jacob explained as if to a child. "They're left to wander, confused, and maybe even vengeful. So how do you propose you help me with that?" he asked in a snide voice, looking more at Alex than Mavis.

"Don't be such a jerk, Jacob," Mavis said planting her legs wide with her hands on her hips. "Don't talk to me like I'm stupid. I know Alex and I can't perform ceremonies. It would be like asking someone on the street to perform a Catholic mass. But we can do plenty. We can fetch and carry and we can…we can look for people."

Alex was proud of Mavis for standing up to Jacob. She gave him the strength to try, too. "Jacob, we can build the wooden gravesites," Alex chimed in. "We can paint the graves and add the names. There's plenty of physical labor we can help with and not interfere with what you need to do. We can even be a house ahead or behind so you can have privacy if you need it."

Jacob nodded his head. It was not in him to delegate…or easily acquiesce. But he was running out of time. The three of them could indeed accomplish more than just he could alone.

***

The next day, Jacob greeted them formally, like a mortician at a funeral. He handed them each a packet of silk dyed with indigo, wrapped in red ribbon. "This charm will protect you from disease and misfortune and from any stray spirits out for trouble. Wear it close to your heart and no harm will come to you while you perform this most valuable service to the *lwa*." His voice was solemn, un-Jacob-like.

By the third day, they had completed twenty-six burial ceremonies on thirty-six people. Alex sometimes assisted Jacob, both of them silent. Alex eventually learned to anticipate Jacob's needs for gauze, cotton, potions. Some families, Jacob buried together. He joined the Miller family in a group embrace, the father protecting the mother, the mother cradling her children.

The vignette reminded Alex of an ancient grave found by archaeologist, David Soren. *History repeating itself. Families warned too late or not at all about pending natural disasters.* In Soren's dig, mother, father, and baby had been killed in an earthquake in the port city of Kourion, Cyprus, circa AD 365. They were found in death as he imagined them in life, protecting each other. Alex thought of string theories, the universal mind. No matter the distance of time or how alone they felt, humans were all connected. He gained a new respect for Jacob.

"They'd rather have it this way," Jacob said with a mixture of sadness and homage in his voice. "Every time any of the Millers saw each other, they hugged, even if the kids were just off to a neighbor's yard to play. That's how they were." There was a catch in his throat, but he overrode it. There was still too much left to do.

The trio honed it to a fine science. By now Jacob didn't need to look anymore. At every house he stopped, they found bodies. He told Alex and Mavis how the little souls of the children called him, how sometimes he could hear their footsteps following him home as he left too early to save them, one house shy. He didn't know if Alex believed him, but Mavis did. Either way, it didn't matter. It just needed to be done.

Once Jacob found a house, he and Alex tore walls and roofs apart to locate the victims. Once bodies were located, Alex went outside to prepare the gravesites. Mavis laid out the ritual tools and potions, the clothes and sheeting. She located appropriate sized pieces of wood and applied a coat of fast-drying latex paint. As soon as it dried, she lettered the names of the deceased for the surviving families, if Perry had found them in papers or the temple's directory. She also added the street address for the authorities. Once the graves were completed, Mavis took photos of the graves.

At the end of the first week, Alex sank down onto an upended cabinet, its folkloric hand-painted flowers still visible. Jacob stood with his dreads plastered to his head and shoulders, sweat dripping from his brow. He went to wipe his forehead with his arm, and then thought the better of it. He gave a little smirk.

"Look, thanks for all the help this week." Jacob found a seat on a swing set, miraculously intact. "But, man, I gotta tell you. I need more."

"More? What do you mean?" Alex asked.

"You don't think you're here just to do physical labor? Here without a mission?" Jake sounded surprised.

"Mission? Geez, Jacob between you and Mavis…," Alex said half to himself. He wiped his face off with the bottom of his T-shirt. He was exhausted, thirsty and hungry, nevermind filthy. The last thing he wanted to talk about was any so-called mission. "Look, I'm not in a mood for any mind games or bullshit," he said to Jacob, his voice blunt, final.

"When I called you down here to New Orleans," Jacob said as matter of factly as if discussing a vacation invite, "I knew there was a perfect place for you in this supremely imperfect landscape."

Alex considered walking off, but he had no idea how to get out of this rabbit warren of the damned. "Jacob," he said in a tired voice as if to a bothersome child. "Jacob, I called *you*, or, rather, Laney did, for the interview. Remember? I came down here on my own."

Jacob ignored Alex's bad attitude. "Well, if it makes it easier for you to accept seeing it that way, who am I to argue?" Jacob shrugged his shoulders. "Look, Alex, it's not just a lark."

Alex considered his stint in New Orleans the furthest thing from a lark. If his legs and feet hadn't turned into lead, he'd already be hoofing it back to a shower and a pitcher of beer at Bad Jacqui's

"I need you," Jacob said interrupting Alex's vision of a hot shower.

Jacob leaned forward on the swing. "I really need you." His tone was suddenly desperate, raw and ragged like a ripped open scar. "I need your skills. You're an anthropologist and now you've seen firsthand what's going on down here. You can write the book this country needs to see. You can write the truth. You came with the expertise, the credentials, and now you have the insight you get only by living it."

Alex wasn't sure if it was his exhaustion or Jacob's mood influencing his perceptions, but the area became gloomier, as if a cloud had covered the sun. But when he checked, the sky was, in fact, the same hideous cerulean blue it had been all day. The air felt heavy, not the ordinary heavy damp of New Orleans, but somehow weighted with a world tension, as if waiting, as if more was to come, more was at stake than a conversation between two people in the middle of a government-funded landfill.

Jacob stood up. "Wake up, man. I need you to be witness. Aware. Observant." Jacob's voice was staccato. "I need you to tell everything you've seen."

The day jerked back into its offensive brightness. Alex wondered if he'd been hypnotized.

"Have you totally forgotten the anthropologist in you?" Jacob asked him, his brow furrowed in a look of disbelief. "Are you so busy playing squire-in-the-gutter that you've forgotten everything you believe in?"

Alex stood up, too. Jacob's word's finally struck a nerve, a painfully awakened nerve. "No, Jacob, you're right. Mavis accused me of avoidance once. And I guess it was true. But to tell you the truth, I don't know if I can do the anthropology gig anymore. I've lost all sense of perspective. Let me think about it. I know what you say is right. But I'm not sure if I can analyze, write, or even see the truth. Everything's in chaos. My mind's buried under Katrina mud."

Alex sighed a breath of relief as Mavis walked up. "Whew, I'm finished photographing the new graves. I'm hoping you guys are discussing calling it a day." Her entrance let Alex off the hook for the time being.

***

On the third day two Indian *krewes* found them. They asked to be put to work, fifteen men altogether. Jacob gave them indigo packets then showed them the routine. Some helped pull apart buildings, others set out erecting the graves and painting the makeshift mausoleum lids. The unlikely team upped their production by thirty rituals that day. Every day more people showed up to help, until Jacob was forced to jog to perform rituals. Sometimes Mavis or Perry assisted with the simple steps. By the second week, they'd honored the deaths of over three hundred people. From time to time, even Catholic priests came to officiate at combined services.

It was on the 27th day all hell broke loose. Jacob was interrupted as he completed the initial stages of cleansing a child's body. "Can we have a minute to talk to you?" He heard a voice behind him. Jacob jumped, the real world intrusion of a strange voice jolting him out of his trance, even deeper than normal due to the victim being a child. Jacob turned, still on his knees in the muck.

Two uniformed police officers stood over him. Shit, Jacob thought, just what I need.

"Can we ask what you're doing here?" The one watching his back asked.

"I'm burying the dead," Jacob said simply. He was glad Alex and Mavis, leading two separate teams, were up the street and out of sight.

"And by whose authority," the second officer asked, as he slid around to Jacob's right to get a better look at what he'd been doing. Jacob looked up and recognized him as Frankie Coster. Jacob knew most of the cops in this area.

"I'm burying some of the remains left to rot in the open. For the families." Jacob said pointing to the partially decayed body of the little girl.

"Is the coroner aware of this?" Coster insisted.

"The families haven't had any luck reaching the coroner, despite many calls," Jacob said in his most official sounding voice. "They haven't been given a date when anyone is scheduled to come on recovery duty."

"Is the CDC aware of this?" Coster's partner asked.

Jacob stood up and turned around to answer. "Well, if it isn't Jezze Breazeale." Jacob smiled and held out a muddy hand. The officer pretended not to see it. "When was it the last time I saw you, playing drums in Trotter's Zydeco band?"

Brezeale nodded his head. "Coupla years back. Been a while, Jacob." The officer shifted on his feet, wondering why of all the people left in this no man's zone, he had to run across Jacob Laguerre.

"Now, Jezze," Jacob said, smiling. "Let's stop goofing around." Jacob scrubbed his hand vigorously on his jeans and held it out again. Jezze looked to the sky for assistance, found none, so shook it. "You know me and I know you," Jacob continued, "and you know perfectly well that I'm not in touch with the CDC. You wanna arrest me for burying your friends, your neighbors? Then go the hell ahead." Jacob didn't reveal that he also knew Jezze from the temple. Jezze didn't come often, but he'd played drums there on occasion. Jacob figured the white patrolman might not be privy to the fact that his partner, Jezze, was involved in *voudoo*. Jezze knew exactly why Jacob was burying bodies.

Coster looked over at Jezze. "You know this guy?"

"Yeah, we're both musicians." Jezze admitted. "Look, maybe sometimes we gotta look the other way, you know? This guy's a friend of mine. A good guy, a good man. These people were our friends. He sees a need and he fills it. What's the harm in giving these poor souls a little dignity? Would you want your mother and sister lying out in the open, decaying without a proper burial?" Jacob knew Jezze had pulled a low blow. Three months ago, Frankie Coster had buried his mother and sister, following a long ordeal of red tape getting their bodies back from the morgue in St. Gabriel, Mississippi.

"Well, yeah. But it probably is against the law." Coster said.

"Do you know if it is for sure?" Jezze asked.

"Naw."

"Then what do you say? We go back to the station, find out, and quietly take it from there." Jezze suggested.

"Yeah, okay. You're lead." Coster was visibly relieved.

"Look, Jacob." Jezze handed him a card. "I'm off on Thursdays and Mondays. Give me a call, let me know where you are and I'll come help. I know two or three families still missing. Maybe we can find them."

"Thanks, Jez." Jacob was grateful, so much so that he was shaking. This thing that he started, whatever it was, was getting bigger and bigger. "That means a lot," Jacob said, with the first flush of real hope in his heart.

***

By the fourth week, Jacob was helping the Catholic priests bury their dead from the rolls of the missing within their parishes. The divergent religious approaches were no longer an issue, and between the Tribes, the freaks, folks from Bad Jacqui's, neighborhood followers, French Quarter survivors, and the Catholic parishioners and people from the temple, they had over two hundred workers fanning out and helping.

On the 31st day the situation took another unusual turn. Someone at the *Times Picayune*, one of the reporters who regularly walked the Ninth Ward, got wind of it. He wrote an article.

On the 38th day, CNN helicopters flew overhead.

"It appears the people of New Orleans have now taken things into their own hand," announced Albert Grossman on the cable news show, *365 days*. "Hundreds," he continued, "maybe a thousand vivid white graves have popped up in back and front yards of the Ninth Ward. Residents say the coroner didn't have time and the federal government hasn't helped the survivors, let alone the victims. It's now been six months. Something needed to be done."

Jacob, Mavis, Alex, and Lily watched on the huge flat screen at Bad Jacqui's. Laney and Perry joined them. The footage showed the graves bold and bright against the blighted landscape, hundreds upon hundreds of glaring white dots and dashes, a desperate SOS from a city of the dead and the dying. Jacob knew then he didn't have to worry about the dead coming to life; even the living felt barely alive. The people of New Orleans and all over the Gulf coast were now the walking zombies, the tired and the distraught, the shell-shocked and permanently scarred.

"God, it reminds me of all the crosses at Gettysburg," Alex said. "I can't believe we completed that many."

"You've created a memorial, Jacob." Mavis said. "The Ninth Ward is now a memorial, a cemetery." Jacob nodded, knowing it was time to erect the cross to Baron Semedi. His work was nearing an end.

"The graves seem to be of all religions," Grossman stated in a static-filled report, the whirr of the helicopter blades in the background, "all faiths, yet they're all oddly similar, as if designed by a grand plan. Drew Rickman of the Investigative unit for CNN has been on the ground at the scene. We'll turn it over to him."

"We're here at the Katrina Ground Zero," Rickman reported in front of a backdrop of discarded household belongings, a small row of graves to his side. "On interviewing people we found in the Ninth Ward, no one would admit to knowing how it all got started. Many said they saw a crowd working and just volunteered to help. So we've contacted the Coroner's Office here in the City of New Orleans, and Assistant Coroner, Les Valois, is here to address the strange occurrences."

The camera panned to a close up of a child's grave. Mavis' hand-painted penmanship showed up on the screen: *Audrey Tillotson, 8-21-2000 to 8-29-2005*. "Here's an example. Audrey, a little girl, just eight days shy of her fifth birthday. What do you think of this, Les, is it against the law to bury one's dead?" Rickman asked.

Les Valois: "Well, it's highly unusual. The folks at the CDC, as the go to authority, were concerned. The CDC doesn't want anyone hurt in buildings which could collapse. They don't want to see volunteers or families contract diseases. As a rule, everybody goes through the morgue first. But we received word the graves were meant to be only temporary until something final could be planned. We were sent photos of each body and each grave along with identification, address, as far as they could tell and names of relatives."

Rickman: "So this is not the case of relatives burying relatives?"

Valois: "No, not in every case – well, actually not in many. The relatives are in Texas or other parts of the United States and don't have the funds to come here, let alone the funds or a place to stay here while they see to burial."

Rickman: "So nobody knows who is responsible?"

Valois: "Well, in most cases, it's the officiating clergy of the church, synagogue or temple of the victims."

Rickman: "But all the graves look similar. Do you have any idea who started it all?"

Valois: "No, that we don't know. Just some grass roots effort, we gather."

Rickman: "And the photographs and family info, you don't have any idea who sent that to you? There was no return address?"

Valois: "No."

Rickman: "Well, that's quite a mystery here, along with all the other grassroots efforts and mysteries which are fast becoming legend during the rebuilding and recovery effort in New Orleans. Back to you, Albert."

CHAPTER THIRTY-ONE — THE DROWNING POOL/LAKEVIEW

Lily knew all along the coming days – her future – as well as Jacob's, Alex's, Mavis', even Perry's and Laney's would forever be altered. Katrina or post- Katrina. Slack governments and money-grubbing conglomerates, corrupt politicians, and even global warming would all be pulled taut. Around Jacob all the strings would gather together on a fulcrum erected, months, years, and decades ago. Yet, she didn't know the magnitude or direction; could never have imagined it, given the nature of chance and the diverse psyches of those in question. Perhaps, if she'd known, she might have changed her course. But nothing can change the whimsy of nature when played out on a planet raped and fouled by man, wobbling its way through distorted seasons.

It was a night for secrets and revelations. The old ways would foretell or forestall the future.

***

Jacob, too, was not sure if he wanted to see what was to come. For one of the few times in his life, he knew he'd have to step out of guise and reap the consequences of all the puppeteering. He now doubted the outcome of everyone involved. Free will, he wondered, or just bits of subconscious energies ready to run amok? He realized he perhaps was the most unaware of them all. His grand scheme might simply be a front for his own inadequacies; his manipulations a game to avoid playing a real part in this crazy dance of life and death and love. Now the roles would be exchanged in this distorted square dance. Facades would be blasted, safe havens wrenched from their moorings, and dark truths exposed like fissures beneath the crust. The earth would crumble beneath their tired feet in their dirty boots. They would witness all they had denied.

Alex and Mavis walked up the drive of Laney's temporary quarters in Lakeview. Jacob could see they were unsettled. He felt a tinge of remorse for his betrayal of Mavis, thinking it was for her own good. But where on earth did he get the gall to think any of this was for the benefit of any of them? Perhaps it was all just a game played out by his run-amok ego.

He led them to the dock. A wind, sudden and aggressive, rushed off Lake Pontchartrain, assaulted them. They all adjusted their stance to navigate the tilting of the dock. The wind lifted Jacob's scarf and was so forceful it agitated his dreads. He welcomed the violence of it, after so many days of dust and death. *Winds of change.*

The water lapped the edges, greedily, noisily. "Enough of this," Jacob hissed under his breath. He took a step back, suddenly unnerved. Tonight he would have no *lwa* to aid him, no miracles, no wishes answered. Everything might topple as New Orleans had and then all would be lost. But there would be no answers without confronting the questions.

After Jacob and Alex unloaded the truck, Jacob started a small fire in a copper fire pit. Mavis tended a hibachi where they cooked steak on sticks and halved eggplants. All three dipped into a cooler filled with beer.

Laney pulled up in his jeep. As the tall black man, barely visible, headed toward the dock, Jacob could see he wasn't alone.

"You know this is a private party." Jacob yelled out to Laney.

"This is not a party," a woman's voice said. "Let's put away the pretense."

The hair on Jacob's neck stood up. He was suddenly cold, despite the shirt stuck to his back, soaked with sweat. *Lillian Catherine,* Jacob realized from the voice alone, her features still indistinct in the distance.

He walked towards her. "Cate, I didn't know you were in New Orleans."

She kept walking. Mavis and Alex stood in unison.

"Cate!" Mavis said as Lily walked into the circle of firelight.

"Lily!" Alex said walking toward her. But then it hit him. He stopped and turned to Mavis. "Do you mean Jacob's Cate?"

"Is this your Lily?" Mavis asked, her face a white moon in the night, her mouth a crater of shock.

"I'm afraid so." Lily said to both of them. "One and the same."

"Why didn't you tell me you were coming?" Alex asked, the tremor in his voice echoing the question in Jacob's mind.

"I didn't know where you were," Lily's voice was not condemning. "You never called me back."

"I tried the house a number of times," Alex, obviously unsettled, tried to make up for it by offering her a lawn chair.

"We had an ice storm." Lily sank down. "We lost power. But by then I wasn't living there anymore." Her voice was matter of fact.

"I didn't know you had plans to come back to New Orleans." Jacob interrupted. At least he wasn't the only one in the dark. He looked at Laney, wondering what was up. *Had his professor friend master-minded this little twisted party? And if so, why?* Jacob could tell Alex was even more unsettled. He wondered who Laney was trying to unnerve more.

"Laney called," Lily explained to Jacob. "He said you needed help."

As if saving up his anger while trying to register what was going on, Alex was up and out of his seat. "What the fuck is this? How do you know Jake?" Then he turned to Mavis. "Why did you call her Cate?"

Lily looked from one man to the other, sighing. "I know there's a lot of explaining to do." Lily pulled an empty lawn chair near Mavis and sat down. "Yes, Alex, I've known Jacob for years." Her voice was strained, tired. "We were lovers years ago, before I met you. He was someone I didn't talk about."

"But you kept in touch?" Alex was angry, his voice riddled with disbelief. "And you didn't think you should tell me about him?"

"It's really complicated." Lily sank back in her chair, accepted the beer Jacob handed her. "There's a lot to tell. But it appears there's a lot to tell from your side, too. I don't want to get into a blame game here. Not until you hear it all out."

For a long time no one spoke. The wind aggressively filled the gap, whipping the water around the dock into a froth. The wind lifted and twisted – branches, hair, fabric – distorting shapes. It raged, as furious as the four sitting in the midst of nothing, a place removed, erased…so easily erased.

Alex looked down, his elbows on his knees, the beer in his hands ignored. The dock bobbed up and down with the movement of the water. In another time, another place, it would have been adventurous, romantic. But here, now, the motion made him sick. What was this game being strung out before him? It was all unraveling now, this labyrinth of lies, this primrose path of patches and paste-ups. Who wore the masks, who wore the dunce cap? Alex stood up, his hands balled into fists, staring at Jacob; almost shaking, he was so mad. "How long has this been going on?" he asked quietly through clenched teeth, hissing, reptilian.

"Look, Alex, calm down." Jacob said in an even quiet toner. "It's not what you think."

"When did you ever consider I could think for myself? Stop placating me, Jacob. Stop lording it over me, manipulating me, lying and stealing from me." His voice was iron, rusted iron curled into a fist tighter than Alex's own. And so it was when Alex finally opened the fissure, flung back the gates, and reawakened the emotions vanished for security, society, tenure, he kicked the fulcrum so cleverly concealed in a copper fire pit. He launched his body across the dock, his arms clawing forward like a target-hungry raptor, his face skewed to the side, screaming obscenities. To Lily he was unrecognizable.

And the firepot, quite happy to disgorge its illuminated contents, was eager to take more than center stage. Even before Alex's body could stop mid-hurtle and navigate a clumsy two-step sideways, even before Mavis or Lily could stand or Jacob could execute an evasive maneuver, the dock erupted in a burst of flame. In seconds the fire split the dock in two. Figuratively and literally.

Alex was denied his grasp of Jacob. The fire drew the line. Lily, reacting, unaware of movement, grabbed Mavis, the closest object to her. She yanked her back across the divide, not meaning to take sides but to save lives. Now, Alex alone in his rage-induced territory, found his anger subsumed in shock. The dock disintegrated in a rush of fuel and flame, spilling him into the toxic gumbo. His slide into the murky water, not so dark now as the surface erupted in flames, his descent seemed slow motion to the observers who stood transfixed watching the vignette through the fire, a contortion of an action film, and a distortion of reality no one believed for a few moments.

Jacob yanked both Lily and Mavis, duplicating Lily's move but doubling it, pushing them both onto the landed part of the dock. Before they could get solid footing, Jacob, mid-leap, was thrust backward. What was left of the water borne dock slammed back down, casting his silhouette against the backdrop of flame, a puppet dance, hand play indicating the shape of flight, an Icarus, a heron, a fallen angel, and then it was gone, a David Copperfield trick, a joke of illusion, *trick the eye and fool the mind*. The splash was barely audible against the noisy gluttony of the flames. A series of events flashed faster than Lily and Mavis could absorb. A fast forward slide screen instead of slow motion.

The remaining dock, now bereft of first Lily and Mavis and then Jacob's weight, reacted in a dramatic high five. Its upward tilt flung the copper fire pit into the air in a spinning discus. Just as Jacob surfaced it made impact. He had little time to react. The water dragged, and the shiny metal, still hot and red, made contact seconds before his arm broke the surface. There was the unearthly sound of metal forcing its way into flesh, and the copper disc, now the instrument of the eclipse of Jacob, winked at them in a triumphant sideways smirk before sliding into the black.

The women on shore, paralyzed in horror, watched as Jacob disappeared. Alex bobbed and weaved in the water, trying to avoid the Katrina debris popping and exploding in flame around him. His own personal terror was replaced with horror as he watched the spot where Jacob went under. Jacob did not come up. The flames left the place alone. Black thrashing water closed over the spot, a black hole, as if to proclaim Jacob never existed.

"*Jacob…*" high-pitched and frantic echoed across the lake. The word sounded strange to Alex on Lily's lips.

He swam forward, the observer side of his brain calm and analytical even though his muscles rebelled. *Hades. Hell,* he thought…*if I believed in such places.* The water was vile and heavy. Obstacles he could not identify, except in varying degrees of hard and sharp, assaulted him. He inched forward in his clumsy half crawl, half breast stroke, struggling to reach the area where Jacob went under. *What a joke. Jacob's the sailor, the man comfortable with water, and here I am, a backyard pool dabbler, trying to reach him through what feels like a bad disaster movie.* If he didn't need every inch of his energy to keep going, he'd laugh. Commentary via *Mystery Science Fiction Theater Three Thousand* went through his head. *Weird, the things you think about when you're about to die.*

He hit an object he recognized. It gave where everything else – wood, metal, plastic – in this cesspool didn't. Human flesh, Jacob's torso. There was a sickening thud, a give. Alex grabbed hold of him as best he could, the weight heavier than expected. Jacob did not struggle or move. Alex headed for a small incline, a boat ramp he remembered to the right of the dock. He knew he'd never be able to lift Jacob over the steeper banks. Besides, the whole dock area was in flames now, vivid curling fire hungrily fed on every ripple of petroleum product coating the surfaces.

He reverted to a one armed dog paddle. His arm was too exhausted to lift for a good stroke. He thought of the arthritis commercial as he strained to lift his arm. He couldn't arc it any higher than a ninety-year old man's. It seemed as if the bank retreated with every effort. As his arm grew heavier and heavier and a stitch intruded in his side, he considered giving up. *How much easier to just sink under, to stop, be done with it all?*

But this was not to be his choice.

In the time it took for him to blink the water out of his eyes, everything went black, disappeared, including the air from his lungs. He was so disoriented he thought he'd gone under, might be dead. *So this is what's it's like after all. Kudos to the atheists.*

But, no, unfortunately, he realized, he was alive, just no longer in control of any part of his body. He lost all sense of physical presence as he was drawn up, forced forward by a blast with the thrust of a jet engine, flipped, rolled over and over, worse than the day the monster wave had caught him at Rye Beach, tumbled, and then dashed him to the Atlantic seabed. He collided with debris in a virtual rock tumbler. His body was unable to recoil. He absorbed impact after impact in sharp angles of pain, random brutal hits as his limbs twisted in awkward gyrations, all muscles ignoring his commands, powerless beneath the assault of forces erupting from heady mixes of elements not meant to be connected. He held Jacob for a moment. Then the unconscious man's body was yanked away.

Alex had no sensation of falling, only impact, water as concrete and then dividing, opening up to take him. If he hadn't witnessed Jacob fall, too, he would have let it take him.

Jacob thrashed in wild contortions. Alex caught his breath. They'd been dumped miraculously close, as if a school principal had banged their heads together in anger and tossed them together onto the floor. Only this floor had no bottom.

"What the fuck?" Jacob yelled, frantically treading water, trying to orient himself. Over his shoulder, Alex saw the glint of hope, the boat ramp, its white cement calling out, a welcome mat to life on the other side of hell.

"Jacob, calm down. This way. Here, let me help you." Alex reached him, caught in a crossfire of relief and disbelief, his sides aching.

Jacob's eyes were vacant, then angry. But he let Alex take hold of him. When they reached the shore, Jacob was able to halfway haul himself out of the water. They both collapsed, rolled onto their sides ,and listened to each other retch as the combined pollutants of American society streamed from their lungs and stomachs.

"What just happened?" Jacob asked after what seemed like hours, sounding more alert than Alex felt.

"I have no idea," Alex attempted to sit, then gave up. "But I'm gonna kill whoever's responsible."

CHAPTER THIRTY-TWO — THE MORNING AFTER

Lily woke up on the couch in the waiting room of the hospital. Sunlight streamed in through the window. Birds were singing. Had it all been a nightmare? But, no, the bruises and the flashbacks told her it was real. It was all reaffirmed when she looked up at the clock – she'd nodded off for four hours. No doctors had come out yet. Jacob must still be in surgery. Perry sat at the table wearing the same clothes from last night. She was just as fashionably dressed. She was glad Alex was back at Laney's with Mavis after being released from the emergency room. She couldn't handle both of them here at the same time.

"Well, at least now we have an answer," Perry said, walking to a nearby coffee machine.

"What do you mean?" She asked as she headed to the table, hoping the straight backed chair would help her aching back.

"There were tornadoes last night." He handed her a steaming Styrofoam cup. "Three, to be exact." He sat down and picked up the *Times Picayune*. She was close enough to read the date: Feb 3, 2006. Perry's dark eyes pinned her for a moment as if to emphasize what was to come. He looked away and read, "It's been 24 years since the New Orleans area has had an F-2 tornado and last night we had three. They took out part of Louis Armstrong Airport, damaged the Ochsner Clinic Foundation, and took down a State Police radio tower, not counting demolishing whatever houses Katrina didn't get the first time around. Here, I'll read it to you. 'The strongest one reached wind speeds exceeding 113 mph and cut a 2 ½-mile swath from the eastern edge of Metairie through Lakeview to the lakefront.'"

"So that was it, a tornado. And Jacob will probably think it was him." Lily's voice was sarcastic.

"My, my, aren't we feisty this morning?" Perry asked, shocked. "Don't you have any compassion for the poor guy? After all, his face is scarred for life and he may lose his eye."

She slumped in her chair. "I'm sorry. That was out of line. No, I do have compassion. I was terrified last night. And it's going to be rough. I'm so tired of all this. All this drama, all this tension."

"Now who is blaming tornados on Jacob? It's not like he planned it," Perry said.

"No, I know. But if he hadn't started this whole thing, this whole plan, none of us would have been out here." She was exasperated.

"You weren't supposed to be here, as far as Jacob knew." Perry folded the paper as if any more news would be too much. "Maybe Laney misjudged in calling you. For some reason, he thought you'd be an equalizer."

"It is all my fault. I didn't tell Laney or you everything." Lily admitted. "For some stupid reason, I thought I could protect Alex. I knew it would be hard for him, learning about Jacob. But it's going to be even harder when he learns the truth about the ritual. I misjudged Alex. He's been so passive before he came here. I had no idea he'd actually attack Jacob."

"Maybe that's what he needed," Laney said as he walked towards them, his voice was calmer than the rest of them, considering the consequences. "Maybe Alex had to be kicked into feeling alive again. And maybe Jacob knew the risks by agreeing to the cook-out. He didn't figure on you. But you have to remember, he and Alex have had their own differences lately. Despite what was obvious on the surface, Mavis knew the tension was growing. Sometimes we need an equal adversary before we can come to learn our true capacities."

Lily wondered how long he'd been listening to their conversation, feeling as if everything was a muddle and no one had a clear idea of what the others were thinking or the complicated histories they reacted to. "Maybe," she said, the exhaustion fraying her voice as much as her hopes, "but now there's too much going on behind the scenes. Too many hidden agendas."

CHAPTER THIRTY-THREE — STONE EFFIGIES

Later that afternoon, Alex stood in the hospital room and watched them both sleep. Lily, exhausted, slept in a chair, her head on folded arms at the side of Jacob's hospital bed. The image on the pillow was much more disturbing. A thing from nightmare or the subconscious. Jacob's face was gray-blue, the color of thunderclouds, smoke. He was drained of any color close to human. A huge gash was stitched from the center of his eyebrow down over his cheek – a lightning bolt of red anger slashed across the once perfect features. It was a mask, more bizarre than any he'd seen. If not for the tubes, the steady beeps, it would be a death mask. Alex remembered a statue he'd seen in a gallery when he was an exchange student in Norway. Loki, one eye missing, his face scarred. Alex hadn't noticed the resemblance before. The same cheekbones, the same grim smile. How odd. Punished now, marked. The symmetry slandered, the spirit drugged. The Lord of Chaos undone – at least for the moment.

Alex couldn't believe he'd been the cause of all this. He'd leave if he had the guts; leave this hospital, New Orleans. But he couldn't make his feet move. Couldn't pull his eyes away from the effigy on the bed. Jacob's body seemed shrunken, broken. He'd been larger than life to Alex. Jacob's personality, his vision and passion were too large for such a small frame, so they burst out in a series of supernovas.

Lily stirred, mumbled in her sleep, "Jacob." Alex leaned against the door jam, exhausted. A feeling of desolation washed over him. When had they failed? When did the connection between him and Lily dissolve? He could see it had all collapsed, maybe years ago. They'd led parallel lives for so long. Not lives entangled, enmeshed as the four lives were now. He'd lost part of himself somewhere and left her behind along with it. They'd functioned like ghosts with each other, talking but not communicating, loving but as one loves the dead or the distant, as only an image of the people they'd once been. Now they were both so different. He felt no jealousy, even as she said Jacob's name. Only sorrow…deep loss and sorrow, that things had gone so wrong.

Had he and Lily been bad for each other? She'd lost some of her vitality, and he as well. He'd found it again with Mavis in this god-forsaken town, and with Jacob, too. He had to acknowledge it…with Jacob, too.

Lily raised her head slowly, looked around as if forgetting where she was.

"Alex, how long have you been here?" She rubbed the sleep from her eyes, swept the tangled hair from her face.

"A while. How's Jacob doing?" He didn't want to say how bad he thought he looked.

"Not good, but better. They finished the second surgery about 3:00 a.m. They finally stopped the hemorrhaging, but they had to take the eye. They couldn't save it." She looked thoughtfully at Jacob, and then turned to Alex. "Jacob's tough, he'll be okay. Different, but okay."

"He needs you," Alex said, realizing a truth he should have seen all along. He'd never needed Lily and she hadn't needed him. Mavis did need him and he realized how much he needed her. And Jacob certainly needed Lily.

"Even more so," Lily said her tone serious, determined, "he needs you."

"What do you mean?" Alex fidgeted. It was time to leave.

"There's a lot you don't know." Her voice was tired. "Let's just say he was preparing you for something. He'll have to tell you himself. Please don't think about leaving." She looked at him hard, accusatory, reading his mind. "We both know you have this way of leaving when things get complicated. Alex, for all our sakes, please wait this one out. Mavis will help you. She's strong, you can lean on her." Lily nodded her head, a strange little motion, a sign of approval. There were tears in her eyes.

Alex realized they were meant for him, for him and her in the grief of the end of their marriage. For all their distance, Lily did know him better than anyone on this planet. But for a long time he didn't act true to himself around her. Something illusive stopped him, as if she knew him better than he did himself, and so he erected a façade to keep her out, to keep her from knowing all the parts he'd disown.

But with Mavis, he just didn't care. Everything here in this city was stripped to the bones, more real. Nothing but the truth could live in this barren place, this lost world of broken lives and crazy dreams. He realized how he'd bought into the system back home. The programming ran his life until he became a shadow, a robot, where Lily couldn't reach him. She retreated into her head, into her own world. Here in New Orleans there was no place to retreat but to the core. All pretense was torn away and now he could see it all as a blessing. *A weird second chance of being fully, vividly alive.* He knew now he'd always been meant to work in the field. Yes, there would be horrors and things beyond his control – maybe most of the time – but now he could see it was the only way he could be himself. *Tingling with fear but always in awe.* The system, even the university, had stolen that from him. But this town, this second chance, had given it back.

"We blew it, didn't we, Lily?" The lump in his throat strangled the words.

"Yeah, Alex, I think we did." The tears fell freely. She didn't wipe them away.

"Did you ever love me?" He couldn't resist asking.

"You know I did. Still do." She was openly sobbing, her face red and blotchy, her shoulders shaking. Unashamed. "But I don't think I ever stopped loving him." She looked at Jacob. "It was different. I can't explain it. I loved you each as deeply as the other, but in different ways. With you, there was a meeting of the mind, a gift of ease in being with you, until...," she looked down. "Until you changed. You sort of just drifted away, lost in your career, chasing something I never could see. I felt that if I followed you, I'd lose my way, but I didn't know how to bring you back. I wasn't strong enough or aware enough."

"And with Jacob?" Despite everything, he had to know.

"Jacob and I were catalysts for each other. Sure, most of the time, there were just huge explosions and we couldn't see what happened for the fallout. But I always came away knowing myself more, learning from him, even when he was a harsh and cruel teacher."

Alex nodded. "I know what you mean. He does it to me, too. Mavis does it, too. I guess we each need someone who has the guts to challenge us when we get too comfortable with the charade."

"Bingo," she said, sounding like Jacob.

"I'm going to leave now, Lily. But I'm not going away. This time I'm going to stay and pick up the pieces. Jacob and I need to talk...when he can." Alex looked at the figure on the bed. He wondered how different Jacob would be. He walked over and kissed Lily on the forehead, wiped away some of the tears, sorry there'd been a need for them. "Take care of him for us, okay? I think we all need a little hope right now." Alex turned and crossed the room in rapid steps, not wanting her to see his own tears.

CHAPTER THIRTY-FOUR — A CHALLENGE FROM THE MOUTH OF THE CURSED

A month later, when Alex stepped into the entrance room of Perry's Courtyard, he felt as if he were attending a wake. The room was full of flowers, as a florist's should be, he told himself. But none of these flowers were of the FTD variety. No happy birthday bouquet with their garish balloons, no VIP centerpieces with trailing tendrils and dramatic arrangements, no vases of long stem red roses or Easter baskets filled with daffodils and tulips. No, the walls were lined with cemetery bouquets, some live, some silk.

Jacob emerged through an archway of lilies and stood for a moment watching Alex as he lifted his nose from a hyacinth. He needed the smell of Easter…spring, fertility, new beginnings.

Alex stared at Jacob, hoping his face didn't reveal his reaction. Jacob stood in a crooked man stance – or was it the face? Alex couldn't tell. Jacob had decided against plastic surgery, Mavis had informed Alex. The eye had been sewn shut. But the scar ran from above it down past the cheekbone as if lightning had hit it or an earthquake had erupted in his flesh. There was no other way to describe it. *In this time of laser microsurgeries and miracle flesh, what the hell happened here?*

"The mark of the gods," Jacob said as if reading his mind. "Kind of melodramatic, don't you think? But then you know how much I need all the attention. This guarantees it."

Jacob walked into the room. He was indeed crooked.

"Why are you walking funny?" Alex asked, ignoring Jacob's question but glad to see he still had the old sarcasm.

"It's not so much from where my thigh was injured, although I'll always have a limp." Jacob began.

"But you're crooked."

"The doctors say I lost my perception when I lost the eye." He grinned. A weird perfect grin on a very imperfect face. It was out of place, and for a moment Alex thought the mouth should have been altered, too, for symmetry, for a strange anti-aesthetic.

"But most everyone who knows me would say I lost my perception a long time ago." He headed for a chair. "They said it should even out in a while. I'll learn to compensate with the good eye and get around fine, except for stairs."

Alex watched uneasily as Jacob nearly missed the chair. It was disconcerting to see him so out of control. Alex remembered the languid ease, the way Jacob once moved his body through the atmosphere with a sublime grace, while Alex tripped and stumbled all over the place.

Alex found a bench hidden in the greenery and sat a short distance from Jacob. The position put Jacob in profile, the unharmed side facing Alex and, for a moment, before Jacob turned, he was perfect again. Whole and elegant. But he did turn and confronted Alex with the damaged side crumpled in on itself, still raw in places from the third degree burns. The skin was pulled taut over those prominent cheekbones, giving a distinct skeletal resemblance. The missing eye was the least disturbing of the gestalt. It was the slash that got to Alex. As if something had tried to split his mentor's face in half. Alex was appalled but still couldn't stop looking.

"It's a ball buster, ain't it?" Jacob asked. "You're damned if you look and damned if you don't. We actually had a couple of options. They could have relaxed the skin a bit here." Jacob gingerly dragged his fingertips along his cheekbone as if to confirm it was there. "But then it left me with this kind *happy-to-know-ya* look. And I thought the menace was better. Despite all my joking around, I couldn't see going through life laughing all the time."

At first Alex didn't know what to say so he just blurted it out. "How are you taking all this, Jacob? How's this affecting you? God, I'm so sorry. If roles were reversed, I'd be wringing your neck right now."

"You gotta look at the bigger picture, Alex. Don't you see? You were just an observer in a play of meaningful accidents. You've heard of meaningful coincidence, right?"

"Yeah, Jung, from Lily – well, I guess, your Cate." Alex replied, hoping Jacob would pick up on the concession.

"Well, this was a meaningful accident. I should have seen it coming but my arrogance got in the way." Jacob stood up and walked awkwardly through the rows of flowers, a thorn among the blooms, a threat on the horizon, a thunderbolt charging across the flesh. "Along with my perception, my perspective needed changing. When you go from two eyes to one, there's only one answer. Now I must see only what is important to see. No distractions, no confusion. And besides, 'In the land of the blind, the one-eyed man is king,'" Jacob quoted.

"But, Jacob," Alex said, almost too tired to argue. "Humans need two eyes for correct vision. It takes two to see what's out there."

Jacob laughed, a derisive laugh, laden with sarcasm. "Don't ya see, man?" His voice rose. "I'm not meant to see what's outside." He flung his free arm wide. "What's outside is human – what me and you and everyone else with limited vision, limited imagination have left after our cycles of greed, war, destruction. This is not the world I choose to witness. It's already fuckin' lost. Can't you see that?"

In his unsteady gait, Jacob stormed up and down the paths of flowers. A crooked man in a rampage among the cascades for the dead. His gestures were wild, unstable. Plants were deflowered; blooms fell to the floor or were flung in the air. The reek of broken nature filled the room. Jacob couldn't stop moving.

"Geez, Alex, after all this time. Can't you see the world I know is inside? It's the world of the spirit. Something to fuckin' transcend this trash heap left by consumerism, capitalism, and the rape of the planet. All that's left now is the spirit. The spirit can rise above it, live beyond, outside of it. And if you can't see that...then it's just too fuckin' late for you, too. Even if I took your eye out now."

"Jacob, wait, you got me wrong." Alex jumped up and followed the agitated pacing. He avoided the fallen flowers, not knowing why.

Jacob turned on his heel. His face was inches from Alex's. Alex could see all the striations of color radiating from the scar.

"The only reason I was left with one eye was so I can spot the folks who wanna join this second string street parade. I thought you were one of them." With that remark Jacob turned on his heel. In one of his illusive disappearing acts he vanished through a cut in the foliage. Alex could hear him singing *Stairway to Heaven*, his voice not too far off from Robert Plant's. *"There are two paths you can go by and in the long run, it's not too late to change the road you're on."*

This time, Alex watched his back for only a few moments. It was Jacob's final insult. *I have no more time for you,* he seemed to say, the swaying of that long black coat speaking the words for him. The retreat into the *Vieux Carrè*, the Lower Ninth Ward and now a world Alex couldn't enter. Alex finally understood why Lily and Mavis needed to paint. If Alex had the talent he'd paint a collage of Jacob's back, Jacob's dismissals of him. Maybe that way he'd understand.

Jacob entered the courtyard, what would be the makeshift center of the temple in a few short days. How could he manage the ceremony? He'd never doubted his physicality before but now the vehicle he needed to drive his spirit was failing, hindered by the consequences of his mistakes. He stood in the center and imagined it as it once was, filled with people, the drums playing, the flags rippling in the breeze, the *lwa* speaking to him and through him. No matter what they'd done to his body, he remained intact, a happy observer. Could he still serve them? What if he was broken by their passion, their anger?

"I know you can still do it." He heard Lily's voice, quiet, confident from behind him. "You're not having doubts, are you?"

"I'd like to lie and say no. But look at me; I'm an old man in a young man's body. I don't know if they'll even use me anymore." Jacob stood before her, leaning. He reminded her of her step-brother, Francois Burgogne. She hadn't seen him since she'd left France. It was eerie, the same tilt. She noticed the similarity, as an artist, detached, as if working out a composition. If she photographed each of them and layered the photos on top of each other, as she did in her art journals from time to time, how close would the images align?

"You know for yourself from Maman Simone, age has nothing to do with it, or your physical state," she returned to the conversation, trying to discount the image. "Haven't you always taught how it comes from here, and here?" Lily touched his forehead, his heart place. "But you may have to admit it's time for you to pass the baton. I know you haven't wanted to give it up. But not all your roles are public."

He turned and looked at her, his head cocked to the side. "How do you know these things about me?"

"I pay attention to the signs," she said pulling him to a bench beneath a magnolia. "Besides, you told me so yourself a long time ago. Don't you remember when we were first at the temple? When Maman Simone laid the tarot out on the table? The fool was about to walk off the cliff." She pointed at him and smiled broadly. "You laughed and said, "Is that me? Am I the fool?"

"And Maman Simone reminded us," Jacob said. "'Respect the fool. He's the part of us who begins the hero's journey. He'll take all risks for what drives his heart. He'll step off a cliff for his dreams. Without the fool, there can be no Magus, no Hermit.'" Jacob finished the recitation and sat with his head down. She couldn't believe he'd remembered it all word for word. He'd positioned himself so only the untouched side of his face was visible to her. Lily wondered if he did it to protect her, or more from shame, fear. Sunlight flickered; the wind played among the banana leaves, causing a shift, an illusion – a trick of the light beneath the shade. Lily swore she watched Jacob's face age, crinkled with worry, the skin like old parchment, yellowed and brittle.

"It's time for me to give up the Magus and step into the role of the Hermit, is it?" He walked a little way from her, towards the shed which housed his altar, as if he'd realized the vision she'd just witnessed. Or had she willfully imagined it? Sometimes she couldn't tell.

"Only you can judge that." She stood up to go, aware she was being dismissed. She no longer knew his boundaries and couldn't bear to make him more uncomfortable.

"You knew even before you sent him to me, didn't you?" He tempered his accusation with sensitivity, as if his purpose was understanding and not blame.

She nodded. "Maybe that's my gift, as yours is in communicating with the *lwa*".

"You're the seeker of fools then?" He finally smiled, an old Jacob smile.

She laughed, too. "It would appear that way."

"Then call Laney." Jacob said, standing up, taller and straighter than she'd seen him attempt since the accident. He laughed. "It's time for an awakening. Send in the Fool."

"What's this all about?" Alex asked as Laney showed him to a chair in front of a large computer screen. Alex had arrived at Perry's with mixed feelings, knowing everyone would be there, hoping it was a forgiveness invitation. He was uncomfortable without Mavis, who had to work at Bad Jacqui's, but the dinner had proven cathartic, awkward at first, but as the alcohol flowed and jamabalya and red beans and rice were demolished, the atmosphere turned into one of those joint survivor reunions where unsaid fears dissolved, and exhaled sighs and emotional pauses in conversation were fully understood.

"There's a little film I'd like your opinion on," Laney opened the file and started the footage. Alex was the only one still seated, trapped in the computer chair by the rest of those who watched over his shoulder. It gave him the creeps, invaded his personal space. He realized the film was of the ritual. It replayed Jacob's movements. Alex recognized the antics of the great *lwa*, Baron Semedi, talking through the front man. Alex watched in renewed awe as the ritual was displayed in a different perspective. His spine tensed once again, perhaps even more so than it had that night.

The uninjured Jacob sang in his uncanny voice, his movements odd but graceful as he enacted his salute by circling around the fire. He shook the stick with red ribbons, hitting high notes, falling to notes in minor keys, causing chill bumps even now. The old Jacob that was. The odd Jacob-mix of ancient and streetwise, carney man and demi-god.

But then the camera shifted to the onlookers, panned the faces in awe, in various states of ecstasy. *Union with the spirits.* Alex spotted himself in the crowd, apart, hanging back two rows. It was unnerving. Then he watched in shock as the Alex onscreen stepped out from the crowd and walked forward. "This isn't what happened," he said in a low, voice, as much to himself as the others.

Alex could barely take his eyes off the footage to turn and look at Jacob or Laney. "What the hell is this? Did you edit the film?" he asked, incredulous. His voice was raw with emotion, even as his eyes flicked back to the screen. He watched in horror as the Alex onscreen stepped into the circle around the fire and mimicked Jacob's movements to the drums: dancing, twirling, lifting his head and singing. *It was unbelievable.*

"Wait a minute...." Alex felt even more trapped. He'd clenched the armrests without even being aware of his actions.

"Stop the film," Jacob told Laney. Alex twirled around in the chair, not caring who he dislodged from their observations. He searched their faces. "I don't believe this. Where did you get this? How did you doctor this film?" His voice rose at the lack of response from any of them, not even Mavis. "I never left the crowd. What the hell are you up to?"

Laney leaned down. He peered at Alex. His eyes held nothing but frank disclosure. "We did nothing to this film," Laney said, his deep baritone words laden with finality. "I took it with my camera phone, just as a record of the ritual, for research, for documentation. I had no idea you would play a part. But, Alex, believe me, what you are about to see all happened. You can check it out. There is no way we could alter or create the following scenes on a computer. You may believe it or not."

"Of course I don't believe it. I was there! I know what happened!" Alex was almost out of the chair, but Laney placed a hand on his shoulder, not threatening, more paternal, but he still made his point.

"As you'll see," Laney recommended, "if you have the patience to watch, from this point on, you were possessed by the *lwa*. I realize it's hard to believe and a shock. As soon as we're done, you can take the DVD to an expert and see if it was manipulated. Will you at least watch it? I've been your friend a long time, Alex. You know I don't play games with my research."

"I'm not sure I know any of you at all," Alex hissed, trying to unclench his hands, but unable to.

Alex turned to Lily, his face pleading, desperate. He tried to stop the rapid breaths threatening to unbalance him. "What? What is this?"

"Maybe you should watch and find out if you have the courage to see." Lily said, her voice quiet, solemn, firm.

"They choose who they will, whether you're ready or not," Jacob said quietly as he backed away and sat on the couch, leaving Alex a path and the option to leave. "Watch this if you can. Perhaps it will say something about your role in New Orleans, your new life."

Alex shook his head no, but despite his doubts he couldn't leave. He had to see, even though he still refused to believe.

Laney restarted the film. The onscreen Jacob shook his stick and smiled. Then he stopped singing and stepped back from the circle. The Alex of now watched in horror as the Alex of the ritual began a lewd dance, laughing and grabbing himself, imitating the motions of intercourse. The camera panned to the people. They were laughing and singing. Their faces were radiant with happiness. Some yelled out. "Yes! Welcome Baron Semedi. Tell us what you have to say!"

The Alex on the film grinned at them then stopped. He walked to a nearby table. He fashioned a hat out of gold metallic paper and placed it on his head. As he danced and laughed, he snatched a bottle from the Baron's altar and drank, as if he was in a drinking contest and the liquid was only draft beer. But the off-screen Alex remembered the taste, dark rum. The sensation was shocking, as intense a jolt to his sense of reality as the image onscreen. The Alex on film ignored his discomfort. Instead, with obvious pleasure he egged the crowd on with odd motions. The hat resembled a mix between a dunce hat and a parody of a golden crown, like something from theater or carnival, Cirque de Soleil. The voice erupting from his mouth was not his own. It had an accent, part Creole, part street thug.

"This is my new instrument. He is a fool," it said.

The crowd agreed in loud affirmations.

The filmed Alex/Baron leaned over in a conspiratorial manner and pointed his finger at the crowd, circling in front of them. The front line shrank back, afraid to be picked out. "Respect the fool," the transformed Alex said in a voice so deep it could best the strains of a cello. "Respect the fool. He has the courage to go where you do not. He will lead you to your better selves, your better lives, despite the dangers. He will go with innocence in his heart. He carries loyalty and courage on his shoulders, for I shall ride with him all the way. He is my instrument to bring you to your senses, awaken your strengths. Do not take his role for granted."

The Alex/Baron of the ritual raised his arms in the air on either side of the dunce cap. He spun around slowly watching everyone. "Now we shall sing and dance, for there are duties which lay upon us and great sorrows to amend. You have a second chance, my friends, those who have survived. You! You! You all have missions. Together you will rebuild what has been destroyed by ignorance and greed. You shall remember the names of the *lwa* and call upon them to help. From the refuse of the winds and water, you shall rebuild the altars. Do not forget who protects you. Feed us well, for we are your *lwa*, your guides, and we will repay you in ways you cannot imagine. Release the souls of your friends who have died so they may come to *Ginen* and join their ancestors. Release them from this place. This is home to them no longer. Now I go. Guide this fool on his first unsteady steps and then see how fast he leads the way!"

With those words still ringing in their ears, the four crowded around the computer screen. They all watched, mesmerized, as the Alex/Baron fell to the ground and writhed as if in a fit. His hands and feet curled up, his breathing harsh and rapid. Finally he went limp. On screen, Jacob and Laney entered the ritual circle and picked the barely conscious Alex up beneath his arms, the fool's cap falling to the ground, as if no longer necessary. The shaman and the professor half-walked half-carried him to the back of the room. They sat him on a sack of coffee beans.

The Alex of now recognized the actions of the Alex on screen, as the de-capped figure came to and wiped the sweat from his brow with the tails of his shirt. He looked around, slightly out of sync. Alex vividly remembered how unsettled he'd felt back then, as if he'd been coming out of a fever or a fugue.

Alex leaned back in the computer chair, still not believing what he'd just witnessed. He needed to feel justified in his role as victim, but strange things filtered back into consciousness. The way he'd felt hypnotized as he'd fallen and ended up sitting on the bags of coffee beans, the odd taste in his mouth. No, more than remembered; he tasted it again: a strange and strong rum. And all the time he'd chalked it up to the strange aromas in the room, the powders Jacob-as-Magus had thrown on the fire.

"Do you realize what happened?" Lily asked softly, sitting down beside him, her arm protectively on the back of the chair. "You were possessed. During your first ritual you were possessed. It's a rare thing. But it happened."

Alex didn't answer. He recalled once how he'd suffered a blackout after a drinking binge of Aftershock. He'd woken up, confused as to the clothes strewn from the living room to the bathroom. It was morning, but all the lights in the house were still on, the curtains flung open, the stereo playing. He and Lily both couldn't remember what happened, but the telltale signs were there. He tried to connect the alcohol blackout with what he watched on the computer screen. He tried to recall facts to discount it, but they only corroborated what he was afraid to believe. The day after the ritual he'd found a huge bruise on his hip. Had it happened when he fell to the ground? How could he have lived for more than six months with no recollection? *It was all too bizarre.*

Alex turned to Jacob then, swiveled the chair around. Lily's arm flew off. "If that really happened, why didn't any of you tell me?" He spat out the words; the anger bubbled in his throat. He glared at Jacob, his mentor now turned tormentor.

"We were hoping you'd find out some way for yourself. We thought we had time." Lily said cryptically, without emotion, as if she ignored Alex's distress.

"Time for what?" Alex asked. "More tricks? More lies?"

"No. Time to prepare you," said a voice from behind him. He flinched in recognition, afraid as he turned and watched as Mavis walked into the room.

"You're in on all this?" his voice was ragged with shock, disbelief.

"It's not like that," she said. "It's not how you think."

Alex sat with his head in his hands. "I'm such a pawn," he mumbled through his hands.

"No, Alex. You're not a pawn. You're gifted. You're chosen." Jacob's voice was gentle, considerate. When the *lwa* sits on your head, especially Baron Semedi, you are the messenger, the vehicle. He chose you for a reason."

"Chosen? How can I be? I don't even buy into your whole voudou religion. I just study it. My God, what the hell is going on?" He got up from the chair, found himself pacing, and then realized the action was a shadow of Jacob's movements that day at Perry's, in the greenhouse. He forced himself to stop.

"I need to think," Alex announced. He wanted to tear his hair out or punch someone or grab both Lily and Mavis and shake them. He felt so out of control, out of his depth. Totally unbidden, he recalled his own words, as if they'd been planted in his brain.

...*a weird second chance of being fully, vividly alive...meant to work in the field...there will be horrors and things beyond your control – maybe most of the time – you'll be tingling with fear but always in awe.*

"Arrggghh," he yelled.

"Do you believe it now?" Laney asked him, eyeing him harshly, polishing his glasses. Alex bolted out the door.

***

A short while later, Bad Jacqui placed a menu in front of Alex. "How're you doin' Alex, my boy? You're looking a little green around the gills. What will it be? Your usual?"

"Not tonight, Jacqui. How about a double shot of vodka?"

"Nothin's wrong with you and Mavis, is it? You didn't have a fight, did you? You know if you hurt that girl, I'm gonna have to hurt you." Jacqui sat down across from him and motioned the bartender to come over.

"No, everything's fine with Mavis. She's wonderful." Alex sighed, worn out. "Things with Jacob have gotten so weird. I'm so far out of my depth I don't know which way to go. I'm at my wits' end." He reached for the first shot and downed it, then wrapped his fingers around the second.

"Jacob has a way of doing that to people. But I heard from Mavis he was in bad shape, what with being in the tornado out at Lakeview and all."

"He is. Yeah, he is. He's a different man. But he still has a way of getting to me. And it's not just him. Lily, I mean, Cate, the girl you know as Cate, is back in town."

Jacqui's head snapped up. "Cate?" My God, I haven't heard that name in years. Why hasn't she been in to see me?"

"I couldn't say, only that I've known her as Lily and we were married. We lived together for the past seven years," Alex reported in dismal sarcasm. *The layers of betrayal were unbelievable.* He downed the second shot.

"Well, I'll be damned. I knew it was too quiet lately. I knew it would all have to crack open sooner or later." Jacqui shook her head and signaled for the bartender to bring more drinks. This time there were two instead of four. "On the house, and I think I'll join you."

"Is it more of that *voudoo* shit?" Bad Jacqui asked as they clinked glasses, not in celebration, but in mutual realization.

"You could say that." Alex said dismal.

"So is the shit gonna hit the fan?" she continued as if the liquor didn't affect her or burn her throat. "I warned Mavis to stay out of all that. She's got a good head on her shoulders but she always did take a shine to Jake. Unfortunately, everyone did. And he knew how to use them to his advantage. He even had me suckered in for a while."

"Yeah," Alex looked at her. "Yeah, *voudoo's* part of it. But I'm not sure if that's why things are so messed up. It may all be just me, ready to run away again. I've been known to vacate the premises when the soup gets too hot. And y'all know how to brew a spicy gumbo down here."

"That we do." Jacqui put her hand on top of his. "That we do. But we also have some of the toughest, smartest, most spirited women here, too, and you can make that work for you. Lean on Mavis, Alex. She's strong, and what she doesn't have in book smarts she's got in street smarts." Jacqui stood up. "Why don't you drink up and go on home and talk it out with her."

But before he could finish the fourth drink, an odd lopsided silhouette blanketed the door. The figure leaned on the doorjamb. Alex didn't know if it was for support or a staging for drama. Then he entered the room. Alex was sure Jacob could hear the gasp from Bad Jacqui when she saw his face.

"Well, Jacob. You sure do look a sight, but you're up on your own two feet, and if I know you as good as I think I do, you're gonna work this new look into your act."

"That's exactly what I had in mind, Jacqui. Glad to see you. Been longer than I liked. But I think Alex and I have some things to work out." Jacob hugged her, and then shuffled over to Alex's side of the table. Alex stood up, like a kid to an elder, then thought better of it and sat down quickly. He didn't want to emphasize Jacob's state.

"I thought I'd find you here." Jacob sat down awkwardly, the wooden chair threatening to tip over for a moment. "Before you scamper off, let me apologize. I know all of that back there's a shocker. I can't say it wasn't a shocker for me the night it happened. But we couldn't figure out any other way to let you know."

CHAPTER THIRTY-SEVEN — IN THE ALEMBIC WITH A BROKEN WING

"It looks like you have plans to stay," Lily guessed.

It felt odd to Jacob to be here. It had been weeks since he'd seen Lily, or the woman he'd prefer to call Cate, but that woman seemed lost to him now. He hadn't seen any others of the cross-wired group, either. After he'd left Bad Jacqui's, Jacob had gone into hiding, his own hermitage. For many reasons he couldn't explain to the rest of them…for what he'd done to them and to himself. He had to find a way to sort it all out. He looked around the third story apartment Lily had found off of Magazine Street, not far from where they'd lived years, no, lifetimes, ago. "When did you decide to move out of Laney's?"

"I only stayed there a few days." Lily moved through the apartment, her back to him. It could have been fear or dismissal, Jacob wasn't sure, couldn't read her anymore. He thought of all the times he'd turned his back on Alex, on her, never realizing the impact. He'd often only meant to get away.

"So Mavis convinced you to come see me?" Lily asked.

"Yeah, I went to see her at Bad Jacqui's. Find out how everyone was doing." Jacob admitted.

Lily turned to him with a weak false smile and motioned him to a small rooftop porch, as if she were a reluctant hostess. As he moved through the three small rooms, he could see little of Lily in the furnishings. They must have come with the place – an evacuee who decided to stay away. It seemed out of place that Lily lived here. The rooms were bland, lacking her touch. Their own homes years ago had always been filled with her findings from thrift shops and flea markets. Assorted hand-thrown pots, small oddities she collected: a marble statue of Alexander the Great, an alabaster one of Diana, trinket boxes filled with old fountain pens and inks. He ducked beneath the overhang to get to a niche carved out between dormers. The small veranda was so overrun with plants and vines he had to hunt for a place to lean on the balcony. He looked out over the city and for the first time saw an aerial view, revealing a viable reality very different from filmed montages he'd seen on the news. The actuality was terrifying – the sheer magnitude of it. The wasteland below echoed his inner state.

"Pretty grim, isn't it?" Lily took a spot beside him.

"Why'd you pick this place?" he asked, shaking his head.

"The contrast, the counterpoint. The way all the greenery came back on this patio, in defiance of the devastation out there. As soon as I saw it, I knew it was the right place, a place where I could learn balance."

He turned to look at her. She gave him a sly look and shrugged her shoulders. "I keep drawing the two of pentacles."

"The one who juggles," he pronounced, thinking of the figure balancing two crystal balls. Her favorite card in the Morgan-Greer Tarot deck. His dark eyes confirmed her interpretation.

She nodded her head as if aware he'd remembered. "To really comprehend it all," she said. "I have to keep reminding myself this is real. In our time, we're witnessing the destruction…if we're lucky, the rebirth, of a unique culture. Personally, at this point in my life, I can't afford any type of complacency."

"None of us can." Jacob looked off, his one eye negative space as he turned inward, going to a place he could not invite her, even though his words harkened back to earlier times, more innocent times.

"*Solutio, purgatory*. When will it all end?" He spoke more to himself than to her. "I knew all along the levees would break, but it never dawned on me what an alembic New Orleans was."

"The perfect vessel to purify the sludge of our country." Her voice was low, resigned. "Where else could the *prima materia* be so easily deposited? But now, what to do? It seems the *sublimatio* and *calcinatio* weren't enough."

He looked up, remembering their debates, the easy flow of ideas. He almost smiled, grateful in the midst of this grim diagnosis, to see how her mind charged his. His usual witty comebacks seemed shallow in light of the deep intuitive insights he realized in her presence. Their minds were like two halves of a whole, working better because of the uncanny connection to the other; a wireless network of shared data impossible with anyone else. *How had he forgotten?* "Now we're into *coagulatio*." Alchemy was a safer way to view the deeper implications. "The stagnation of the half-baked base matter; it only can mean one thing." He couldn't look at the city anymore. He turned his back and leaned on the balcony. "We'll have to repeat the stages again until the wolf conjointly burns with the lion."

"Another hurricane? Another natural disaster?" she asked.

"I'm not the only one predicting such things, whether they be instigated by natural or societal events." He tossed his head to the side, as if he could cast the thought away. "Enough of that. I've had enough doom for one day. Let's change the subject." He left the rooftop garden and walked back inside. "Have you painted here?" He hadn't seen any artwork or even her usual jumble of canvases, empty frames, open paint tubes, and brushes standing at attention in pewter mugs.

"I've rented a studio not far from the Quarter. Bad Jacqui told me about it." She looked away, unsure.

But just before she did, he caught the shift, her eyes clouding from emerald to malachite, like an opaque veil attempting to hide the moon. A shift he remembered well, her own inward turn as she disappeared, as skilled as a dancer behind a silken veil.

"I've worked some, but what with everything going on, I seem to be in transition." She peeled off the fingerless gloves she wore to protect her skin from the pigments. She must have returned from her studio just minutes before he'd arrived. He wondered why she hadn't invited him to come there. He smiled at the sight of her multicolored fingertips, remembering meals they'd shared where he couldn't take his eyes of those hands, hands like a melusine, always fluttering as she talked, reflecting the leftover teal and copper, phthalo blue and ochre found only beneath the depths of the sea.

"Well, tomorrow is the day of answers," Jacob said, his voice restrained, reluctant. He knew he was avoiding the issue of the two of them, but he'd accepted her invitation for a purpose. He needed her to talk to him into going through with the ritual. It was an old need, an uncomfortable one, but for the first time in many years he was actually afraid to be in front of the public, even if that public were his friends and the congregation.

"It will work out," she accepted the lobby, as eager to avoid the awkwardness as he was. "Can you look at tomorrow's ritual as an obstacle to test your resolve? You can't really be worried the *lwa* has abandoned you?" She hoped he didn't read the shock on her face. It disturbed her to view Jacob without his usual confidence. His natural ease had exited with the accident. Sure, she'd seen him vulnerable in their days together, more vulnerable than she'd ever expected, but this was a Jacob she hardly recognized. Images of their early days reminded her of his duality, the public Jacob and the highly private Jacob. When they first lived together, she remembered how alarmed and isolated she felt. Following passionate and tender lovemaking, he'd slept next to her on his back, his arms folded on his chest, his ankles crossed. He rebuffed her when she attempted to touch him. She alternated between crying and biting her tongue. Then one day, during a round of the thrift shops, she'd found a strange figurine. It was a red devil with one angelic wing and a forked tail, its head and one wing broken off.

Jacob had taken to it immediately. "Well, that's me in a nutshell, take it or leave it," he'd said in a moment of candor.

"I'll take him," she'd said, winking at Jacob, turning to the girl at the cash register.

Outside the shop, they'd walked along Magazine Street. "Does this mean you accept me as I am?" he'd asked.

"Of course. Isn't that what love implies?" She'd said simply, studying the figure in her hands, an amulet.

"But I'm mixed up." Jacob had stopped and put his hands on her shoulders. He turned her to him. She was forced to look at him. His eyes had probed hers; their depths beckoned, like the need of the free-divers, the need to go deeper and deeper, despite the risk. "I'm the bad boy who wants to do good, the attention grabber who wants to make something of it." He had forced her to pay attention, perhaps as guardian of his depths.

They'd walked for a long time circling the Quarter along Canal Street. He'd led her into St. Louis II, slowly escorted her through the narrow aisles. He'd indicated a tomb, and then turned toward her. "That coffin sleep of mine," he looked at her out of the corner of his eyes, as if he were afraid she might bolt, "it hurts you, doesn't it?"

For a moment she'd wondered if this was all staged and, if so, how long had he waited to bring her here to discuss their distance? She'd felt shut out as if a stone vault, stained with the rust and oxidation of her tears, had conspired to keep her from knowing the core Jacob. "Yes, it does. How you can be so tender and loving and then shut me out?" she remembered saying, her stomach in knots.

He'd taken a seat on the tomb. "Lily, it's not you. It's everyone. I don't do it to hurt you. I've slept that way for years. Ever since the first invasion of the *lwa*. Despite all the good it represents, it unhinges me. I can't trust my body to be my own," he'd confided. "So I learned not to trust. I can't trust myself or how I might act and I can't trust others who might do something to me while I'm under the influence of the *lwa* or asleep."

"But without trust, there can be no intimacy." Lily had said, hopeless, filled with a deep sadness. The same sadness which permeated the cemetery.

After the revelation, it took many nights of patient small steps. There were times she thought his inability to trust and open up would destroy any intimacy they developed during the day. She'd even considered leaving. Their pillow talk had turned more and more to past incidents of pain or hurt. With those quiet talks she saw his trust begin to grow. Sure, there'd been arguments. Great rages when she'd gone in too deep, opening scars with knifelike precision. He'd stormed from the bed, knocking over lamps and pacing around the room, railing at the world, at the loss of his dad and the abandonment of his mother, at his lack of faith in himself. She'd talk him down, trying to remain calm herself but often failing, bringing up her own losses and torments. Finally, when she'd end up crying, he'd soften, return to bed and hold her. Eventually, he learned to trust her enough to sleep more naturally. Once he'd allowed himself to become vulnerable, the love she felt was tinged with the responsibility to protect him.

Even now she still felt that responsibility, fourteen years all told. How could it be that long already? She pulled herself out of the memory, back into her new apartment, the post-Katrina winds blowing in from the balcony, as it to emphasize life was nothing but adaptation to change.

Jacob followed Lily as she walked over to an antique dresser, vintage '20's, much like the one Ensie had.

"Look what I still have." Lily went to a small shrine on the dresser. It was encrusted with plaster and Tibetan skull beads carved from bone. Small hand-carved crucifixes of every design completed the collage. Inside the shrine hung the devil/angel figurine. It was the only example of Lily's art Jacob had seen in the apartment.

Seeing the small shrine gave him the courage to bring up a huge doubt. "I've had to think a lot lately – not something I'm accustomed to doing. And it dawned on me that Ezeli must be pissed." Jake walked back out into the tiny garden, turning his back on their past. He lowered himself onto a bench

Lily sighed and followed. In the aerie garden he looked much like a Green Man...all he needed was a beard. Unattainable, she admitted to herself. "What? What about Ezeili?" Her words were sharper than she'd planned. She was angry at him, even angrier at herself for not having the guts to confront him. And now the moment had passed. The vulnerable risk was for nothing.

"Yeah, it occurred to me – with the whole copper fire pot business." He continued as if their previous conversation had never happened. "The lwa was trying to tell me something. And wouldn't you agree only a female would get mad enough to throw a pot at someone?" His lips curled up in a wicked smile.

"Well, despite all my feminist dismay at stereotypes, I'd have to agree." Lily said. "But you've never been involved with Ezeli. Why should she get jealous now? And from all Maman Simone taught me, Ezeili is a spirit who doesn't expect anything until you ask her favors, get her to interfere in love matters. Otherwise she may not know you exist."

"Perhaps the Baron sent her – she's better at fast anger than he is. He prefers the slow turn."

"Ezeli is not known to do anyone's bidding, lwa or otherwise," Lily said. "But you do have a point. Flinging pots is not the Baron's style. Not at all. If he wanted to get your attention or even punish you, he had a million opportunities while you were completing the burial rituals."

Jake looked at Lily with new eyes – well, one eye, he thought to himself. When he'd first met her, she'd resembled a Modigliani woman, long-necked and innocent. Now she was more like Munch's Madonna or Vampire, wilder red hair and a look which implied she gave no quarter. She could go from ecstatic to ravenous in moments. He wondered when the change had occurred. Recently? From the tales he'd heard and the night of her art show, her transformation was not accomplished on the footsteps of her life with Alex. No, it had been recent, sometime during her hermitage, and, he realized, perhaps for the first time, she was a force to be reckoned with alongside the Baron.

Lily turned to view Jake again, ready for another argument, maybe a decisive one this time. But the image she witnessed kicked her out of the mundane, back into the world they'd both once known so well. Timing, synchronicity, connections…whether they be the universal mind of Jung or the string theories of the quantum neo-physicists, now offered another glimpse of serendipity. The sun setting in the Quarter eerily surrounded Jacob's head. The sunset a new sight now, blocked for 200 years by the intrusions of buildings and foliage. But now many of the trees had been removed, relocated to the landfills by the hand of Special K, relegated to what might become the lasting memorial: a mile-high dump, a testament to the abandonment of a city by its own country. Thanks to "The Thing" as New Orleanians called Katrina, portions of the sky were now again visible.

The disc of the sun positioned itself directly behind Jacob's head. He was a bas relief in silhouette, a perverse St. Francis of the Renaissance paintings, or a showman's ploy, like her autographed photo of Trent Reznor as he posed in front of industrial-sized gears. The nimbus surrounded Jacob's head, fiery light streaked with the pinks, oranges, fuchsias and purples only seen in the 21st century, a gift of pollution radiating out, overstated like a child's drawing or a vision of mystics.

Tears welled up; of thanks or fear, she didn't know. And for a moment, Lily thought this might be what she'd been looking for all of her life. He wasn't a saint, far from it, but her Catholic past reminded her how all saints had once been sinners. Even though she'd cursed her religious upbringing for years, she knew bits and pieces had never quite left, embedded seeds which grew, changed, and twisted to mingle with every new revelation she discovered in the depths of Thomas Moore and James Hillman, Joseph Campbell and Marcello Ficino.

Jacob thought he'd been broken by the accident, but the sight of Lily's tears broke him even more. Now he crumpled on the inside. A tension built, filled his body, threatening implosion. One eye was not enough for all the tears he should shed. He felt ready to crumble to dust or burst into a flock of crows like in the movies. Now he knew where that image came from: all the black tension needing to wing away.

He jumped up, strode as if he'd never been injured and grabbed her into his arms. She crushed herself to him, held him to her. Her hands followed the lines and shapes of his body, remembering, discovering the changes. In many ways it felt like she'd never left his side. The years disintegrated, pressurized by too much pain and even greater need. But then her cheek caressed the scar, her hands discovered a broken shoulder blade, two inches off-kilter, the bone jutting at an awkward angle out from his back. Her fingers traced the ridges of it, questioning. *How could there be things I don't know about Jacob? How could the years have stolen such knowledge from me?*

"This is from your car accident in Haiti," she said in shock. She could hardly believe she hadn't touched him like this since he'd walked away seven years ago. She tried to think back, but her mind was rushed, panicked. *I haven't touched his back in all this time? Not in the apartment after the art show, not beside the lake, not in the hospital?* Silent tears flowed without her consent.

"The gods must have been angry that time, too." He laughed.

She looked over his shoulder at the angel/devil in the shrine, struggled to regain her composure before Jacob could see how she'd lost it. A stray breeze enlivened the figure, animating it, as it swung to the tune of the Tibetan wind chimes on the porch. The figure of duality's spinning dance mocked her, reminding her there was only one wing. If the figure owned a head it would be grinning, implying *you should have guessed all along.*

"They ripped the wing right off your back," she whispered.

"You never knew?" he asked.

How could I? She almost flung the accusation at him, but then realized the anger was aimed at her own false assumptions. She recognized in an instant where she'd gone wrong all along. What if the figure's mockery offered a gift, like the insight Jacob gained with only one eye? Now she had to view things differently. It was time to merge the splits she saw in Jacob. It was time to love the whole being, neglecting neither the human nor the divine.

CHAPTER THIRTY-EIGHT — REPLAY THE RITUAL

A breeze blew through the potted citron tree, stirring the purple and black ribbons, the offerings hanging there. The fire was already burning. Laney positioned an iron bar in the center. Perry hung a small wooden sailing ship from the awning near the altar room while Jacob festooned the huge black wrought iron cross with more purple and black ribbons. Lily placed the items he would need: red brick dust for the *vever*, the rattle on a small table near the circle they'd created with plants in white pots positioned in the courtyard.

"Hey, Laney, come here. I need help with this." Perry was nearly forced to the ground by a massive tree trunk. Laney and Jacob rushed over to help erect the *potomitan* at the center to represent the *axis mundi*, the tree of life, the way to *Ginen* – or the underworld, depending on the mood of the spirits.

They'd been surprised how hard it was to find a tree trunk they could use thanks to Katrina, but one night Jacob pulled it out of the old bus, without a word about how he found it. In preparation for the set up, Perry and Lily had painted all the colors of the rainbow in spiral bands for *Ayida-Wedo*, the female, the protectress of the cosmos, the serpent and the rainbow. Perry nodded his head once the trunk was set up. "Now we have the link between sky, earth and *Ginen"* Perry stood back and nodded approval. The *lwa* will be pleased and able to come here easily."

The altars were ready. People were already starting to arrive. Hundreds of white pots created concentric rings around the *potomitan*. The Fibonacci principle, Lily thought, harking back to her arts training. She stood on the sidelines, trying to hide her anxiety for Jacob, as she waited to function as one of the flag bearers.

As the people filed into the courtyard, there was an air of expectancy, of fear and hope. Many came in, looking around in surprise, in awe.

"Newcomers," Perry said.

After everyone had arrived, Jacob moved slowly to the center of the circle. He carried the wand in one hand. Lily sucked in her breath as she watched the newcomers look at each other at the sight of his face. Perhaps they wondered if he'd worn a mask or makeup for the ceremony. Jacob looked to Lily. He'd noticed, too.

He flashed his lopsided grimace at her, looking for a moment like the old Jacob, a wry look, an inside joke. But the joke didn't spread to his eye. She winked back, hoping it would summon the full-blown trickster, the true representative of Baron Semedi. But Jacob was something else now.

Older, burdened, as if he carried a sack of stones on his back, one stone for each body he'd buried.

There was no breeze, just an eerie stillness, as if the crowd had all sucked in their breath at the sight of him, leaving the place without sustenance. But in moments, as if the entire world must let out a sigh of relief, the red ribbons on the wand fluttered in the air. Jacob's gait was slow and measured, the limp more emphasized on uneven ground. His shirt and hair were plastered to his body with sweat, even though the evening had become temperate for New Orleans.

Almost broken, but still shuffling through the dirt, he made his way to the place he'd been most at home. He took up the machete from where he'd stashed it, and, in a surprising act of agility, slammed it into the ground. The crowd reared back at the sudden act of violence.

After, he began to sing, a slow song, a dirge. Deep and resonant, it brought the crowd to tears. Baron Semedi was still not present. Lily realized the song was private, internal. Jacob could care less that a congregation was present. This was his personal act of sorrows. Lily looked at him and shook her head; *this is not the time, not the place.* But he didn't notice her, even when he moved close to her to lay the machete on the table and retrieve the sacks of dust. He slung the long narrow inkle-woven bands over one shoulder, across his chest, rainbow threads of silk Lily wove for the ceremony, the bags hanging against Jacob's hip on his good side.

He moved in slow awkward sliding steps, dipping his hands into the sacks, drawing out handfuls of dust. Pouring white chalk, and then red brick dust, on the ground, he drew out the *vevers*, formed elaborate curlicue patterns – more complex than he'd done before. It took over an hour. He was oblivious to everyone else present.

When he went toward the fire, Lily could feel a sense of release rise from the crowd. *Now things will get going. Now we can all participate.*

But no sooner had the fire taken hold – the sticks of kindling flaming each other, like passion, like anger – when Jacob looked around, as though surprised anyone else was present. The shock was evident, even on those distorted features. He shook his head, as if shaking off a dream, and began to dance, or try to dance. His natural rhythm was lost. Lily could see his lips moving. She hoped he wasn't cursing himself for not having the guts to practice. He'd told her he thought it would all come back, like riding a horse or bicycle. It didn't. His feet refused to obey his brain. He needed a cane to execute the simplest steps, but his cane leaned against the wall in the greenhouse. He tripped at one point, like a drunkard. The wand tip scraped the ground. It was a makeshift but inadequate cane, leaving trails of red ribbons in the dust, erasing the designs, like rivulets of regrets. He nearly fell into the fire before catching himself. Then he circled again, becoming at ease in body, but disoriented in time and space.

Lily willed him to remember back to the early days when his body moved before he could think to command it. Now it moved on twenty second delay, a miniscule stretch of time in the grand scheme of things. But, then, events and history are frequently altered on the pivot of a second, she thought.

When Jacob went to move again, he stumbled, looked into the fire as if he'd find answers there. His look of disorientation vanished. With a grimace of firm resolve, followed by relief, he stepped straight into the flames, as simply as walking through a doorway. Screams of shock erupted from the crowd.

Lily, Laney, and Alex all moved at the same time. Lily and Alex reached Jacob first. They grabbed his shirt and arms and pulled him back from the flames. He turned his head to look at them, his eyes clouded with grief, with loss, with anger, as if they'd snatched him from a place he'd rather be.

Perry stepped into the circle and took up the ritual as Jacob was hustled off into a side room. His shirt was singed and smoking. The pungent smell of burnt hair invaded the room. Alex led Jacob to a chair, but the shaman flung Alex's arm back.

"I am no invalid!" Jacob turned on his heel and exited the room before they could stop him. He glared at them from beneath the shadow of a banana tree.

Lily returned to her spot, picked up her flag and shook off the dust. Alex circled the courtyard, found a place as obscure as Jacob's.

Perry went through the complicated steps, adequate but uninspired. The drummers beat out their complex rhythms, but the *lwa* did not appear. Perry drew more *vevers*, some Lily could not place. The crowd grew restless, as if they were being fooled, used. They needed this ritual for closure and now it was shredded to tatters.

Jacob looked up before everyone else. Alex followed his eyes. A great staggered shock of lightning sliced the sky, like a staircase ripped in the fabric of the firmament. In the blink of an eye, before the thunder, a cascade of rain, heavy as a waterfall, crashed down upon the ceremony. Some shrank back, wondering if the staircase were for them, a call for them to leave this life. Within minutes everyone was soaked to the skin. Fire tenders rushed to the fire and piled on more kindling and sticks, torturing the coals, imploring them with chants to stay alive.

Some turned to leave the circle. But Jacob strode in, barely limping, standing tall and straight. He danced a radical jazzy two-step, shuffling like a tap dancer in the Quarter, a parody of skill.

And then he stopped. The wand was held high in the air as if taunting the lightning to come back and fight, ignite the wand if it could. The red ribbons hung down his arm like blood, like lava, liquid fire.

"There must be great times of change." A voice, an accent, not Jacob's own, but issuing from his mouth, bellowed. He winked at those in front of him. A lewd wink, a joke. Jacob's movements held little grace. His body jerked as tragic-comically as a vaudeville dancer. His shoulders squared off as the demeanor of an African, a full black, not an Americanized mulatto, took over. To Lily, Jacob's eyes were no longer grey, but blacker than the stone she'd put in his pocket, the *zemi*, the thunderstone, where she hoped the Baron might live. Never had Jacob been so completely not himself. He was once again, and for all time, the Baron Semedi in full guise, in full regalia of twisted mocking shaman. The Lord of the Dead. The King of *Geude*.

Lily winced. She hardly recognized Jacob. Never before in all the years of service to the *lwa* had she ever seen anyone so transformed. Jacob's stature as the Baron grew. His physical body ate up more space, his strides longer, his movements so grand and powerful she knew she was witness to the full force of the god.

"I will break this body no more," the Baron/Jacob pronounced, "for he has been a most loyal servant." The Baron, like an interior puppeteer gaining prowess in technique, manipulated Jacob's body and took a huge step towards the crowd. It appeared the man Jacob walked totally out of his skin, leaving it fully to the Baron. Lily could see nothing of her lover left in the form. Even the scar was dimmed by the animated facial expressions of the speaker. Gone was Jacob's wit and intelligence. Instead a figure comfortable in its massive physical stature and power took hold. The face and voice were coarser, rougher, more confident than she had ever seen Jacob, even onstage playing music.

"Now I will need three," the thickly accented voice called out. "Three it will take to replace him. For this horse of mine has other missions. He has proven his worth. This horse must carry our words to those who fear us, who will not come here as you brave and eager ones have. He must now go out to the greater world, to those who have no *Ginen*, to offer them peace."

For the first time Lily saw wholeness, completeness. Spirit and body as one, not spirit driving a body. It was like flame and fire, one and the same, whole in its energy and voracity, individual fingers of flame, yet aligned as an element unto itself.

"Who is there among you who will step forward?" The Baron peered into the circle of faces.

No one moved. The rain fell in sheets, in slides of water thick as a heavy Katrina-sluiced curtain. Fog rose from the heated ground cooled by the rain, a fog where they all wished to hide.

Laney stepped forward. Alex looked on in doubt and surprise, knowing how much Laney could lose in his diligently nurtured career. Then Perry stepped forward, too, a big grin on his face, knowing he'd wanted to all along.

The courtyard was filled with stillness except for the thrust of the rain. Water danced in puddles; mad sprites sought mayhem. Baron Semedi peered through the fog. He pointed a blunt finger towards a dark corner. Alex shrank back.

"And you," the Baron said, "you, my horse, you who I rode at your first ritual. Will you not stand forward?" His tone questioned, but left little room for denial.

Alex didn't step forward. He didn't speak. He only shook his head side to side. Laney and Perry watched. Everyone in the crowd could see the intensity of the Baron's eyes, and for a moment the Jacob-as-Baron returned, sought Alex out from the other side of the *houdan*. The shadows and fog couldn't hide their ambiguity.

CHAPTER THIRTY-NINE — THE REFUSAL

Hours later, they sat in the dark in the middle of the temple, now simply a courtyard again. Exhaustion lay on Alex like a pall, as heavy as the air laden with the damp of the passing storm. It was not over. He was learning to smell it, the precursor to more storms, more trouble. The confusion left him angry and at a loss of any safe foothold.

Too much had happened in too short a time. He was unsettled, overwhelmed. It was a case of sensory overload and emotional conflagration.

Lily had left with Jacob to settle Laney and Perry in the quarters where they were to be trained for their new roles in the temple. Mavis had gone home alone, respecting Alex's wishes to stay behind, to talk to Jacob in particular. Alex had no explanations, no feeling in his gut. But he'd felt no calling, either, even though the pressure from the Baron and the congregation's anticipation was fraught with more tension than the storm.

When Jacob finally entered the courtyard, Alex stood. It was a natural reaction, without forethought. Alex noticed Jacob's walk was different, more at ease, nothing like his old self, but more relaxed, more comfortable in his new skin. However, he was profoundly tired, as Alex was. Jacob sat wearily next to Alex on the bench, awkward for only a moment, almost like the early days, as if the past few months had not occurred.

Jacob leaned back and sighed.

"What happened to you at the fire?" Alex couldn't stop himself from asking.

The mulatto's eyes quickly drifted away, as if the lure was too great to resist, "The ground was not where I'd envisioned it. For a time, I thought I was in Haiti. And I had this feeling, that everything was false. I knew that if I stepped into the doorway where the fire had once been that I'd pass through to a better time, to a place of answers. So I took a step...and I was right."

"I'm just not inclined." Alex said, speaking out into the night, sounding like an archaic pastor refusing an invitation to tea, as if he'd rehearsed a safe answer to elude a confrontation. Inside he was in turmoil. He snapped. "I just can't go there, Jacob. I can't let go like you do. It's terrifying, let alone dangerous. Even if I did feel a calling, as you seem to, I'd run away from this all as fast as I can. It's too much for me. I can't do it."

"You misread me, Alex," Jacob said, calm, perhaps resigned. "You don't need to explain anything to me. I'm simply relieved. It's been a very long day." He looked into Alex's eyes as if searching for answers himself.

Alex was surprised to see the gray lucid gaze instead of the black hole look the Baron had thrust at him, as threatening as a machete, during the last moments of the ritual.

"There's not much left to say, is there? I don't care what you choose, Alex." Jacob got up from the bench. "All I care is that you have a choice."

Alex watched as Jacob's back merged into the steamy night. He sat on the bench many hours after Jacob left. For the first time in their relationship, Alex didn't feel abandoned.

CHAPTER FORTY — THE ATHANOR

The drive to Lakeside brought memories rushing back. Blurred and confused, but vivid. It had been many months now since the accident, since the ritual. Jacob had avoided everyone, had left town. It came as a surprise for him to hear from Lily with an invitation to her relocated studio.

"I have an idea," Lily said on the phone, "and I need your input. I'm not sure I can pull it off." Her voice was more urgent and needy than he remembered; a different Cate/Lily yet again.

"Why me?" Jacob asked, feigning nonchalance.

"Let's face it, Jacob, you know me better than anyone else. If I do this wrong I could hurt a lot of people, but I have this feeling I might be able to pull it off. Can you just come and look?"

"Why can't you ask Perry or Laney?" Jacob wondered where his role would fit in this new pattern of their always changing, often filtered, kaleidoscope.

"They're already involved. Laney's all for it, at least from what he's seen. Perry hasn't been here much, too busy with the temple. I wouldn't have asked for your input if it wasn't important." She was adamant. He agreed. Agreed beyond his better judgment, because he still felt like he walked a precarious line between coping and not coping. The past months had been empty.

When he drove through Lakeview, much of the area looked the same as it did following the double sucker punch of Katrina and the tornado. The Army Corps of Engineers wouldn't meet their deadline of having the levees and the pumps finished in time for hurricane season on June 1st. The stalwart went ahead and rebuilt anyway. But they were few, and the rest of the homeowners, at least the ones who returned, delayed rebuilding until they felt safe it was worth the trouble.

Jacob expected to overreact on the walk up to Laney's house, where Lily explained she'd fashioned a studio of sorts. The view of the lake behind it disturbed him, but he wasn't flooded with the expected rush of emotions or regrets. Everything was so different, he felt as if he were somewhere else. The house had been completely rebuilt, with a second story added. Flowers bloomed in shady areas alongside trees and shrubs Perry replaced. The renewed garden offered a welcome of a peace he hadn't known in a long time.

He followed a narrow path between budding camellias and gardenias to the back of the house, just as they'd always done, instead of the more formal approach to the front door.

Jacob rounded a corner where he found her, near a circular stone structure, half as tall as she was. The bottom half glowed white. He stopped short before Lily could see him. He was unprepared for how much the back lawn stretching towards the lake had been transformed as well. As opposed to the clean serene lines of the front, this area was a littered scrap yard.

He wiped his brow. He could feel the heat thrown off by a circular furnace, a fire pit of ancient design, a 15th Century illumination come to life in 21st Century New Orleans. Lily, distracted and busy, was dwarfed by the structure as she stood on a small scaffold a few feet high.

She cussed and leaned over deeper into the pit, straining to the point where he feared she'd fall in. He took a step forward, and then thought better of it. When he decided to move again, it was too late. Her actions changed from awkward struggle to a mastery of her materials. She talked to herself, or to the depths of the pit, and gently stirred the fire with a long iron rod. Sparks and smoke erupted from the disruption. She brushed them aside. Jacob considered creeping back to his car.

But, instead, he stayed, aroused by her casual approach to danger, by the changes in her, by her unawareness that her seclusion had been breached. Jacob didn't know if her scene worked on the gods, but it worked on him. He inched forward, careful to stay obscured by a camellia.

But then she looked up, her mouth set in a grim smile, a knowing look and a sentient gesture of her head. In seconds, she paid heed to the pit once more, dismissing him. Just as abruptly, she called out, "I hoped you would come." She looked directly toward the camellia, his traitor.

Jacob stepped from behind the greenery. "I had to see what you were up to. It appears quite a bit."

She waved at him. "I have to keep an eye on the temperature. It's at the critical stage. I have to get it to 550 degrees," she said as she checked a gauge hung on a pole.

Her voice and attitude were so different from the last time he'd seen her. The smell of burning wood flared his nostrils, made him think of other times when fire wasn't a threat.

He was flooded with an old feeling, something he remembered from Paris when they first knew each other and portents of regrets were not evident. She climbed down from the scaffolding and began to dress in what looked like winter garb, fit only for a blizzard or a trek in the Himalayas, bulky oversized overcoat and overalls. She put on a similar heavily quilted hat with ear flaps, like he'd seen the lumberjacks wear in Maine, and completed the bizarre costume with a welder's mask. Sidestepping the scaffolding, she entered the structure through a small opening in the wall. He tried to gather his thoughts, unprepared for such a sight, all the imagined scenarios cut loose, leaving him drifting in a vague and confused mindset.

She picked up a shorter pipe, this time copper, and leaned over a heavy vessel; a dyer's pot, a potter's kiln, or a witch's cauldron? She dipped the pipe into the center as if to stir it and its illusive contents. She manipulated a foot peddle and inflated a huge bellows which blasted air on the wood burning beneath the cauldron.

To his surprise, the copper pipe was not a stirring device, but a source. Eventually it shrank as she stirred. He realized she was melting it in the pot. In a few moments, she picked up a large crucible on a long handle. While her right hand managed the copper tube, her left dipped the bowl of the crucible in and out of the caldron as the last of the copper disappeared. She deftly transferred her energy and focus from the left hand to the right. Sidestepping once again, she lifted the heavy crucible with its steaming contents and poured the glowing liquid metal into a row of brass molds which formed a semi-circle at her feet. He could feel the heat from his position as the sole spectator. Jacob thought of the Waterhouse painting, *The Magic Circle*, as if he, too, witnessed a current-day sorceress at work. It was an absurd scene, the atmosphere archaic and threatening, but more than the eminent danger of scalding, it was perverse, as if the act was one of creation from fire instead of matter. Spirit – not physical reality. It held the sense of threat he'd felt in the air all day.

After she poured all the copper, Lily approached him, removing the mask and hat. She looked different. Transformed by the physical exertion, she glowed from inside, despite the soot on her face. Sweat beads covered the surface of her skin, still pale but flush with heat, activity, and something he envied – purpose. Her hair, haphazardly pulled back, had fallen loose in many places, unkempt, like a wild woman of the woods from an old fairy tale or myth.

She struggled out of the rest of the suit. Beneath it she wore only a slight tank top above gauzy pants more fitting for the New Orleans weather. They looked highly flammable, as if she'd not only force the elements to serve her, but taunt them, as well.

"Is this a foundry?" Jacob asked, not masking his surprise, but trying to hide how dangerously entranced he felt.

"In a way. The design is based on an old depiction of an *athanor*, a furnace the medieval alchemists used for their work. I've been working with copper ever since I came here. I've wanted to do it for a long time but never had the guts. One day, I walked back here and here were all the materials for the project. They'd been strewn about in the floods, some left over from the rebuilding, but they held a pattern. Even on the ground I could see what to make with the bricks and cement blocks. There was plenty of dry wood, bits and pieces of metal. It was like a gift. Ever since then, I felt responsible to recycle the materials, put them to some good use. And now it's taken over my life. Perhaps the talk you and I had about alchemy set it all off, I don't know. I haven't been able to stop since. It's what I wanted to show you."

Her hands and face were smudged with soot. Jacob couldn't remember ever seeing her so free, so unencumbered by what was going on in her mind.

"This physical life seems to suit you," he said.

"I think it does." She led him to a shed down towards the small building located closer to the lake. "It's strange. I've been sort of driven, maybe a bit demented. Come on, you'll see."

It took a long time for his eyes to adjust to the darkened interior of the studio. Shelves lined the walls but were empty. Mounds of clay lay untouched on a worktable and another table was splattered with the stains of the hardened metal.

"Here, let me guide you. I want you to see what's in the next room." She pulled aside an old curtain and led him into an annexed building, a room very different from the practical workspace.

It took a while for his eyes to take it all in. "What is this?" he asked, his voice dropped now to a whisper.

"I'm not sure." Lily said from behind him in a voice as quiet as his. "I was hoping you could tell me. I need a place to put the assemblages when they're all finished. This is just an example. There need to be many more."

He had the oddest sensation that time hadn't passed. A strange shift in consciousness, something like *de ja vu* but also entirely different. It wasn't a memory, but a foreshadowing or, more frightening, a glimpse of a parallel reality, a path not chosen. He had the odd feeling he and Lily had never been apart, that indeed they'd even married. As strange as this whole new side of her was to him, it was almost as if a part of him had known it all along, as if he'd been living with her when all these concepts became actions, as if he'd shared in the experience. Yet, he knew full well he hadn't. The awareness such a vision of commitment was already lost prompted him to an immediate reaction, even though it required a dedication he'd been incapable of for a long time.

Jacob shook his head seeing it all fall into place. "I think I have just the place. Westwego."

"But that section of town was closed off, totally abandoned." Lily looked confused. "Every night there's another fire."

Jacob turned to her. The scar was part of him, like a knot assimilated into the landscape of an oak, not imposed upon him from the outside.

"In many ways you're right," he said. "It is pretty much a wasteland. That's where I live now."

CHAPTER FORTY-ONE — OF JOURNEYS AND FAR FLUNG PLACES

It was a month of reunions, remembrances. Jake walked down the street in awe of the changes and repairs, but saddened at how much more remained the same. Mavis' house looked much the same from the outside, tilting, the paint flaking. It didn't stop Jacob's fears. For these past months he'd avoided all contact with his previous life, but Lily had been insistent.

"Alex has called you many times," she'd said. "You should call him, see him. You'd be proud – of both him and Mavis."

"What was the name of his book again?" Jacob had asked.

"*A Comparative Study of Mongolian and Voudou Shamanism,*" Lily had said. "He came up with the idea after he reunited with a professor he worked with in Mongolia. He was only gone a few weeks but it appears he's reconnected with something he lost."

***

Indeed, the evidence of the couple's travels were everywhere in the shotgun house. Jacob couldn't tell whether Mavis' paintings or Alex's cultural mementos took up the most space.

Mavis moved paints, a Mongolian drum, and a basket of totems from a chair so Jacob could sit down.

"When did you return?" Jacob asked.

"Just two days ago." Alex handed Jacob a glass of wine.

Jacob walked through the open rooms, examining each piece of art at length. "I saw some of these paintings at the Katrina show at the old Iron Works. They really make an impact. I'm glad the gallery put together the program. People need to know."

"Getting those walls out of the attic was one of the first things we did after…well, after …you know." Alex said.

"Alex cut each one of them out and then backed them on fresh wood to preserve them. I didn't have a clue they'd travel." Mavis sat on the couch next to Alex, tapping his thigh in an intimate affectionate gesture.

"Did you go on tour with your show?" Jacob asked.

"Only for a short while. When I received the grants, I arranged for the artwork to be shipped. If I'd gone along with them, I never would have time to get any painting done. Besides, I wasn't quite in people mode, if you know what I mean."

"Yeah. Yeah, I know. I'm still not in people mode." Jacob stifled a nervous laugh.

"Jacob, that sounds odd to me – the way you loved audiences and how they loved you back." Mavis said, hoping to trigger memories of a past pre-Katrina.

"So, how long were you in Boston?" Jacob's obvious change of subject was not lost on Mavis or Alex. They went along with it, as much to protect Jacob's nervousness as well as their own.

"We were there sixteen days," Alex explained. "We were supposed to be home a week ago after my colleague and I met with the publisher. But Mavis got booked in some museum shows and galleries in New England so we attended those openings, staying longer than expected."

"It sounds like you've found your paths – both of you." Jacob toasted his glass toasted his glass in their direction.

Mavis nodded her head in thanks. "Once Alex finished the final copy edits, he started another book," Mavis said quietly, stating a fact as opposed to bragging on her husband.

"I didn't know you were so prolific," Jacob said.

"Neither did I." Alex stood and picked up an item Jacob knew well. Jacob's old wand. The ribbons, charms, even the voudou figure were still intact. Just touching it brought back a whirlwind of memories. He looked over at Jake and saw he, too, was caught up in the past. They exchanged a look of co-conspirators once again. For old time's sake? Alex wondered. *All is forgiven? How many nights does this wand recall? How many changes and prophecies? How many warnings? How could our roles now be so reversed?*

Jake returned the look with his own mindset of questions. Alex read them as they passed across his features, like clouds over Lake Pontchartrain, revealing random patches of landscape exposed to the light. The light flashes revealed a nakedness, an emptiness unbearable to witness.

Alex broke the spell first. "I was very surprised to receive your wand in the mail, especially since I didn't accept a place in the temple. I thought Perry or Laney deserved it more."

"They were the ones who finalized my decision to ship it to you." Jacob detached more quickly than Alex could. Their shared knowledge was lost, blanked out by a slow blink of the one eye, as if someone had pulled the shutters on a *Vieux Carrè* street level window, saying *private. You are not welcome.*

The way Alex handled the wand reminded Jacob of Lily. It wasn't an association, but counterpoint. Lily, copper pipe in hand, had risked peering deep into the pit, stirring up its contents. Women were more comfortable with vessels. While he and Alex had waved the wand around, drawn symbols with it, eventually each, in his own way, had put the implement down before the work was completed.

"When did you decide on going back to cultural anthropology?" Jacob asked Alex, veering away from the topic.

As if on cue, Alex looked at Mavis. "Mavis helped me decide. One night, we listed the top five things which made us feel one hundred percent in the moment, alive in every fiber of our being. For Mavis it was her art. For me it was my research and writing."

"*Soror mystica*, the mystical female to enhance the work of the male alchemist, necessary for the completion of the *chymical wedding*," Jacob intoned. "For in every aspect, it takes opposites, dualities, paradox to complete the wholeness. One could not see fruition without the other. The great trick is to hold them in balance." Because of Jacob's role in playing the observer, he saw the meaning as clearly as if he gazed into a mirror pond. With one interchange of current, energy, and light, every hidden detail was brought into stark clarity. Not so much male and female, as in personas, but as symbols in motion – the wand and the vessel, the active and the passive principle, the observed and the observer operating simultaneously: the ultimate goal.

Mavis raised her eyebrows, a disarming grin on her face.

"Alex, when your papers were published about the work we did in the Lower Ninth, I realized why you denied the Baron," Jacob continued. "Your mission was more far-reaching. I realized you were doing as much for the *lwa* as Laney and Perry were in their daily lives…well, you with Mavis in hand. It appears the wand should be meant for you both."

Alex held the wand. "The experience at the temple meant a lot to us, as well. It opened me up to so many other possibilities where I can still support Mavis in her work. I see things with different eyes, more open perspective. That whole experience since I came to New Orleans, with you, is the stepping stone for what I envision for my next book."

"What's that?" Jacob asked.

"The death rituals of our time. There's a need in every culture to honor the dead. For the past few generations, especially in America, veneration for the psychological power of dealing with death has been stifled in obedience to productivity and getting on with life. Our consumer society won't allow the gears to come to a halt. But I've seen a shift back to some of the old ways; new ways to keep the spirits of the dead alive in the souls who remain behind."

Jacob smiled, even as felt the tears well up. "You've turned out to be one of my most accomplished pupils."

"And you my staunchest teacher."

Jacob smiled, noting the sly look in Alex's eyes. The statement could be read many ways.

"And what of you, Jake?" Alex probed. "Where are you living? What are you doing?" Alex was persistent

The resigned man sitting before him was nothing like the shaman he'd known, the man who served as both uncomfortable catalyst and inspiration. Alex couldn't hide his need for reassurance. "We haven't heard from you for too long."

"I live in a place not far from here in miles, but very distant in, shall we say, customs. I never come to the city. New Orleans is not the same to me. At first I thought I could build a new life there. The people I've met share my views. But recently, my way hasn't been clear. Since I left the temple, I'll admit, I've been lost." He shrugged his shoulders, an un-Jacob-like move, as many of his new mannerisms were. "From chaos and confusion evolves the new order of things," he continued. "I'm trying to be patient."

"So where is your place?" Alex looked at Mavis. "Can we come see you?"

"For the moment it's not wise. It's a place in transition, as I am." Jacob looked over his shoulder out of the window, like a seeker looking for the promised land. "Westwego is where I live now; some there call it the land of the lost."

A line of cars snaked over the Mississippi, crossing Luling Bridge from one side, heading down Clearview. Others crossed the Henry P. Long Bridge to I-90 until they converged on the Westbank Expressway and entered the closed off lands, feeling their way through the darkened streets of Westwego. Headlights searched the wreckage. Two years gone now and the place was too decayed to sustain or rebuild, but alive enough to feed the anger of the forgotten. *Purgatorio* they called it. And to many it was home. But on this night of nights, those brave enough to penetrate the darkened gulf between the reincarnation of New Orleans and the forgotten land were tempted into the wasteland by a triangle of sacred paper.

The cars, filled with people, their necks craned, inched their way out of the relative comfort of the Quarter into the Netherworld, the industrial underbelly sided by the Mississippi. A variety of vehicles followed each other on a quest, each trusting the one before them to know the way, the hazards and dangers. None of them knew the rewards. But they hoped. Word had passed quickly from bar to apartment, bookstore to record store, and over the internet, speculating in whispers of the things which might take place on this night. If only one had the courage. They passed gutted factories, industrial complexes, docks, and sleazy bars. Some were gutted, others, as the cars rolled by, were on fire. Alligators had burned and the Aragon Shipyard sprouted flames, as the night was punctuated by sirens speeding towards the Moon Suite Inn, 6613 Westbank, where the Marrero-Ragusa Volunteer Fire Dept struggled to put out the blazes. After Katrina, this area was given the role of the keeper of anger, hoarding the flames of outrage. Symbols Washington, D.C. still ignored.

Shrimp boats still sat lodged on rooftops. The line of cars, lengthening even more, was forced to pivot around a boat lying on its side straddling the median. Dark underpasses harbored the secrets of Westwego, Bayou Segnette, now the land of the lost. The sounds of the Mississippi lapping at the docks, once comforting, now only echoed

Loss

    Loss

Gone were the fishermen and boat builders, machinists, and dock workers; imports and exports; coffee, corn, oil, and trinkets; histories and futures. Even legends were mired in mud. Story tellers sat in tract houses scattered over a country that forgot there was such a land the waters of the Mississippi kissed.

Passengers winced as they passed acres of tall fencing, Davidian style. Huge shells of buildings, hulked, barely visible, as if smudged in charcoal against the dark. The glint of broken glass reflected their discomfort.

Twenty minutes later, the nicotine sky was punctuated by explosions, first one, then a series. The riders jumped or hunched into their leather jackets. They looked at each other to gauge reactions. *Should I be worried, should I flee? Can we leave now?* Their eyes said more than their guts would allow. No words escaped from mouths shut tight against screams at the back of throats.

What type of place is this?

Finally, the first car pulled into an abandoned complex. What buildings remained lurked together, like a gang, holding a grudge, the taste of sludge still in their mouths. Doors and windows were painted with symbols of the lost, the found – those who knew and protected the truth. The onlookers worried, *were the symbols invitations or threats?*

The first passengers left the safety of their vehicles. Laney stepped out of the dark, a moving figure in cast in relief. The light from the incoming headlights flared off his glasses, winked, an SOS or lewd summoning. His own demeanor was not so flippant.

"Welcome guests," he bellowed, his deep voice in full accord with the acoustics of cement and night.

"We'll wait for everyone and then I'll lead you inside. Thank you for leaving the safety of your little nests. I know how far you've come in your survival, but one lesson we all need to learn is to avoid complacency. This is the one place in this country where it will and can not happen."

He smiled. Only the closest witnessed the grim set of his lips, the sly look in his eyes. They squirmed and telegraphed their uneasiness to those walking up to the entrance of a factory.

Laney turned and indicated a massive brushed steel door. Unlike the rest of New Orleans, it carried no telltale rust, no evidence. It was only the first of the blatant lies. The tricks and temptations.

"Take nothing for granted." Laney warned.

When everyone had assembled, he pulled back a lever and the door slid silently, effortlessly, as if they were on the set of a high tech SC FI epic. But a few steps inside revealed no planetary landscape, no comforting alien sleekness.

No. The portal led to the place Katrina and time had thoroughly buried. The place of no return, the horrible days after beforetime.

"Purgatorio." Laney announced as he craftily disappeared, leaving the disoriented visitors to their own remembrances.

The uneasy visitors walked into a vast room. A sound of wind resonated through the higher reaches, and in front great lengths of filmy gauge danced and sighed in the breeze. Spanish moss fell in waterfalls, cascades of mermaid hair, sheets of broken twisted fragile lives, strung together in vague dreams and mysteries.

The onlookers wandered about looking up, feeling ahead, forgetting the others. Vague sounds filtered through the gauze and moss. No one could identify it – voices, a strain of a melody, the sound of hearts breaking and loving hands being pulled apart.

Some were crying. It was only the beginning. The first and most stalwart, a tall thin boy named Adam, stepped through the frontline of gauze, then stopped in his tracks. Before him were the images he wanted to forget.

 Marble slabs – or where they altars – held white shapes of human figures. They could be sleeping. Or were they bodies? He forced himself to move forward to see. Once beside the first of hundreds, he couldn't resist reaching out and taking its hand. A cold hand, but not dead – never alive except in the mind of its maker. Leaning close, he peered through the diffused light. The body was whole, not mutilated or decayed, but not at rest, not asleep. Oxidation stains of muted verdigris and dusty vermillion, sienna browns and raw umbers played upon the surface, parti-colored graced with a subtle overlay appropriate for the grave, the tomb. Because, Adam realized, this was a tomb, or a replica, a reminder.

Not a graveyard of mud and sludge, broken sticks, bits of metal and telephone wire, but a tomb, a proper tomb, for on each slab beneath the rendition of the body was the name and a birth date. And on each slab birthdates were all followed by the same date, August 28, 2005. It was a tomb, a memorial for all of those who would never be found. And now he knew why he had received the strange ATC invitation.

It only took him 20 minutes to find her. And there she lay, reborn, a sculptor's image, a person forgotten no longer. The hair was her color, and although the face had a hint of her discernable features, a hint of what might be viewed through a veil of gauze, the spirit of her was there. His mind, needy, filled in the details. The height and weight were correct. He swore he'd seen her lay this way two years ago when he'd step into their room hours after she'd gone to bed because his book had to be written and he wrote better at night. Strewn around her were dried sprigs of a plant. He could smell the fragrance as he lifted one. Tied to each sprig was a small piece of parchment. The words, Remember Me, were written in a fine calligraphy hand.

He looked around to find Lucretia. She'd know what it was. He didn't remember them being separated after they'd passed through the metal door. He threaded his way through the kids and found her lying with her head on the marble, as if looking into her ex-lover's eyes. He couldn't be jealous. He'd just dealt with the same sense of lost futures.

Lucretia turned and saw him, as if she'd heard his footfall, but she couldn't have over the ringing tones of wind chimes. She sat up slowly, not letting go of the hand. Her face was red from crying.

"You found some, too," she said through her tears. She held up a similar sprig. "It's rosemary for remembrance. Do you think they mind…us finding each other?" she asked, full of doubt.

"No," he reassured her, and he believed it, too. "We've learned a lot of things. How we'd have acted differently if we'd known we'd have such little time. I don't think they'd want us to be alone. I hope they're glad we found each other and can help each other through this. At least, I know Adrienne would. She had such a big heart. She'd like you."

***

Up in the plant manager's booth, Laney watched the scene twenty-five feet below from his stance behind a tempered glass window.

"They look like sleep walkers" Laney said, his hands gripping the metal guard rail.

"I never knew how they would react," Lily said, "even until right after the installation. What if it's too much?" she wondered.

Perry, with one hand plastered to the window, stood with his forehead resting on his arm. "Poor kids. They've been through so much." At first he could hardly watch. He knew this was a necessary step, but he feared the display was too extreme.

"It needed to be done," Laney said. "We had to know they'd understand before anyone else saw it."

"I know," Lily said. The sense of poignant awe was palpable, even behind the glass. It was like watching a somber funeral procession. She believed those who'd withstood tragedy needed to gather together, if not to understand the enormity of an event so uncontrollable in their everyday worlds, but to see how others had survived, too. She hoped they realized, how despite the depth of their loss, there was reason to embrace life.

Perry turned his face away from the comfort of well-washed cotton and scanned the crowd moving slowly through the room below. He relaxed his shoulders even as he watched. "Without this, there would be no memorial. Maybe this can be closure for those kids down there and their families when they bring them," he said. "I'm amazed at the reaction, how moved they all were, even though it's what I predicted, despite my conflicting fears, all along." He walked away from the window and took a place beside Jacob.

"But more importantly, we need this to be an opening to the rest of the country," Jacob said from his place against the wall. "A way to make them open their eyes and look at what they've done. How they've abandoned their fellow countrymen."

Lily wondered what his detachment hid. Fear of the strain of the survivors' grief on what he must do later, a calculating stance to avoid the fear that their plan would backfire, marking him as one instrument of additional pain, even more dangerous than what her role could have caused? She wanted to hold him, reassure him, now she felt assured her concept could be healing.

"Yes, these people needed closure," Jacob continued, "but maybe they're the lucky ones, because at least they're human and now tragically aware of the truth. It's the rest of the country that's blind to how safe we are. They still think they're protected by the Declaration of Independence and their government. What a joke. Those are the people we have to reach."

"I was so worried." Lily leaned against the rail, the weight of it all finally hitting her. "It felt right all these months, but I didn't want to hurt those kids anymore."

"You didn't hurt them any more than they've been hurt. You're helping them to heal." Jacob said. "I guess I'd better go and get ready. My turn's the one I'm worried about," he admitted.

After Jacob left, Lily collapsed in a chair. "This is almost too much. I thought all the pressure and doubt came while I was making the figures. But now, it's worse. All this responsibility. I don't know if I was ready, those people...Jacob."

"You have to trust," Laney said sitting down, putting an arm around her bent shoulders. "You have to give grace a place to grow. You have to trust that you've done your part and let the universe unfold the rest. Those people will heal, as you have in your process. Don't expect it to be linear. Healing, growth, insight, none of those come from linear living. Leave some room. Stay true to yourself and other energies will enter to assist you. You've known that all along. How can you have a crisis in your beliefs now?"

"But what about Jacob? He still seems so lost. What if it's another night like the ritual?" Lily asked.

"He has his path to follow and we have ours," Laney said. "There are never guarantees. We just have to prepare and take the risks. Would you rather not try and just succumb to a life of feeling numb or plastic? No matter the outcome, hasn't the effort all been worth it? Don't worry about Jacob. You and I are slow, deep learners. He's a quick-change artist. He may surprise us all."

Laney took her hands and encouraged her to view the scene below. Some cried, some wandered about touching hands, some spoke in quiet whispers or brushed a cheek or lips with theirs. They passed through the huge vaulted room, passing one figure after another, all different; some bore the colors of oxidation and moss, others were black fired or glazed with walnut gels; still others bore a sheen like gasoline on water.

"I'm so grateful to the other sculptors who came forward to help. She slumped back. "There were so many victims – and all so different. They deserved a memorial. I can't speak for the other artists, but it was healing for me."

The trio in the glass booth watched as the people below moved through the room. Lily recognized some of the sculptors, as they witnessed the full effect the first time, saw the work of other artisans, and understood the purpose of the last two years.

"I need to get my heat suit on," she said. "I should have left a while ago. It's not fair to have the others do all the preliminary work."

"I assure you, they don't mind." Laney smiled a benefic expression. "After all, you started all this. I'd call that the preliminary work."

***

Eventually the people wandering the great vaulted space moved toward the end of the room where a dark tunnel, carved in stone, was hung with variegated green moss.

"I smell flowers." Lucretia said, catching up to Adam and grabbing his hand. "I know this smell. What is it?" She wracked her brain, knowing the fragrance, but unable to name it out of context. Then she remembered – the breaking of the branches and hauling them home, stripping the leaves and frothy blossoms to throw in her dye pots. The strong aroma as the leaves and blossoms simmered. "Its mimosa. I recognize it from my natural dyeing. It turns the fiber yellow. The smell is overpowering, but only when the plant is blooming in June."

"The mimosa evokes a feeling of security and assurance..." Adam quoted quietly. "...the assurance that death is only a metamorphosis and not the absolute end."

Once again, Lucretia was amazed at his encyclopedic memory for references and connections. "Who is that you're quoting?"

"*Cavatore,*" Adam said, citing the author in a reverent voice. "I can smell it, too."

"They must have dried the leaves," Lucretia speculated. "That's the only way they could reproduce the smell out of season. It would take a hundred trees to fill a place this big with its fragrance." Lucretia realized this would be a night of fear and wonder.

The sound of falling water drew them, accented by a blue light, a soft blue light. Those who entered barely noticed, but the light pulsated, sixty pulses per minute, the times the heart beats per minute when its bearer is in the zone, the Zen state, a meditative rest. The pulse of the speed of electrons as they begin to pass through the particle accelerator; the pulse needed to begin the slide through copper tubes on the way to split the atom. Quantum physics and individual peace. Cat state, static, yet acting at the same time.

Adam, along with others directly behind him, noticed the shift in the tunnel from rock to copper. At first the copper was dressed in its guise of verdigris but then eventually emerged in its true color just a few steps before they stepped into a room three times as large as the last, lit brilliantly by living flame. Adam felt the heat of it even before the shift from stone to metal, but chalked it up to a fluke.

He couldn't believe the scene before him. The room was divided into two sections, separated by a huge wall of glass. Behind the glass, four, five stories high, he could see huge caldrons or vats. Flames burned in in-ground pits fed by figures dressed in oversized asbestos suits. Others used gaffs and hooks to tip the cauldron. Out of the vessel flowed liquid copper, more vibrantly red than lava, alive and hungry for release. The metal handlers steered the flow into long tubes, tubes to handle the acceleration of electrons and protons, tubes to be shipped to CERN, SLAC, Hadon, metal to unleash subatomic particles, the pathway to energy, the disruption of matter.

On the stage four figures stood dwarfed by the copper smelting, silhouetted against the flame and molten metal. One wore what appeared to be Marilyn Manson-esque makeup, only it wasn't contrived. The jagged slash on one side of the singer's face stood out in harsh counterpoint to the white of the opposite side.

Three were musicians. The music they played, unfolded, bursting to bloom or sparks, pulsating, held together with the dark undertones of a cello. Jacob did not sing for a long time, allowing the audience to adapt to the shift in scene, in senses. Quintessence – five senses. *To fully be alive we must live through all five senses.*

Lily, even through the asbestos, experienced through all of her senses, as well, but her sense of time was altered and her focus refracted as if through a prism. One part of her brain visualized the complex technique she needed to work in tandem with the other smelters. But another part of her brain was constantly aware of Jacob, even when he'd been on the sidelines waiting to go onstage. Among the hundreds of people present and the demands of the malleable, almost alive copper liquid, Jacob was the most vivid image in the room.

The onlookers could feel only a semblance of heat from the smelting copper through the double-paned thermal glass, but the psychological effect took hold. They took off their leather jackets. Some broke out in a sweat. Adam, like the others, tasted the copper on his tongue, the taste of blood and tears. He patted the paperback in his back pocket. *Lost Souls,* by Poppy Z. Brite, another New Orleans survivor, tortured by Katrina but resolved to stay. Adam turned to his companion. "It's an altar," he said. "The stage is an altar."

"An altar in the pit of hell," Lucia replied, taking his hand. "Do you taste blood?"

"The altar isn't in hell, Lucia, remember? *Purgatorio,* the man at the gate said." He squeezed her hand, a gesture of pain and hope. "And what we taste is copper. Copper tastes like blood."

The bass-line built the tensions, subliminal, pervasive. The drums pounded out their heartaches, the stress of clenched fists. The cello echoed their loss, a minor key aural weaving of browns and burgundy, an undercoating to the pain, the color of old blood. While the guitar wove throughout and above, in cries or voices of hope, the melodies pulled the audience's life strings taut. Jacob stepped in, at first in the emptiness between time changes, clear and bright as a bell, a bell of copper. And his voice enticed them, invited them to look inside, take the ride.

The universal messenger, the Thrice Great Hermes in the guise of half man/half monster, by virtue of his change, became the repository for all their broken dreams, their angers and fears, their hopes and disillusionments.

Kids stage-dived, rode the hands of their companions. Many moshed, pounding their untouchable enemies into the cement with beat-up Doc Martins, stamping their anger out in rituals known to man since the earliest need for ceremonial release. Others stood to the side, removing T-shirts, wringing the sweat and then tying the limp fabric around their forwards before heading back into the fray. Tears and sweat mingled. No one knew who was crying, who was not. No judgments prevailed. Those who had never grieved were watched over by those who had.

They released their frustrations in the bosom of those suffering side by side. They played their loss out in wild awkward moves, unyielding... knowing they were safe, knowing they were with kin of the spirit.

Jacob rode the crest of their emotions, fed it back to them in kind, leading the band in time changes with the smallest of tell-tale gestures, a flick of the wrist or nod of the head. The band was tight, in sync like never before, as if mentally connected to each other; sixty beats per minute escalating along the copper tubes of their memories, racing toward splitting the atoms of their fears and dashed hopes, washing their loss in the non-glow of anti-matter. Exploding all that was pent up in a safe and secure vacuum.

At one point Jacob stopped singing, lifted his right arm into the air, and stood still with his head hanging down.

"What's he doing?" Perry asked Laney.

"I'm not sure, but he looks the like the Magus from the Morgan-Greer Tarot.

Eventually the audience stopped and watched as well, wondering. Adam swore he saw a sliver of light slide down from the rafters into Jacob's hand and down his up-stretched arm.

Jacob was just resting, the necessary pause, a moment to regroup. It was not one of his usual stances, a measured drama to orchestrate the show, guide the audience. It was a moment of peace in the midst of whirling emotions crashing alongside rampaging music; he needed to think, must be able to connect somehow, maintain the balance, ride the edge.

And then Jake was Jacob again, the shaman of the community, the mage who harnessed elemental forces and guided them towards his will – all for the benefit of his people. It was like the *Houdan* rituals but deeper, different, because he was possessed by no one but himself and the electric/static connection to something universal, so much larger than one pantheon of gods, bigger than the gods, bigger than religion, bigger than quantum physics. He was not the horse being ridden now, but one of the riders.

And it was his place to lead the rest to sanctuary.

"Correspondences," Lily whispered to Jacob after his performance. "You did it. *Conjunctio.* Copper ruled by Venus, the conjunction, the striving towards art, beauty, music, friends love. You were Hermes, Thoth, the magician. You've taken their grief and fears and led them through the fire, the melting and smelting, so now they can transform. Oxidation, verdigris, liquid fire." She was excited, talking all in a rush. Her voice danced in the stage lights.

"Yeah, and Mercurious the trickster will appear shortly for comic relief." Jacob strode past them towards the dressing room, "And his sidekick Loki is waiting stage left to pull the rug out from beneath us. We can't afford to get cocky."

"Don't be such a cynic, "Laney said, "Lily's right, you were a master. You had them climbing Jacob's ladder, believing there's a stairway to heaven."

"We all know heaven doesn't exist," Jacob looked at them as if they were fools. His voice was dire, flat, final. Then he turned his back to them both, ripping off the wet shirt, toweling himself down. The distorted shoulder was emphasized by the green backlighting onstage, as if someone had traced out the punishment with a highlighter.

Lily cringed and looked away, not wanting to buy into his distemper. "Perhaps it does," she said, "as a state of mind."

"But one must pass through *Purgatorio* first," Laney acquiesced with a knowing smile. "Scars are the badges of our tests. We must be broken and broken down before transformation can take place. The true alchemist's goal was never the philosopher's stone or literally tuning lead into gold. It was the processes, the processes that led to transformation, taking all our denied faults and melding it with our comfortable bits producing the gold of our true inner core."

"Instead of looking into the light, we have to look into the shadows." Jacob's one eye caught her, unflinching, reversing the role of a minnow darting away as it had for the past month. No, this time it was stripped of guile or pretense, flaying the skin to the bone as only an intimate can do. It was a confrontation not without its merit but devoid of compassion. "Perhaps that's where the truth lies," Jacob added. "And right now the shadow's bigger than anyone can imagine."

She tried to read his reaction but it was like attempting to observe herself in a defective mirror while someone stood over her shoulder. If she focused on the unharmed side of his face, she sensed the distorted side out of the corner of her eye. If she lost it and looked at the scarred part of his face, all she read were reflections of her own fears.

It had taken her years to learn to read his face beneath the many masks he took off and on at will. Now she would have to learn all over again.

He turned and grabbed a carpenter's yard stick left leaning against the wall. At first she thought he would shake it or draw patterns like he did with the wand. She shook her head at the memory of Jacob as he had been. It seemed ages ago. But instead he held it across his body in both hands, as if ready to execute a soft shoe. He winked at her. In a deft move, smooth as a snake charmer, he touched the stick to ground and leaned on it as a cane.

He flashed her a Jacob-as-shaman grin. "Don't forget how delicious it is to dance in the dark." With those words, he turned and walked back onstage for an encore.

About the Author

Gail Gray, a native of Lowell, Massachusetts, now lives in Greenville, South Carolina. She has been a photojournalist, professional astrologer, teacher, magazine writer, costumer, Middle Eastern dancer, event planner, music publicity copywriter, deliverer of telephone books, barista, editor, publisher, and has flown hot-air balloons.

She edited *The Howling* and *Fissure* magazines and was arts editor for Edge Magazine. Her short stories have been widely published in international magazines including *moonShine Review, Morpheus Tales, Pear Noir!, The Foliate Oak* and the *Cover of Darkness anthology*. Her poetry has been featured in both the literary and avant garde press including: *Asheville Poetry Review, Counterexample Poetics, Sein und Werden, Being, Deep Tissue, Shoots and Vines, ditch, Main Street Rag, Sisyphus,* and the *Zygote Abstract Libertine* anthology, and her nonfiction published nationally including *Magical Blend* and *Parabola*.

Her previous books include: two short story collections, *Memories and Monsters* and *Dark Voices*, in addition to five poetry books, *Planetary Tensions, The Hazard of Waking Up, Spirals in Copper, Eye on the Universe* and *Storms from the Edge*.

When not writing or working on her micro press, Shadow Archer Press, she enjoys painting and making assemblages, textile arts, making cordials and gardening. Her paintings, drawings, weaving and assemblages have been displayed in art shows throughout the southeast.

She has completed a second novel, *Shaman in Exile*, the sequel to *Shaman Circus*, and is working on a third novel, *Interference Equation: Fireworks*.

To learn more about Gail, visit her website at:
http://www.freewebs.com/gailgraystudios/index.htm